THRILLER

WILLEMS & DIERCKX

THE VIRUS

Nowhere are you safe from online danger

Lannoo

*It's not a faith in technology.
It's faith in people.*
– Steve Jobs

*Our entire much-praised technological
progress, and civilization generally, could
be compared to an axe in the hands of
a pathological criminal.*
– Albert Einstein

Prologue

**A2 Motorway, direction Amsterdam, near Utrecht,
13 February 2034**

'That many?' Jan Goethals exclaims. He's sitting in his self-driving car, a bright blue fifth-generation Tesla. He has his security expert colleague on the phone.

'Yes, Jan, you heard me right, and the attacks are aimed mainly at large companies', he hears Pieter say. 'Right now we don't yet know whether a virus has managed to penetrate somewhere.'

While his colleague continues talking, Jan mutes his own sound with a simple wave of his hand and orders his on-board computer: 'Butler, find numbers on computer viruses 13 February 2034.' With the same hand movement, but now in the other direction, he unmutes and continues the conversation. All kinds of articles on the subject he asked for appear on his virtual cockpit. Jan Goethals studies the data and they seem to tally with what a colleague's telling him. When, following this, the fake news filter also estimates the truth-level of the data as very high, he swallows hard a moment.

Within an hour he'll be addressing the BeNe Security Congress in Amsterdam, with a presentation on a very specific type of computer virus. He frowns, realizing he can't ignore these recent numbers.

'Pieter' he interrupts his loquacious colleague, 'thanks for calling, but I have to go now. I just want to prepare quietly for my presentation, you understand?'

Pieter understands fully and Jan ends the conversation. He leans back and thinks. 'Not a good sign, that increased frequency of attacks over the last twenty-four hours. We've seen it before in the past. But what lies behind it? It could be a manoeuvre to divert attention from a larger imminent attack. Or perhaps a collective attack by several small players in the black economy who've decided to join forces.'

He stares straight ahead and thinks about how he'll process this information into his speech. The sight through the windshield is so familiar. Four rows of very similar-looking vehicles all driving, as if by magic, exactly the same distance apart. As he thinks about his speech, he suddenly starts up. The little hologram of his Butler, traditionally in the centre of his austere dashboard, vanishes from one second to the next, as if shattering. Fortunately, the Tesla continues calmly on its way. Jan heaves a sigh of relief. Like all other drivers of self-driving cars he knows, he's never had to take the wheel himself. The system has been working perfectly for years and the fact that the network is monitored by NATO is one reason for this. Jan determines that, while the hologram has disappeared, the onboard computer is still functioning. That comforts him. But then his mouth falls open.

A hologram appears on his dashboard again and this time it's not his Butler. It's the image of a woman. This is exceptional: years ago several women's movements protested against the derogatory practice of using women all the time as virtual assistants.

Immediately after the woman appears, a text is projected onto his cockpit. John stiffens.

'Pay 10,000 crypto or we'll crash your car. This is not a joke.'

Not a joke? This can't be anything but a joke, can it? How should he react to this?

'Butler, phone Pieter,' he orders.

Nothing, no response. He brings his wrist with the implanted chip close to his mouth and requests again.

Nothing.

'Butler, change route,' he tries. 'Take route home.' No answer. Could it be true then? Has his car been hacked? He, a well-known security expert, what an irony that would be. All kinds of thoughts flash through his head. What to do? Jumping out of a car travelling at a hundred and forty kilometres an hour is not a good idea. Still, he jerks the handle. No movement, it's locked of course. He can't get the window down either, the sensor seems to be deactivated. Sweat pours down him. Against his better judgement, he grips the steering wheel and tries to turn it. It's stuck fast. Meanwhile the car is thundering down the highway, straight ahead, tailing the other cars closely.

With a start he sees the virtual text on his windshield shrink and, to his horror, be replaced by a countdown clock. It starts at five minutes. This must be malware, he realizes, malicious software that has taken control of his car. There's only one thing left for him to do, although he and his colleagues always advise against it: pay. He can't take the risk. His despair is heightened when he sees pictures on his windshield of his wife and his two-year-old daughter, smiling at the camera. Damn it, he thinks, they've hacked my personal photo library too. There's no option than to pay if he still wants to see his family again.

There are almost two minutes left on the countdown clock when he instructs the banking app in his chip to transfer the requested amount to the account shown on the windshield. Discouraged he lowers his arms. That money, almost all his savings, gone in one fell swoop. Just like that, damn it, in a few seconds. 'You're going to pay for this,' he hisses through his teeth.

Then he notices the countdown clock again. It's still counting down and is now at one minute. When's it going to stop? A cold shiver runs down his spine. That clock's not going to stop, he realizes. They're going to make me crash!

'No, I've paid!' he screams and his voice breaks. 'Stop the car, I want to get out!'

At that moment, loud music begins to play, like someone's trying to drown him out. Panic grabs him as he yanks the buckle on his seat belt to remove it. It doesn't move an inch. It too, he realizes, must be blocked remotely. He begins to pummel the windows with his bare fists to shatter them, but that soon proves a vain hope. With tears in his eyes, he looks for something with which to smash the windows. But in the midst of all the touchscreens and digital gadgets, he detects nothing that can serve as a tool.

A quick glance at the countdown clock tells him there are still thirty seconds left. He puts both feet down hard on the brakes and too bad if another car runs into him from behind. But deep inside he knows this won't work. Fifteen seconds left. He lifts his long legs and desperately kicks the windshield a few times, but that doesn't flinch either.

Five more seconds. He's trembling all over and the tears are now flowing freely. He realizes he's going to die. His gaze moves to the photo of his family he's always been so proud of.

One second left. The last thing he feels is the car veering sharply to the right. Then the black hole.

Driving to Brussels, one day later, 14 February 2034

'Luis, are you serious now? Really?'

Righard Zwienenberg, a lanky Dutch IT security expert with years of experience in the sector, cannot hide his surprise. His colleague has just got into his car and told him he needs to practise his presentation. Luis Corrons, a lot shorter than his colleague, looks at him half-guilty, half-smiling. The third man in the car, Eddy Willems, also an experienced security expert, looks on with a chuckle. The Three Amigos, as they are sometimes called in their industry, are on their way to a well-known antivirus conference, where they will each give a presentation.

Righard shakes his head indulgently and turns to his on-board computer. 'Butler, Avenue Lambermont 1, Brussels please.' Every time he utters that last word, he wonders how many people say 'please' to a computer these days.

The fully self-driving electric car starts moving, and with a slight humming sound, course is set for the RSA Virus Bulletin Conference, to be held this year in the Belgian capital. The three men turn their chairs towards each other, which makes it easier to talk.

'Luis, isn't that the same T-shirt as last time?' asks Righard, who is not wearing a traditional shirt, but is sporting a red polo shirt and black trousers.

Luis looks down in surprise at what's printed on his black T-shirt: 'Hard Rock', in big, bright yellow letters.

'Oops, forgot,' he says.

Righard, who has known Luis for over twenty years, sighs deeply. 'I do have a few T-shirts in my suitcase, you can wear one of those.'

Luis thanks him and quickly changes the subject. 'Terrible what happened to that Jan Goethals.'

'Yes, horrible, he leaves behind a young wife and daughter,' replies Eddy.

'What a drama. Is it true his Tesla was hacked?'

'Well, you know I work regularly with Europol, and they contacted me immediately after the incident yesterday,' Righard says, not without some pride. 'I immediately went there with my colleagues to look for traces of a possible virus in the crashed car's operating system.' He shifts position and rearranges his long legs.

He's more than happy to have paid a supplement for this wider version of the Polestar.

'It reminds me of last year's virus that got NATO into trouble for a while,' Luis says thoughtfully.

'Larry Lane,' Righard replies immediately, at sixty-seven still as sharp-minded as he was thirty years ago. And certainly when it comes to his sector and expertise. 'Yes, I'd already thought of it,' he continues. 'Fortunately, that man is safely tucked away in a cell somewhere. We can only hope he hasn't inspired anyone to continue his work.'

There is silence in the car as the three men remember the incident from a year earlier. Larry Lane, then CEO of Bio Dynamics, a company with a dubious reputation, had managed to get a virus into the NATO network, then already responsible for worldwide Internet security. The breach had happened in an original way, via the smart contact lenses of a marketing agency employee. She had been invited to NATO as part of a collaboration, but that turned out somewhat differently.

'That was your son's assistant, wasn't it Eddy?' Luis Luis. Eddy nods. 'Correct. She worked at Frank's communication agency. Worked, because after that incident she resigned, and Frank never saw her again.'

It was Eddy who then found the solution to undo the hostage-taking of the NATO system. Ultimately, Larry Lane was arrested and received a long prison sentence.

There was silence in the car until ten minutes later the Butler informed them that they had arrived at their destination. The three men had spent the entire interval thinking about that unsavoury affair, without knowing what was going to hit them later that day.

RSA Virus Bulletin Conference, Brussels, 1.30 pm

After Luis had donned another T-shirt, much too large of course, the men walked from the parking lot to the building where this year's RSA Virus Bulletin Conference was taking place. This conference, attended by an average of a thousand experts and business people, had been held every year since 1989. It was the rendezvous *par excellence* for IT security professionals, with not only debates, but also sharing of crucial information in the fight against malware and hacking. That made this conference unique. This year it was again well attended. The parking lot was almost completely full and the few landing places for flying cars were almost all occupied.

'I'm curious to see if anyone will provide more insights into the recent proliferation of malware attacks,' Righard suggests. 'No doubt,' Eddy replies, looking up at Righard as they move up a second escalator. 'That's the great asset of our community. While the black economy is very divided, we form a close bloc with all the experts. For us, no commercial considerations play a role in our decision-making. Each of us wants to save the world, so to speak. Some may call us idealists, but for me that's the only right way.'

Righard laughs. 'You've hit the nail on the head!'

They pass a long line of people waiting at the entrance. As speakers, they are allowed to use another entrance, one of the few advantages they enjoy here, in addition to free parking and a decent lunch. The three men don't care that they're not getting paid for their presentations and all the preparation work. The respect they get for it and the added value for their own network are much more important.

After being thoroughly vetted at a side entrance, to their amazement without any human intervention, they step inside and stop for a moment to take in the new event hall. They admire the construction of the capital's largest and newly-inaugurated congress building, hemisphere-shaped, with the highest point of the ceiling at least twenty metres from the floor. Everywhere on the walls are large video screens, right now showing advertising. Soon they will be displaying experts or companies who are unwilling or unable to be physically present today, and who will attend the event or participate in the panel discussions via streaming. In the centre of the room is a series of round tables and chairs. On every table lie trendy multifunctional earphones. In this way attendees can listen to the presentations in their own languages or replay a specific keynote. On the white wall right in front of the entrance, a giant screen catches their eye. None of them has ever seen such a format before. On top of that, the resolution is incredibly sharp, even with fast-moving images. Visibly, the Dome's owner has invested in the most modern technology available. An enormous stage has been erected under the screen, where a colleague is currently giving a presentation. To the left and right of it are two more stages, smaller but still impressive in size.

A hostess rushes to them and offers them badges and slender metal glasses. Righard and Luis thank her, but both politely decline the augmented reality glasses, which would give them information about all conference attendees based on facial recognition.

'Thanks, miss, but I'm far-sighted,' Righard jokes, and all three move on.

A young man approaches them from a group of conference attendees. 'Excuse me, may I introduce myself? My name is Jorgen D'Hondt and I'm a great admirer of your work.' He doesn't look older than eighteen.

Eddy responds first. 'Hello Jorgen, do you know us?'

The boy nods enthusiastically. Like them, he's dressed super-casually, in T-shirt and jeans. 'Yes, I've studied almost all of your articles and presentations. And how you solved that incident from last year, just amazing!'

Luis pats Eddy on the shoulder. 'For that we have to give credit to our friend Eddy here, because he was the one who came up with the solution.'

'Why your interest in our profession, Jorgen?' Righard asks.

With blushing cheeks the young man tells his story. 'I was able to finish my studies faster than usual,' he says without a trace of arrogance, 'and that gave me time to focus on other things. I happened to stumble upon an article a few years ago about computer viruses and antiviruses, and it never let me go.'

'Do you already work in the sector?' Eddy asks curiously.

'Most companies think I'm too young, but through a detour I've managed to participate in a few studies. Admittedly as a student, but I don't care about that, I don't do it for the money. Computers are my passion. In my spare time I collect old computer models. I already have one from every era. Those are my personal old-timers, so to speak.'

They continue talking for a while, until the young man has to leave. 'Nice kid,' says Righard, 'with the right attitude. Maybe we'll catch up with him again.'

They continue into the Dome. Righard glances at the badges they've just received. Each includes a small screen, showing the way to the room where the speakers can prepare in quiet. The men join the bustle of busily talking colleagues and follow the arrows with which the miniature navigation badge guides them. From afar they see a large hologram next to a locked door. Righard and Luis look at each other and shake their heads. In recent years there's has been an incredible evolution in new technologies. Their innate curiosity – one of the reasons for their success – keeps them closely following these evolutions. They also *need* to, because in theory every new application can also exhibit vulnerabilities, and is therefore vulnerable to malware or hacking. But sometimes, when they're together without younger colleagues around, they pity people confronted with this tsunami of new products and services. They date from a time when everything was much simpler. With the success of the internet of things, which has led to almost all devices being connected, things are no longer that simple. To be able to thoroughly secure all those small and large networks and the mutual connections between all devices, demands a lot of time and research. And then there are the updates. These follow each other at a frantic pace, because each producer wants to outdo the other with products that are state of the art and that always incorporate the latest options or trends. Security updates are part and parcel of this, but in reality they are a necessary evil for the manufacturers, something they have to offer but don't make money on. On the contrary, they lose working hours and money with it. They prefer to design holograms, such as the one the trio now stands in front of.

'This is an original version of a hologram', Eddy says.

What they see is a female figure on high stilts, who could have come straight from the defunct *Cirque du Soleil*. The light blue image is of perfect quality, without the slightest trace of vibrations, but Luis just finds it creepy. He's not into holograms anyway. When he comes within one metre of the image, facial recognition does its job and a door next to the hologram opens. Righard and Eddy are also recognized at the same time, the latest versions now making it possible to recognize several people at the same time.

They end up in a room that reminds them most of an airport VIP lounge. Here and there other speakers are sitting in comfortable chairs, waiting their turn. For most of them this is routine, as reflected in their easy attitudes and relaxed faces. Some are even stealing micro naps, using their headphones to cut themselves off from the outside world. Luis and Eddy follow Righard, who is looking for a free place in his seven-mile boots. Along the way they bump into Hans Vomp, a Dutch colleague.

'Hi Hans', they greet him. 'Everything alright?'

Vomp, small in stature like Luis and the proud owner of a mop of red hair, smiles kindly at them. 'Well, if it isn't the Three Amigos! Tell me, the how manyeth time is it for you here at the vbc?'

The conference was taken over by RSA years ago and the name was also officially changed to RSA VBC, but the old-timers still just say 'VBC'.

Righard looks at Luis and shrugs his shoulders. 'Let's see, that must be the forty-second time for me.'

'Thirty-two for me,' Luis says briefly.

'Well, that's a lot, you hold the records! I'm just on my eleventh visit. And you, Eddy?'

'Thirty-nine, I think,' Eddy replies, immediately changing the subject. 'Hans, what do you think about that crash with that self-driving car?'

'Yes, a sad thing. I knew Jan pretty well, you know. We worked together several times. A very passionate man and a gifted speaker too.'

'I think so too', Luis agrees. 'I wish I had his talent.'

'For me it's an atypical attack,' says Hans, starting to count on his fingers. 'One, it's a targeted attack on an individual, not a company. Okay, some celebrities and VIPs have already had to deal with it, but that's still a difference. These are people who are in the public eye and who are easy to blackmail because of their image. This was all about a young man who wasn't very well known at all.'

Righard and Luis nod in agreement.

'Two, I heard Jan was supposedly forced to pay to remove the ransomware, which in the end didn't happen. So those bastards took the money and let him crash anyway.'

A bearded colleague who has just passed them looks up in surprise on hearing the word 'bastards'. Righard notices this reaction and leads the others into a small conference room. They close the door behind them. The four men sit down and Hans continues speaking softly.

'Three, so far no-one has managed to take over a self-driving car and crash it. It still needs further investigation, but it's already clear there's someone behind it who has something completely new, and that means that they have a lot of money and resources.'

'Could it be that a leak has been found in the security of that self-driving car?' Luis counters.

'Hopefully we'll get behind it soon at Europol', Righard says. 'But I'd be very surprised if that were the case. Our first hypothesis is that the virus has sneaked into the network disguised as part of the security update. Just like cancer cells that pretend to be good cells and in this way mislead the immune system.'

'That's not very new, is it?' Hans asks.

'Not when it comes to company networks, no. But here we're talking about something much bigger. You have to be well-connected to get in there.'

'You're right,' Eddy says. 'All supranational bodies are continuously involved in the development and security of self-driving car traffic. Believe me, now that 95 percent of all traffic jams have been solved as a result, they'll do everything they can so as not to return to the miserable situations of the past.'

For the older men, the spectre of the endless traffic jams looms again, something they would rather not think about. 'Indeed, the millions of euros of resulting economic damage are fortunately a thing of the past,' Luis says. Money can now be invested in other, more fundamental things.'

Suddenly Luis' badge, lying on a table between them, starts to vibrate. He picks it up and reads the text that appears on it. 'Guys, I have to speak, see you later?'

'I'm coming with you,' Righard says.

They say goodbye to Hans and Eddy, who want to chat for a while, and go to the back of the immense stage. There, the previous speaker is finishing his presentation.

Righard pats Luis on the shoulder. 'Good luck, my friend, you're going to do a good job of it, I'm sure.'

Luis thanks him and ascends the stairs leading to the stage, unaware that this will be the strangest keynote of his life.

RSA Virus Bulletin Conference, Brussels, 1.55 pm

While Luis puts on his microphone and takes the stage, Righard finds a free seat. Which is not so easy, given the large number of colleagues who have shown up. At the fourth row of tables, he discovers two empty chairs and hurries toward them. Along the way, he greets everyone he knows. He has just taken his seat when Luis is introduced by the female moderator as the next speaker. The topic he has chosen is 'New Malware and the Advanced Internet of Things', a very topical theme.

Luis pauses for a moment until the modest applause stops and then addresses his audience with a pre-rehearsed opening line, the only one, incidentally, that he has learned by heart.

'Hello everyone and thank you for coming to listen to me and not my colleagues next door', he begins, pointing to the two other stages, where the other speakers have also started. 'I assume you all have refrigerators at home?'

Ignoring certain raised eyebrows by some, he launches right into his theme.

'As you know, that refrigerator detects that there is, for example, no more butter and milk. But do you also realize that when it orders those products, butter and milk aren't the only things that are delivered to your home?'

He walks across the stage and tries to catch his listeners' eyes.

'In response to such an order, the refrigerator receives a confirmation from the supplier, and that's where the shoe rubs.'

Righard smiles at his old friend and thinks he's off to a good start. The start of a presentation is crucial, you have to immediately get the audience involved and you do that best with an original opening gambit, like Luis just did. Righard is pleased to notice that everyone is listening attentively.

He also notices how warm it is in this room, and he looks around to see if he's the only one to notice.

'Of course, along with the confirmation come the classic cookies...'

As Luis continues talking, Righard nudges his neighbour. 'For eating with the coffee,' he jokes. The colleague smiles politely and then quickly looks back at the stage.

'However, along with the cookies, malware can also be sent, which recently happened in a pharmaceutical company in Great Britain. Their company canteen's refrigerator then received much more than butter and milk. It took weeks to remove the malware that had sneaked in.'

The colleague in front of Righard takes off his sweater, causing Righard to lose sight of Luis for a moment. Someone else getting hot, he thinks. He unbuttons the collar of his polo shirt and looks up at the ventilation, attached to the ceiling, from where the hot air is forced downwards. To his surprise, he feels the sweat on his forehead, which doesn't happen to him very often. It seems like it's getting warmer.

'Hot, eh?' Righard asks his neighbour.

'Yes, and it seems to be getting hotter', he confirms. 'Someone should ask the organization to lower the temperature.'

Righard takes his handkerchief, wipes away the beads of sweat, and tries to concentrate on his buddy's presentation. He's quietly enumerating all the possible dangers that can arise from the fact that all devices are connected. Righard wonders what Luis will suggest to tackle this problem. We can't go back to the devices of fifteen years ago, can we? Then everyone would have to seriously forfeit everyday ease of use. Suddenly he feels something vibrate in his pocket. He hasn't had a smartphone for years now – just a smartwatch – and yet the thought flashes through his mind that it's his phone and he needs to pick it up or read a message. Crazy how that old reflex is still conditioned somewhere in his brain. But if it's not his phone, then what is it? Righard reaches into his pocket and feels a small, flat object fall into his hand. Then he remembers: it's the badge they were given at the entrance. But why is it vibrating? He takes it out of his pocket and glances at it. Where a moment ago the route they had to follow was indicated, there is now a text in large letters. Reading it, he doesn't feel hot any more. On the contrary, he gets a cold shudder.

'Get out of there and evacuate everyone, things are going to explode!'

He reads it again and wonders what this means. Just like Jan Goethals a week earlier in his self-driving car, Righard now first thinks it's a silly joke. Especially as he also likes to play jokes himself. But this one is very far-reaching. What should he do now? And who is this message from? He looks left and right, but no one else is looking at his badge. Is he the only one to receive the message? Meanwhile, the sweat is back on his forehead, but without his knowing whether it's from the heat or from reading that text. He wipes the drops away with his handkerchief and notices he's not the only one. Everyone seems to be bothered by the clearly elevated temperature in the room. Sweaters and cardigans are taken off, and some men and women even leave the hall, perhaps to get some fresh air. If this goes on, very soon poor Luis will have no more audience, they'll all have walked out.

Righard gets up and heads to the side of the room, hoping to find there someone from the organization who can help him. He passes the stage, where his friend is still talking, and he sees that he's sweating himself. What Righard can't see, however, is that Luis has been trying to ignore the vibration in his pocket for five minutes.

RSA Virus Bulletin Conference, Brussels, 2:21 pm

The warm air descending from the ceiling has become almost tangible and Righard can feel it entering his nostrils. Just before he arrives at a small information desk with a grey man in his fifties behind it, Eddy comes running up to him. Righard immediately notices something is wrong.

'Did you get that message too?' Eddy asks breathlessly. 'Yes, you too?'

Eddy nods. 'Righard, we need to get everyone out. I don't think this is a joke.'

'Are you serious? But why don't the others get that message?'

Eddy shrugs his shoulders. 'I don't know, but suppose this is true and we do nothing? And then the murder of our colleague, I don't think this is a coincidence.'

Righard thinks for a moment, but isn't completely convinced. 'Why would someone detonate a bomb here?'

Eddy casts a sidelong glance at Luis, who is still busily talking on-stage.

Meanwhile, the man at the counter addresses Righard. 'Hello sir, is there something wrong?'

'Hello, my dear man,' Righard greets him. 'A little question: is there something wrong with the heating? It's become very warm in the hall.' 'Yes, I've noticed it too,' the man replies kindly, with some beads of sweat on his forehead as proof.

'Could you ask for the heating to be turned down a little, please?' 'Let's measure the temperature first', the man says and he asks his watch to do so.

Because he takes so long, Righard himself looks at the result appearing on the screen: 32°C. 'Thirty-two degrees, that's not normal!'

The grey man looks crestfallen. 'I'm calling someone,' he says firmly, moving a few steps from Righard. After a few seconds, Righard hears him speak softly to someone through his smartwatch. Righard pretends not to listen and moves a little closer with his back to the counter. The fragments of the conversation he hears do not immediately reassure him.

'What? That's impossible...? Turn them off... Why can't they...? And now...?'

Righard doesn't hide his handkerchief any more. It's not warm any more, it's just hot. Eddy too is sweating profusely. The fifty-year-old has meanwhile ended the call and comes back to join them. 'Sir, my colleague is going to adjust the temperature', he says with a poker face.

Righard thanks him and walks away. This doesn't match what I heard him say, he thinks, there might be something really wrong after all. In the hall more and more people are leaving their seats and moving to the exit. Others, like Righard, go and complain to the organizers. Righard hesitates and returns Eddy's look, who is waiting for an answer. Is it up to them to evacuate everyone? The problem may be resolved within a minute.

And then the badge in his pocket vibrates a second time. Righard suspects it's a repeat of the message he's just received, but decides to take a look anyway, as does Eddy, who also reaches for his pocket. Their hearts skip a beat when they see another text on the badge display.

Now Righard doesn't hesitate any more. As well as his old bones will allow, Righard sprints, with Eddy in tow, to the podium where Luis is speaking. In his left hand is a tiny tissue with which he tries to wipe away his sweat. With his long legs, Righard flies up the stairs to the podium and runs towards Luis, who looks at him in bewilderment.

Righard rips the microphone off the discreet T-shirt he's lent his friend, holds it close to his mouth and addresses the audience.

'Attention please!' he shouts as loudly as possible.

Owing to the low-hanging lighting, it may be even warmer on stage than in the hall; he can feel the beads of sweat sliding down his temples.

'There's a problem with the heating, we have to evacuate!' he shouts as loud as he can.

From the hall he's treated to surprised looks. They probably think like he did a few minutes ago that the problem will be solved soon. Just as he wants to repeat the same message again, the microphone is roughly snatched from him. It's the female moderator who addresses the audience, or at least what's left of it, directly.

'Ladies and gentlemen, we apologize for the misunderstanding. There is no need to evacuate, I repeat, no evacuation. Our technicians are working on the situation and within minutes the temperature will be back to normal.'

Righard does not understand why the woman dares to broadcast such a message. She may not even be aware of what is going on behind the scenes.

He places a trembling hand on Luis' shoulder, who looks at him in surprise. 'Luis, look at the badge you got, it should have a message on it. Where's your badge?'

Luis takes the badge from his back pocket in surprise and they look at it together. There are two messages neatly lined up on the screen. But it's the bottom text that worries them both the most.

'Malware in the heating system!'

In the meantime Eddy has walked up to the young woman, who is still trying to calm the audience. Seeing him approaching, she stretches out her arm to him and moves her index finger from side to side, thus giving him the message that she'll not let him take the microphone off her. When Eddy continues to approach, he notices that she switches off the microphone for a moment and that she asks her watch to send the security service to the podium.

Eddy is now standing right in front of her and shows her his badge, which also has the two messages on it. 'This is no joke, madam,' he says as calmly as possible. 'Malware has invaded your network and the heating is currently controlled by the people behind that malware. I repeat, this is no joke.'

Righard and Luis join their colleague and Righard addresses the frowning lady in a cracking voice.

'That's right, madam. You now have the choice. Either you ask everyone to evacuate calmly, or the heating system will explode and you may have many deaths on your conscience.'

The young woman, unobtrusively dressed in a white blouse and a long black skirt, looks at them in surprise. 'Malware?'

Luis sighs and realizes they don't have time to explain to the lady what malware is. But luckily that's not necessary.

'But... our network is very well secured, how is that possible?'

Eddy wants to snatch the microphone from her hands, but suddenly the woman steps away from them. All three run towards her to take the microphone, but stop abruptly when they hear what she is saying to the audience. 'Ladies and gentlemen, for your comfort, we recommend that you leave the room immediately while we repair the heating. So please go outside right now and we'll make sure the conference can start again as soon as possible. We apologize in advance for this.'

Then the three men see her also inform the staff through her watch.

'Message to all Dome staff. Owing to the problem with the heating, everyone must go outside, I repeat, everyone, public and staff. Hall assistants, please evacuate the visitors now.'

Eddy, Righard and Luis look at each other with relief and hurriedly leave the stage. Because of the action and the tension, they have stopped paying attention to the ubiquitous heat. As they descend the stairs, they feel their clothes are soaking wet, as though they had taken a bath with their clothes on.

Meanwhile, the moderator's message does not miss its effect. All visitors have obediently left their seats and are on their way to one of the exits. The old friends also make their way through the empty tables and chairs and rush to the main exit.

They're almost outside when Eddy notices something out of the corner of his eye. Once Luis and Righard are outside, Eddy retraces his steps. He stares open-mouthed at the video screens, which now all show the exact same image. It's a logo of a company he doesn't know. It consists of a strange combination of lines and colours. In the middle of the logo is a word, which must be the name of the company. Maybe a sponsor of the conference? The word seems to be formed with a font he has never seen before, it looks a bit like Chinese.

Just as he squeezes his eyes half shut to read the word, there's a huge bang and he's thrown back by the airflow from the blast. He lands hard on his back and briefly loses consciousness. As a result, he will not remember the deafening noise of the next two, more violent explosions.

Ten kilometres south of Mechelen, two hours later

Anthony Dice is behind the wheel of a unobtrusive silver car. It's a cheap Japanese model, not a self-propelled type, which is very exceptional. It's not the type you would expect to be driven by someone with the position of NATO chief of security. But that's precisely the intention. Dice has left his top-of-the-range self-driving electric Jaguar, with which he carries out his service journeys, in his garage at home. He uses this ugly car only to drive from Evere to Zemst, a rural municipality between Brussels and Mechelen. He calmly follows the traffic at the highest speed allowed, because he doesn't want to get a ticket. Only a few people know he sometimes takes this route, and they have had to sign a very strict confidentiality agreement. They know that if they violate it, they will go straight to jail. Dice is outraged by the attack on the antivirus conference just now. According to the first reports, ten people have been killed. Who's behind it? Why are innocent scientists and experts being attacked? For him that's terrible.

He turns on his turn indicator and leaves the road he has followed for kilometres. Slowly he drives into a dirt road, lined by tall trees. At the entrance of the road there is a sign on which the fishing association 'De Karpervrienden' welcomes everyone. However, Dice has never held a fishing rod in his life and doesn't intend to.

His tyres squeak as he drives over the gravel. That thick layer is not there by chance, there is no way after all you can get over it silently. It comes on top of the surveillance cameras concealed here and there.

Dice drives all the way to the back and then parks the car behind a dark green hedge, so that it's totally invisible from the road. He gets out and looks around. It is always quiet here, except for the noise of the cars on the road. When NATO went looking for a new location for one of its secret bases, it turned out that the house he's now standing in front of met all the requirements. Located in the countryside, no direct neighbours, a large plot. The house dates from the 1990s, but is still in good condition. The wooden windows are perfectly maintained, thanks to the older couple that are allowed to live here for free in exchange for their maintenance work and their discretion. As he steps to the house, he thinks of his own home. He has finally been able to buy what he has dreamed of for years: a modern white villa, equipped with all the technological gadgets on the market today. He has lived there for a year now, still enjoying the luxurious interior and all the amenities every day. The house is, of course, also highly secured. No one who knows him would ever doubt that.

He's obsessed with all things involving security, and that in all areas. It's been that way since he was in school.

When he stands in front of the iris scanner next to the front door, he smiles. The school benches. It's there he met his ex, she was the prettiest girl in the class at the time. And she wanted to date him, Anthony Dice, the little fat kid. He couldn't believe it, thought she was doing it to tease him. But it wasn't. Years later, she told him she already saw great potential in him then. And that she didn't care that she was taller than him. His smile fades when he thinks of the others at school, who often teased him for being rather short.

Frowning, he puts his index finger on the sensor in the front door handle. His fingerprint is recognized and the door clicks open. Where are they now, those bullies, he thinks. Have they achieved more in life than he? Through long studies and hard work, he has become NATO's head of security. Who has done better?

Dice steps into the hallway and shakes his head. Don't think back, look ahead, always look ahead. His steps sound hollow on the stone floor in the spacious hall of the house. The wallpaper on the walls, the stair carpeting, ... time really seems to have stood still here. And that, of course, is the impression NATO wants to create. A postman or a supplier, whoever comes to ring the doorbell here, should never suspect there is more going on in this place.

Dice opens the door under the stairs, which at first glance leads to a cellar, as is generally the case in such buildings. Here, however, that door conceals the access to a small lift, also equipped with an iris scanner. Dice steps in, stands resignedly in front of the scanner and after a few seconds the lift starts moving. There is no need to indicate the floor, there is only one stop, three floors underground. Whenever he stands here, he thinks of Hollywood movies, in which such lifts also appear. Secretly he dreams of a role in such a film. Not like the hero, he doesn't qualify for that because of his small stature, he's sober-minded enough for that. But as the villain, the evildoer who has cunning plans to take control of the world.

When the lift doors open and moments later Dice is searched by a security guard, he is made aware that the reality he finds himself in is just the opposite of that dream. His job now is to rescue the world, to protect it from the evil that spreads mainly through that damned internet. It's an assignment he cannot fulfil alone, but fortunately he can count on a whole team of dedicated employees. It's that team he's come to visit now, and one man in particular: Peter Black.

NATO Headquarters, Evere, Brussels, one day later, 15 February 2034

The NATO building in Brussels was built in 2017 in the shape of two hands, each with four fingers intertwined as a symbol of unity. Its location in a suburb of Brussels, close to the main arterial roads, was a well-considered choice. In those seventeen years, more buildings have been added, reflecting NATO's increasing importance in the world.

In the reception area of the main building, Frank Willems, Eddy Willems' son, places all his electronic items into a so-called 'smart' dish under the watchful eye of a guard. After they've been scanned and found safe, he is let through and has to wait for them to come to him. He's so pleased that he's passed all those strict security checks at the entrance with a smile. This morning, he learned that he and his own communications agency, Frank Talking, will take care of all communications during the investigation into the explosions at yesterday's RSA Virus Bulletin Conference. Or rather, his job is to ensure that as little publicity as possible is given to this incident and to the ensuing investigation. He will learn within a few minutes what exactly the assignment will entail. He has donned his smartest suit for his meeting with two senior NATO officials. The fact that the conversation takes place with them means that as few people as possible are being involved in this case. A year ago, when the Bio Dynamics incident occurred, he was also in touch with Anthony Dice, NATO's head of security, and Meredith Weston, head of communications at the same organization. He will sit down with these two people again to discuss his mission.

An employee approaches and invites him to follow him. Frank, with only a wafer-thin tablet under his arm, follows the man down a long corridor. After passing two more security posts, they arrive at a large conference room. The glass of the wide window is currently dimmed and therefore opaque. There is probably still a meeting going on, he thinks. After a few minutes' waiting, the glass becomes transparent and he recognizes the two senior NATO employees with whom he worked a year ago. There is also a third person present in the room, whom he does not know. This is a slim woman with long, dark hair reaching down to her shoulders. That luscious hair and her light tawny complexion suggest that she's of southern descent.

She towers over Anthony Dice, though comparison with the tiny Dice reveals little about her true stature.

Dice gestures to Frank to come in, whereupon the employee accompanying him quickly opens the door for him. As soon as Frank is inside, he hears Dice say 'Dim!' and the glass becomes opaque once again.

'Mr Willems, welcome', Dice greets him. 'You remember Meredith Weston, I assume, and this is Lara Hartman, from EC3, the European Cybercrime Centre, part of Europol.'

Frank shakes hands with Dice and Weston, then turns to the woman, whom he estimates to be in her early thirties. 'Pleased to meet you,' he says, noting that she, like himself, has green eyes.

'Hello,' she replies with an accent he can't identify immediately.

'Let's take a seat,' Dice says, and sits down at the head of the long wooden table.

Frank runs his palm over the beautiful, smooth wood of the table and admires the attractive grain. He suspects it's burr walnut, a lovely material, but expensive. NATO has good taste, he thinks. As he sits down, it also occurs to him that this wood is used to make rifle butts. That's not so nice.

From an invisible projector Dice has meanwhile projected a large photo onto a white wall. The photo shows a general overview of the central area in the Dome, where the explosions occurred yesterday. Frank suspects the image comes from a drone, because it shows a bird's eye view. The havoc is complete. All the tables and chairs have been knocked over and scattered everywhere. The floor is covered with glass from the large video screens which have exploded.

Frank leans forward slightly to get a good look at all the details. He recently went to the ophthalmologist to buy new contact lenses, because his vision has really deteriorated lately.

His friends had already warned him about this. This evolution is inevitable from the age of 40 and he has just turned 43. The ophthalmologist had advised him to purchase the latest generation of smart lenses. They are very good and they are equipped with augmented reality, which has become a real hype. In the beginning he eagerly took advantage of it, but after a few days he already turned the function off. Everywhere he looked, information about the object in question appeared in the corner of his eye. That was a bit too much of a good thing. He sees that the photo shows many dark spots on the floor and fears these are blood spots. He has learned through the social media that 12 people are reported to have been killed, plus dozens more injured.

Dice says: 'Next', and another picture appears on the wall. This time it's a ground-level photo showing a view of one side of the conference room. It shows remnants of what must have been a reception desk. Apparently it was thrown against the wall by the air movement and flew into pieces. Frank hopes no one was behind that counter when the blast happened. He glances sideways at the Europol inspector next to him. Judging by her facial expression, she thinks the same. Meredith Weston, on the other hand, has a poker face as always. For Frank it has to be impossible to know what that harsh-hearted lady is thinking, but she certainly doesn't seem to be empathetic.

The third photo has been taken not in the conference room, but in a space that resembles an engine room. The floor is littered with pieces of metal, broken pipes and other parts that Frank can't immediately identify.

'The heating,' Dice announces, 'or at least what's left of it.' The photo remains for a few seconds and then disappears when Dice says 'Stop!'. 'The investigation is not yet complete, but the first results indicate that the explosions — there were three in quick succession — were caused by too high a temperature in the heating boilers. They appear to have gone mad, but we don't yet know why.'

Frank opens his mouth to ask something, but the Europol inspector beats him to it. 'How was the heating in that room controlled?' she asks with an unmistakably Dutch accent. Frank feels outwitted; that was the question he was going to ask.

'Fully automatically, of course,' Dice replies, 'but the organizers claim that there were personnel in the control room.' 'Is that control room intact?' Frank quickly asks. He feels the inspector's gaze on him, but continues to look at Dice. Has he now outdone her in turn?

'Yes, luckily, because it's at the end of another corridor.'

'I want to question the staff there,' Lara Hartman says in a tone that brinks no opposition.

Dice gives her a piercing look and appears unimpressed. 'You can, but first you're going to do something else.'

Now Frank takes a sideways glance at the Europol inspector and he sees her cramping. He expects her to protest, but in the end she doesn't.

'I expect a complete embargo on communication about this incident and the investigation,' Meredith Weston intervenes in her deep voice. She points to Frank. 'I want you to have a communication plan on my desk by noon. I want to know how you're going to reassure public opinion and the business world after these two incidents.'

Frank is equally surprised. Two incidents?

'The self-driving car that got hacked,' he hears Lara Hartman say.

Weston nods and looks back at Frank. 'Despite these two facts, we must create the perception in everyone that NATO is still able to perform its function as the guardian of the Internet.'

The perception? That scares Frank. Just the perception? And how are those two events linked? He thinks about it and something starts to dawn on him. 'So... those explosions were caused by outside manipulation?' he asks hesitantly.

The Europol inspector looks at him pityingly, as if it took a whole day for the penny to drop.

'Malware,' says Dice, jumping up energetically. 'I'm convening all NATO member states for an exceptional meeting to discuss this issue. And as for you, I'm counting on you to work well together and that Europol will find the responsible criminals as soon as possible. NATO will provide all necessary logistical support and we'll also make available a whole team of scientists and experts.' He comes to stand next to Lara and addresses her specifically. 'Lara, you've interviewed several people who were present at the attack, to no avail, I understand. I've just sent you the list of all the others present. There are three that you absolutely must interrogate, because apparently they were the only ones who were forewarned. They're currently located here in this building, room 3.2. You can then interrogate the control room employee. To work, everyone.'

The meeting is over for Dice and Weston also hurries out of the room. Only when Lara Hartman gets up and hurries to the exit does Frank go outside, wondering how on earth he's going to get that communication plan ready by noon.

Cyberspace

'Hey.'
'Have any news?'
'Investigation has started. Two persons, a man and a woman.'
'CIA?'
'Europol.'
'Keep a close eye on them. Something else?'

'Three old men are being interrogated. Probably witnesses of the attack.'
'Never suppose. Find out who they are.' 'Okay. And my reward?'
'First do what we agreed. All in due time. Must go now.'
'Okay.'
Hangs up.

NATO Headquarters, Evere, Brussels

Frank and the Europol inspector walk at a cracking pace through the long corridors of the NATO building. Both have their reasons for starting the investigation as soon as possible and solving the case. Frank has worked with Europol in the past and these inspectors are all the same. Driven, tough, ambitious. When they receive an order from above, they go for it one hundred percent. Lara Hartman seems to be no different in that area, although it remains to be seen. Frank himself absolutely wants to keep NATO as a client of his communications agency. You can't imagine a better reference, so he's also willing to go all out. Soon he will call his assistant to instruct him to take care of his agency's other clients. These should of course not be neglected.

Lara stops in front of a lift and steps in front of the iris scanner, under which a red light is on. The colour changes to green and the lift doors slide open silently. Frank lets her in first and then follows her into the lift when she says 'three'. The doors close and for a few seconds they stand in silence next to each other. 'Pleasant,' he thinks, 'it'll be fun working together. I need to find a way to break the ice.'

The doors open again and the inspector storms out.

Frank has no longer any intention of running after her like a lapdog and overtakes her. 'Do I point out to those eyewitnesses at the outset that this interrogation and the entire investigation are confidential?' he asks.

'Okay' is her brief answer. Without a moment's hesitation, she turns into another corridor and knocks on a door above which hangs a display that reads '3.2'.

They enter and find themselves in an old-fashioned interrogation room just like these must have looked in the 1980s. Bare walls and soberly furnished with just a metal table and four chairs. Three chairs stand on one side of the table, and sitting in them are what are at first sight three absolutely normal older men. In one corner of the room is a NATO staff member who was asked to stay with them. Lara shows her ID and gestures for him to leave the room. After he's closed the door behind him, Lara immediately sits down in the only remaining chair. Frank must therefore remain standing. But that doesn't worry him. Without ceremony he goes to the three men and shakes their hands. His father had called him as soon as he could yesterday and reassured him that he was unharmed, as were his two friends. He had also told him that they would be called as eyewitnesses, but Lara doesn't know that, of course. The Europol inspector looks at him quizzically and he introduces everyone to her. 'This is Eddy Willems, my father, and these are Righard and Luis, his colleagues. They helped NATO out of trouble last year with that ransomware affair, remember?'

Lara nods cautiously, and judging by her face, she's made the connection.

Frank addresses his father's two colleagues. 'So you're both unharmed?'

'Yes, fortunately,' Luis replies. 'But your father took a nice tumble. And I still hear a whistling in my ears.'

'They must have been quite some explosions; I've seen the pictures and...'

'Should I get you some coffee?' Lara Hartman interrupts them.

'Oh yes, I'd like a cappuccino, with…' Frank doesn't finish his sentence when he sees the Europol inspector's angry face. He realizes she wasn't really going to get coffee.

'Sorry to interrupt your social gathering,' she says coolly, 'but I have an investigation to conduct.' She activates the recording function of her watch and points at Luis. 'We'll start with you. Tell me everything from the beginning.'

Luis obediently begins to tell what happened from the moment he was in the car with Righard and Eddy. He describes the crowds at the entrance as they approached. How impressed all three of them were with the stunning new conference hall. He recounts their conversation with their colleague in the speakers' area. And then how he had started his presentation, in an ever-warmer room. And then his surprise when Righard and Eddy came running onto to the stage and told him about the messages on the badge.

'After that it all went so fast,' Luis tells her. 'Once the moderator was convinced, we walked to the exit together with a lot of people.' He bows his head and continues. 'Maybe we could have saved more lives if we had urged everyone to hurry.'

Righard gives him a squeeze on the shoulder. 'Then there might have been panic and maybe even more people would have died.'

Luis seems unconvinced and ends his story. 'When we were outside, Eddy stayed behind for a while. I had just turned to see where he was when—' Luis's voice falters as he thinks back to the moment when the sky seemed to fall on him. 'I don't know which came first, the loud noise or the air displacement. But the explosion was huge, I've never heard such a noise. My ears seemed to explode. At the same time, I felt a hard push in my back, causing me to fall forward, just like the colleagues walking next to me. And we were already outside by then, I can't imagine what it must have been like inside the hall.'

He shakes his head and continues.

'I scrambled to my feet with that whistling in both ears and my first thought was that Eddy was still inside. So I walked back to the entrance, and my heart skipped a beat when I saw him lying there.'
He looks at Eddy and he returns his look with a faint smile.
'He was lying face down on his stomach, at first glance I didn't see any injuries. Righard and I squatted next to him and I think we shook him quite vigorously to see if he was still alive.'
'That's right,' Eddy responds. 'You even slapped me in the face.'
Luis blushes and nods. 'I needed to know if you were still alive. You lay there so still.'
'Couldn't you just ask me if I was awake and unharmed?' Eddy jokes.
'I don't think I'd have heard you. But when I felt a pulse, I figuratively jumped high into the air. Unfortunately enough, my joy was short-lived. Suddenly there was the sound of another explosion, immediately followed by another. Maybe they were even louder than the first. But that was difficult to judge because I couldn't hear well at that moment.'
Luis gets up from his chair and paces the interrogation room with his head in his hands.
'My attention was completely focused on my old friend here,' he points to Eddy, 'but when we dragged him a few yards away from the exit of the hall, my eyes opened too.'
Dismayed, he tries to describe the chaos and panic that prevailed at the exit of the Dome.
'The vast majority of people only looked out for themselves. Man or woman, young or old, they all took flight without looking back. Only a few bent over the injured persons lying on the ground. I was surprised to see colleagues still stumbling out of the room. I don't understand how they survived those blasts in there. Some were in a very bad way. I suppose most were in shock, following those in front of them like sheep in a flock.'
'If I'd have been fully conscious, I would certainly have helped,' Eddy says, head bowed.

'I know, mate, I know. I then did my best to help others until the emergency services arrived. Terrible what happened.'

'Thank you, Mr Corrons,' the Europol inspector says. 'Mr Zwienenberg, can you give your version, please?'

'Is that really necessary?' Righard protests. 'Up to the explosions, my story's identical to Luis's.'

'It's important we hear it from your point of view as well. I hope you understand. You weren't with your friend all the time: for example, during his presentation that wasn't the case.'

Righard has to agree with her and sighs. 'Okay then.'

After he's told everything, Lara Hartman fires one question after another at them. 'Did you see any suspicious persons on the road or in the parking lot? People who didn't belong there at first sight?'

The three men think for a moment and shake their heads.

'And in the hall itself? When you looked around and went to that separate room, was there anyone out of the ordinary?'

'Well, we know a lot of colleagues there, but of course we don't know everyone', Righard answers cautiously.

'And what was out of place?' Eddy adds. 'The conference dress code isn't exactly strict, so most of them were dressed casually.'

'Did any people leave before the temperature really started to rise?' was her next question.

Eddy shrugs his shoulders. 'Madam, there were about a thousand people in that room, it was a constant to and fro, just from the smokers going outside.'

Lara nods in understanding. 'What about staff? Didn't notice anyone leave the room early?' Because they did not notice this either, she continues with her interrogation. 'Did that female moderator seem suspicious to you?'

'Because she at first refused to evacuate, you mean?' Righard asks. 'No, she just didn't realize the gravity of the situation. She couldn't, she hadn't received those messages.'

Lara picks this up at once. 'Who did those messages actually come from?'

No one can answer this. 'We don't know, you couldn't see the sender on that badge.'

'Those badges aren't intended for sending messages, are they?' Eddy says. 'I didn't even know it was possible.'

'Me neither,' admits Righard. 'So I was very surprised. I couldn't believe it at first and thought it to be a colleague's joke.'

'Do you have any idea who the messages might have come from?'

Luis, Eddy and Righard look at each other. 'A fellow security expert,' suggests Luis. 'But then I don't understand why he sent them only to us.'

'Are we the only ones who received the messages?' Righard asks.

'So far,' confirms Lara. 'I've put that question to many survivors and until now the answer has always been negative. We've not yet been able to interrogate some of the injured. All the stories we've heard match what you've been through. The gradually rising temperature in the room, the moderator calling for evacuation, and the three explosions.'

'The badges were handed to us by the organizer', Frank tells her. 'It should be able to provide more information about that.'

'I already checked that this morning,' Lara announces. 'Indeed, that type of badge has a message function built into it, but it's rarely used. I discussed this with some Dome employees. None of them knew how to send a message with it. At least that's what they claimed.'

'Can we trace the origin of that message in the history on the servers? Like you can trace the IP address for an email?' Eddy wonders.

'The computer room where the servers are located has been seriously damaged by the explosions. It's not possible to investigate there. My cybersecurity colleagues are currently searching the cloud history, but that'll take some time,' Lara announces.

'It could also be the perpetrator of the attack itself,' Eddy thinks aloud. 'Maybe he didn't want to take victims.'

'What did he want then?' Righard counters. 'Just destroy the Dome? For what reason?'

'No, I rule that out,' Lara says. 'If that had been the case, he would have warned you earlier. There was no time to get everyone out.'

There's a moment's silence in the small interrogation room while everyone present thinks about the case.

'What could have been the motive behind this attack?' Lara asks. 'Could this have been a targeted attack against certain experts? Maybe because they were onto something?' 'Gosh, you could be right,' Luis replies. 'But most experts don't play detective. In the security industry, our job is to respond to new malware attacks as quickly as possible. The method is always the same. Everyone sets to work immediately, analyses are made and shared, so that a patch or an update is developed very quickly that can neutralize the threats.'

'It's of course a fact that the security industry helps NATO to keep the internet malware-free. If you look at it that way, this could well be an act of revenge', Eddy thinks. 'Then this could be the first in a series', Frank says. 'Because this is surely not the only conference of its kind?'

'No, that's right, but it's a very well-known one, and one that's been running continuously for over forty years.'

'So this could be a warning to anyone working in the cybercrime world along the lines of 'Don't work against us or else...', Lara concludes.

'If that's true, it's the first time physical violence has been used against us. Until now, the battle has always been fought on the internet. In any case, we must not let ourselves be deterred by it', Righard says defiantly.

Lara nods, thinks for a moment, then returns to an earlier topic. 'You'll understand we find it strange that you're the only ones to have received the messages.'

Luis and Eddy look at her in shock and Righard straightens up to his full height. 'Do you mean we're under suspicion?' he exclaims indignantly.

'Hey, Righard, no, that's not what Lara means,' Frank soothes him. 'For the time being you're not under suspicion. But you can understand we need to investigate this further, right?'

Lara nods. 'We ask you not to travel for the time being and to be available at all times in case we need you,' she announces formally.

'Righard, they're right. When all's said and done, we were the only ones who knew what was going to happen,' Luis states.

'Indeed,' Lara confirms. 'I have another question for you. The second message stated that malware was used. I know what malware is, but do you know what exactly might have happened there?'

It's Righard who speaks. 'Well… we've obviously already thought about it, the three of us. And maybe all our other colleagues too. We don't know how the malware ended up in the Dome's central network, but that needs to be investigated. In any event, it took control of the central heating system. It was apparently programmed to raise the temperature and continue to raise it, knowing that this would eventually lead to an explosion.'

'For my clear understanding, did this malware do it all by itself?' Lara asks. 'I mean, it's not a type of malware that nestles into the system and allows someone, human beings that is, to take control of the heating?'

'Both types of malware do indeed exist. Further analysis should show this.'

'We can help search for that malware if you wish,' Eddy suggests.

'That won't be necessary,' Lara states coldly, 'another team is already working on that. For the time being, I know enough. Can we exchange phone numbers?' she decides.

Once that's settled, she turns her gaze to Frank. He understands what is expected of him, activates his wafer-thin tablet and opens some documents. He places the device in front of the three men and explains to them what the intention is. 'Given the potential impact of this attack on NATO's credibility, I must ask you to sign a document accepting the confidentiality of this conversation. This means that nothing of this conversation and of any subsequent conversation may be shared with third parties. Not with your family, friends, your own wives and certainly not with the press. Violation of this agreement is punishable by no less than several years in prison. Do you understand that?'

Everyone seems to understand this, for which Frank is grateful.

'Are all three of you signing?' he asks.

Righard puts his hand on the tablet first and holds it still until a soft beep is heard. That's the sign that his unique human characteristics have been recognized by the software. Then it's Luis and Eddy's turns, which also goes without a hitch. Lara gets up, thanks them and steps outside. Frank takes back his tablet and hastily shakes the three experts' hands.

'Thank you, guys, we'll see each other soon.'

As he also rushes out, he resolves to find a way as soon as possible so as not to have to run behind the police inspector like a lap dog.

On the way to the Dome, Brussels

Lara and Frank are sitting silently in Lara's self-driving car, on the way from Evere to the Dome in Brussels, where they question the staff. Lara has her wireless earphones in and is listening to the recording of the conversation of just now. Frank is putting the finishing touches to his communication plan on the tablet, which he has on his lap. Once he's done and has sent it to Weston, he puts the tablet away. He looks at the Europol officer next to him and wonders what kind of person he's dealing with. He will not be able to deduce that from their sparkling conversations, because they have only exchanged a few words with each other. So far, he finds her somewhat hypothermic and very focused on her task. He'd like to make more contact with her. Isn't that more than normal if they're to conduct an investigation together and therefore spend a lot of time with each other? Could she be in a relationship? He doesn't see a wedding ring on her finger, so she's probably not married. What could he talk about to unfreeze her? Europol is known to keep outsiders at a distance as much as possible to avoid any leaks in their investigations. He must therefore make it clear to her that she can trust him.

Suddenly Lara turns her head and looks him straight in the eye. 'What is it?' she asks with a frown. 'You've been looking at me the whole time.'

Frank feels caught and blushes. 'No, nothing, I just thought... we haven't talked much yet.'

The frown on her even forehead does not disappear and she continues to look him straight in the eye. Frank gets hot. Without taking her eyes off him, she removes her ears and lays them on her lap. 'What do you want to talk about?' she asks in a very neutral tone.

'Just what colleagues normally talk about. What we do outside of work, whom we go around with, things like that.'

'Okay, you first', she says, turning her chair towards him.

'Me? Okay, I'm forty-three, single, and have my own communications agency, but that of course you already know.' She continues to stare at him calmly, the corners of her mouth slightly raised and her arms crossed over her chest. 'And outside of work I write a lot,' he adds.

'Oh, what do you write then?'

He's glad she finally seems to be showing an interest in him. 'That ranges from blogs to books, short stories and columns. Do you write too?'

She looks at him in surprise and shakes her head. 'No, what makes you think that?'

'Um, just because you asked. Tell me, what do you do after office hours?'

'Office hours? Are you kidding now? Do you think I'm a civil servant? At Europol there's no such thing as office hours.'

'Sorry, I didn't mean it like that,' he says quickly. 'I just wanted to know if you have any hobbies.'

'Sports' is her brief answer.

He opens his mouth to ask what sports she practises, but closes it again. He no longer wants to initiate a dialogue. He turns his seat away from her and looks out through the large car side window. It becomes very quiet in the car and he doesn't like that. In the past, before the arrival of electric cars, you could still hear the sound of the engine, but that's also a thing of the past.

'You don't do sports, probably?' he hears her say.

He turns to her again, unsure how to interpret that comment. 'Why do you think that?' he replies somewhat indignantly.

'You don't look like the type to exercise a lot.'

He's momentarily flabbergasted. Type? What type does she mean now? He decides to temper the subject with humour. 'You're mistaken, I do a lot of sports. Even more so recently, since here at NATO I keep running after you down those long corridors.'

She stares at him for a moment and then bursts out laughing. Just for a moment, because after a few seconds her face regains its composure, the corners of her mouth drop again and she is all serious. 'You'd better learn to walk faster so you can stay ahead of me,' she says calmly. 'But then you also have to know where we're going, don't you?'

He has no response to that. With that one sentence she made it clear to him that she is in charge of this investigation and that he may well try to take the lead, but that in her view he lacks the necessary information and competences. He doesn't know what to say to that, and he's glad the Butler warns them that they'll be at their destination, the Dome, in five minutes.

Lara points to the Butler's hologram. 'You do know this is the system that was hacked in the car of that security expert Jan Goethals?'

That's right. I've heard no one had ever managed to do that before. Should I be worried now?' he asks.

At that point, the car slows down.

'If it can be done once, it can also be done twice', are her not exactly hopeful words.

As the car drives into the Dome's parking lot, he wonders whether it wouldn't be better to choose a different mode of transport from now on. When the car stops, he gets out and decides to make another attempt to defrost her. Deliberately, he sets a fast pace to get ahead of her on the way to the main entrance of the Dome. He hears her footsteps behind him and rushes to be the first to enter the building. To his surprise, he hears her laughing.

'Well, apparently you've made a decision. I told you, if you want to take charge, you'll have to do something for it. So you take the lead.'

Frank stops and turns around. 'Are you serious? May I conduct the interrogation? No problem.'

Deep inside, he feels much less confident about what he wants to do. He's not a policeman, and he's never interviewed anyone before. But now he must continue.

They arrive at the typical blue and white police tapes sectioning off the entrance to the conference hall. An officer who just before was casually leaning against the wall now comes to meet them. 'Are you from the press? You can't come in today, come back tomorrow', he says in an imperious tone.

Lara pulls out an ID and hands it to the officer. 'Lara Hartman and Frank Willems, from the European Cybercrime Centre. We're leading the investigation into what happened here.'

The policeman, possibly close to retirement, takes the document, digs out a pair of horn-rimmed glasses from the top pocket of his uniform, and studies the document carefully. 'Hm, Cybercrime, hey. What do you have to do with the explosions that happened here?' he says suspiciously.

Lara doesn't answer and looks at Frank, who sees through her. He wanted so badly to be in charge, so now he also has to make sure they get past that police officer.

Frank deliberately looks left and right for a moment and then moves closer to the officer. 'Don't tell anyone about this,' he whispers into the older officer's hairy ear. 'But the attack was allegedly carried out on behalf of some notorious gambling companies. The Dome also successfully organizes gambling games via the internet and because they are a thorn in the side of those other companies, these would have taken revenge.' He puts a hand on the officer's shoulder, who stares at him wide-eyed. 'You don't know this from us, officer, is that clear?'

The policeman is impressed and nods. He hands the ID back to Lara and hurries to hold up the blue and white ribbons so they can pass underneath.

Frank feels his heart pounding in his chest and does his best not to show it when Lara quietly asks him what he said. 'Oh, I promised him you'll have a coffee with him after the interrogation, that's all.'

Lara stops abruptly and looks straight at him. Seeing her expression, somewhere between disbelief and anger, he bursts out laughing.

'Joke', she says angrily and gives him a slap on the back.

Their laughter quickly fades as they enter the main hall. They have already seen pictures of it at NATO, but in reality, it's all much worse. The explosions must have had tremendous force, everything has been destroyed. With the forensic investigation only just completed, it has not yet been cleaned up. Everything is exactly as it was just after the explosions. Frank has to swallow especially because of the dark red spots on the floor that he now sees in real life. 'That's blood from people who were in the wrong place at the wrong time. Who had come here for professional reasons, to learn, to network. Who more than likely had someone at home waiting for them and to whom they never returned. Horrible isn't it, who is behind this attack?'

Lara is standing next to him and from the corner of his eye he notices that she is also affected by what she sees. It's very quiet in the room, except for the two of them there is no one there. There is a strong smell of smoke and it tickles his nostrils.

To the left of the large hall is the sound of footsteps. A lady with Asian features approaches them. She passes a giant video screen that has crashed down, and steps over the remains of a piece of ripped-apart furniture. 'Good afternoon, are you coming to question our people?' she asks.

'That's right,' Lara replies, introducing them both. Just as before, she keeps silent about the fact that Frank is only involved in the investigation as an external employee.

'Welcome I'm Laura Ming, Administrative Service Supervisor. Follow me.'

Lara and Frank follow her through the hall, and the smell of smoke grows even more insistent. They see puddles of water in several places, perhaps from the fire extinguishers. The slim-looking lady with the pitch-black hair leads them down a corridor where the only damage is the entrance door, lying on the ground several metres away. The explosions apparently didn't extend beyond the entrance to these offices, because further down the hallway it's as if nothing happened.

They arrive in a spacious open-plan office at the other end of the building. Large windows that let in a lot of daylight, a bunch of exotic plants and a table football game provide a pleasant working environment here. A group of people is talking at one of the modern ergonomic desks. All eyes are on Lara and Frank, who are approaching.

'Colleagues,' Ming says, 'these are the police officers from the European Cybercrime Centre. They've come to ask us some questions about what happened.'

Frank sees a mixture of anxiety and sadness on the faces of most of those present. One of the women quickly wipes away her tears with a handkerchief.

'Good afternoon, everyone,' Lara starts off. 'We have indeed come to ask some questions. You don't have to worry, there's no need for that.' She points to Frank and continues: 'My colleague here will first have you sign a document in which you declare that everything discussed here is not to be made public. That's standard procedure, and we do it to keep the investigation confidential.'

She nods to Frank and he activates his tablet.

'We are going to do the conversations individually, it goes without saying that you're allowed to talk about it among yourselves.'

After the first employee electronically signs the document, Lara invites her to accompany her to a conference table at the other end of the office space. They sit down, while Frank has the others sign as well. He notices that Lara is waiting for him to start the interrogation. Could she be turning round?

When everyone has signed, he hurries over to her. He takes a seat next to Lara, who is actually looking at him expectantly. Does she want him to ask the questions? All right then. He takes a deep breath and begins with the question that always comes first in an interrogation.

Cyberspace

'Hi.'
'Yes?'
'I've an assignment for you.' 'Okay. What's it about?'
'I'm forwarding the data now.'
Connection ended

The Dome, Brussels

'Name and first name, please?' 'Sarah Lintens.'

'Your position at the Dome?' 'Administrative assistant.'

'Thank you; What were you working at when the explosions occurred?'

The woman nods and lowers her eyes. 'When I heard the explosions I didn't know what was happening. Together with our colleagues, we ducked under our desks out of sheer panic. The building shook to its foundations and the noise was deafening. After hearing three explosions in a row, the worst was yet to come.'

Big tears well up in her eyes as the memories return.

'The moans of the survivors, the cries of people needing help. It was horrible.'

'That must have been terrible indeed,' Lara agrees. 'By the way, I already told another police officer everything.' 'Yes, I understand that,' Frank says. 'But we're looking at doing the investigation from a different angle. Do you know what the European Cybercrime Centre does?'

The woman must be about fifty years old and he's not sure how far her knowledge extends.

'Criminal activity on the internet?'

'Right,' he replies, 'you've got it.'

'So... you think those explosions have something to do with the internet?'

He glances quickly at Lara, who is watching him closely, and then turns back to the employee. 'That's one of the possibilities, indeed.' He quickly asks another question to avoid discussing the investigation. 'What kind of work do you do here as an administrative assistant?'

'Normal things, handling emails that arrive at the Dome's general email address, providing support to the sales team, that stuff.'

'I understand, and...'

'Have you seen any strange emails in the inbox recently?' Lara interrupts him.

The woman, a very different type from Lara, several kilos heavier and classically dressed, gives her a perplexed look. 'Strange emails? What do you mean by that?

'Emails arriving from unknown senders, or emails with strange attachments.'

Lintens has to think about that for a moment, but then shakes her head. 'I can't remember anything like that,' she says thoughtfully. 'Sometimes commercials come in, but I immediately move them to the trash.'

'May we have a look in your mailbox and your waste basket? Not that we don't believe you, you know, but the criminals have become so shrewd that normal people sometimes don't realize they're being tricked.'

'You'll need to ask my supervisor,' she says firmly. 'I don't decide on that.'

Frank sees his chance to ask the question he wanted to ask just then. 'Is your antivirus always up to date, madam?'

Before the woman can answer, Lara gets up and says this matter will be taken up further with the Dome's computer department. She asks her to send another colleague to them. As the woman returns to her desk, Frank sees Lara looking at him with her hands on her hips.

'Antivirus? Serious?' she says scornfully.

Frank has now realized this was the wrong question. After all, it's never the employees themselves whose job it is to update the antivirus protection, the IT department does that for them.

'Yes, beginner's mistake,' he confesses.

She smiles and he finds himself wanting to make a lot more beginner mistakes just to see that radiant smile.

Two hours later they have questioned all colleagues present. No can remember anything strange in any of the mailboxes.

'What now?' asks Frank, drinking lousy coffee from a cardboard cup.

Lara sighs. 'Now we're going to have to check all those mailboxes ourselves. After that, we still have to interview the employees from the IT department.'

They both sit a little downcast at the conference table. Neither of them wants to dive into those mailboxes and look for something that might not be there or that you can't recognize. Just as they want to get up, the first person they questioned, Sarah Lintens, comes their way. Their hopes rise. That could mean she remembers something after all. They invite the woman to sit down and look at her expectantly.

'I've been thinking a bit,' she says uncertainly. 'I've remembered an email from one of our suppliers. It came with an attachment, and when I opened it, it turned out to be empty. I didn't stop to think about it then. I thought it was a mistake and the supplier would send a second email.'

Lara's face lights up when she hears that. 'Do you still have that email?' she asks eagerly.

'Yes, I dragged it into that supplier's folder.' Lara jumps up and Lintens looks at her, startled.

'It may not be what you're looking for,' she says hesitantly.

'Oh yes, I think so, madam. Come on, show me that e-mail, please.'

Lara is already on her way to Laura Ming to ask her permission to examine Lintens' mailbox. Frank goes with the woman to her desk and a minute later Lara joins them, along with supervisor Ming.

Lintens sits down on her all-way adjustable desk chair, looks straight into the camera on her screen, and says one word: 'Mailbox.' A list of mailboxes immediately appears on her screen. 'Let's see,' she says out loud, 'I think it's this one.' She pushes the second one in the row with her finger.

Lara and Frank, standing behind her, look on with hope. The mailbox opens and a large number of e-mails becomes visible. Then the woman presses the 'filter' button and pronounces the name of the supplier. 'Ranson.' In a millisecond, the messages are separated from each other and only the e-mails from this trader can be seen. The clerk finally presses the trash button, looks back at Lara and points to one of the last emails she received from that supplier. The sender's email address is info@ranson.com.

'Can you open the e-mail please, just the e-mail, not the attachment,' Lara asks her.

With a slightly trembling finger, Lintens pushes the e-mail with the subject 'order confirmation'. The e-mail opens and a large white sheet is displayed. There's no greeting, content, or signature. At the top it only says, just like in the subject, 'order confirmation'. At the bottom is the attachment and it also bears the same name. Lara bends over and presses with her fingertip the e-mail address where the e-mail came from. A more detailed description appears on the screen, but the sender's address remains unchanged.

'That's strange,' Lara says to no one in particular.

'What's strange?' Frank asks.

'You usually find a different email address here, but that's not the case here.'

'Does this mean the email really came from the merchant?'

Lara doesn't answer his question, but turns to the employee. 'Do you know that trader well? And the people who work there?'

'We haven't been working together for long, but I'm always in contact with the same man. I don't know him personally,' she hastens to add, as if afraid of being accused of complicity.

'Can you give us that man's name?'

Lintens looks up at her supervisor and she nods. 'Hugo Vandaele.'

Lara dictates that name to her watch so as not to forget it, then asks for the email, along with the attachment, to be sent to her. She spells her email address and Sarah Lintens types it in on the virtual keyboard. When she's done with that, she forwards the email to her.

'Isn't that dangerous?' Laura Ming asks.

'No, as long as the attachment isn't opened, no damage can be done. If there's already a virus in that email, it's always in the attachment.'

'But what's the connection with the disaster that took place here?' Ming asks, frowning.

'Maybe there isn't one,' Lara replies, 'but we need to search all possible avenues.'

'Did I do something wrong?' Lintens asks.

Lara stands in front of her and reassures her. 'Like I said, this may not mean anything at all. And if it had anything to do with it, why would you have done something wrong? You simply opened an e-mail from a company known to you. It's not like you opened an attachment from an unknown sender. That would have been very unwise.'

Lintens is grateful to Lara for that explanation, as is clearly visible on her face.

'So… that email could be from someone else? And we view our supplier as the sender?' the supervisor asks.

Lara can only confirm that. 'That's called spoofing, a well-known technique for misleading people. We're done here, if you think of anything else, be sure to let us know, please.' She hands the supervisor her visiting card and then asks for directions to the IT department.

Frank in turn thanks the two ladies for their cooperation and leaves the office space with Lara. As they walk down the corridor, Lara calls a man named Tim and Frank overhears her asking him to drop everything he's doing right now. She orders him to examine the attachment of the e-mail, which she will now forward directly to him. When her conversation has ended and the e-mail has been forwarded, Frank asks her if they are really on to something.

Lara shrugs her shoulders, not quite convinced yet. 'So far we're not sure whether there's a connection between that email and the attack. It could also simply be a mistake on the part of the supplier. The first thing to do now is to analyse the attachment. It depends on what was hidden in there.'

'What do you mean?'

'There are many different types of viruses and malware.'

As they walk into another corridor, Frank thinks about what to do next. 'After analysing that virus or malware, can we find out who's behind it?'

'Well, dear partner, let's hope so.'

Frank opens the door to the computer department and lets Lara lead the way. Did she just call him 'partner'? With a big smile he follows her inside, for once he doesn't care about coming in second place.

The Dome, Brussels, computer department

The Dome's computer department is located at the very back of the building. It's as if the management wanted to hide it, completely out of sight of guests. Stepping in, Lara and Frank find themselves in a completely different world compared to the offices a moment ago. A less pleasant working environment, because there is no direct daylight here due to the lack of windows, which means the lighting has to remain on all the time. It's also clear that the clean desk policy doesn't apply here. Cables lie on the tables like coiled snakes, computer screens are stacked on top of each other at an angle and disassembled computers display their innards on a long table.

Four people are working and Frank wonders whom to turn to. Lara steps resolutely to the one nearest to her, a broad-shouldered man with a sprawling bald patch on the back of his head who is sitting with his back to them.

'Hi, are you the supervisor here?' she asks, tapping him on the shoulder.

Startled, the man jumps up, causing his chair to fall over with a lot of noise. 'Hey!' he exclaims, startled. When he sees Lara standing there, he seems reassured. 'You scared me,' he says loudly. 'I didn't hear you come in.'

Only then do Lara and Frank see that he has two earphones, which he quickly removes. He puts them away, straightens his chair and looks at them questioningly.

'We're from the European Cybercrime Centre', says Frank. 'We're here because of the attack, I mean yesterday's explosions.' He notices that Lara is giving him an angry look because of that slip of the tongue.

The stout man looks at Frank with half-closed eyes. 'Attack, hm, that's what we thought.'

'Why?' Lara immediately asks.

'Common sense, Mrs ...?'

'Hartman, and this is Frank Willems.'

'Please to know you, I'm Ludo Aerts, head of the computer department at the Dome. You know, the heating system we have here, or should I say the one we had, was top of the range. Fully automatic, economical, sustainable, you name it, only benefits. And then one day it suddenly explodes? No, that there's something else behind it, that we already knew here.'

Frank looks around the computer room, where it's several degrees cooler than in the other rooms they have visited. The three other employees have halted their activities and are following the conversation. Frank realizes he must ensure the confidentiality of the investigation and approaches them with his tablet.

'We also thought at first that there was a problem with the temperature regulation, that the mechanism had run amok. But in fact that's not possible, because that system contained double security.'

'What do you mean by that?' Lara asks.

'Firstly, the temperature could never rise above thirty degrees Celsius. In theory, because that was reached and even exceeded. Normally, a system shutdown should have occurred when that maximum temperature was reached. Which didn't happen.'

'And secondly?'

'The extra security was of a different type. If the temperature were to rise continuously and too quickly, the idea was for a built-in fuse to shut down the installation.'

'But neither of those protections worked?'

The man shakes his head. 'No, unfortunately not. And that's why all those people died here', he says with a sad face. He points to a desk with an empty chair. 'One of our team, Rudy Mommens, was in the large office space at the time helping other colleagues. He never returned. Dreadful.'

Frank joins Lara after having the three computer specialists sign and their manager likewise.

'If the installation didn't explode due to a technical problem, what do you think could have caused that?' Lara wants to know.

'Sabotage' is the brief answer she receives. 'It can only have been sabotage.'

'You mean someone let the temperature rise on purpose? That means that person must have disabled the protections?'

'Yes indeed. Even more than that. There was also a manual control built in, for emergencies. When it started to get too hot in the hall, we didn't feel it here yet. This is because the temperature is always kept lower in computer rooms, and in our case, this is done by a separate air conditioner. That's why nothing happened here.' He points to one of the men who are still listening intently. 'At the time of the temperature rise, Benno was called by an employee in the room where the conference was taking place. Benno, tell me what you did then.'

The man in question, of a nondescript type, with straight dark hair and dark clothes, gets up and comes forward. 'It was Marcel who phoned me. He said the conference guests were coming to him complaining that the room was getting too hot. He himself thought so too. I then called up the heating system data on my computer and I was shocked when I saw the figures. In ten minutes the temperature had risen by twelve degrees.'

'So it was already more than thirty degrees in the room, if I understand correctly?' Lara asks, horrified.

The man nods. 'Yes, from twenty to thirty-two degrees. Unbelievably fast. But as Ludo said, it was a very high-performance installation.'

'Go on,' his boss urges him.

'Ludo wasn't here at the time of the call, and I couldn't reach him, so I had to do something. I then told Marcel that I'd put things right and that he'd soon feel it getting fresher. We hung up and I then did what I had to do by the book, which was to suspend the automatic control program and go into manual control. To my great surprise, that didn't work.'

Lara and Frank see the disbelief on the man's face.

'I tried three times, but couldn't access the functions that were needed. Switching off the installation completely did not work either. It seemed like someone else had taken control.'

'Were you still logged in with your personal details?' Lara asks.

'Yes, but there was nothing more I could do. I think someone with more authority could have taken over the installation.'

'Just to be clear,' Aerts adds, 'I'm the only one with greater authority. And I was neither present nor logged in. That can be easily checked in the log files.'

'Then what did you do?' Frank asks Benno with curiosity. 'I knew there were two automatic safeguards built in, as Ludo's just explained. But in the temperature rise graphs, I immediately saw that neither was working. Then I really panicked. I can still see that arrow on the chart going up and up. I knew I had to do something to avoid a catastrophe.'

There is silence in the computer room as he continues to tell his story, shoulders drooping.

'I warned my colleagues here and I stormed to the room where the cables and connections of all the installations converge. There I searched like crazy for the power cables of the heating system and when I found them, I immediately unplugged them. The power was cut and I hoped that would solve the problem. I came back here, straight to my desk, to see if the temperature had started to drop yet.'

He pauses and swallows the memory.

'I was very happy to see the graph go down, not super-fast, but still steady. Until the arrow shot up again! I literally fell out of my chair when I saw that. My colleagues were standing by and they didn't understand how that could happen. Until one of us remembered. We'd all lost sight of the fact that the heating system was connected to a large battery. The electricity produced by our solar panels was stored in that battery.'

There's a moment's silence and then he shakes his head.

'That meant we also had to disconnect that battery, which is on the other side of the building. We all sprinted to it, but unfortunately we were too late, we only made it into the corridor.'

Aerts puts an arm around Benno's shoulders. 'You have nothing to blame yourself for Benno.' He turns to the others. 'And neither do you. You did your best, nothing more could be asked of you.'

'Thank you, sir, for your testimony,' Lara says, wishing him well.

Once the man has sat down, Lara has another important question for the IT chief.

'Have you been able to verify with which access code the control was taken over?'

The answer is both surprising and disturbing.

'Yes, it looks like the installation detonated itself. No trace of a username or password. We're faced with a mystery.'

Vilamoura, Algarve, Portugal, hole number seven

For the time being, the sun has not yet put in an appearance above the Quinta do Lago golf course, a stone's throw from Vilamoura in Portugal. This exclusive golf club was founded in 1972 and for over sixty years has attracted golf enthusiasts from all over the world. The fantastic location is its greatest asset. On the one side it borders the Ria Formosa Natural Park and on the other side the Atlantic Ocean, offering a great panorama. Green is the dominant colour, in whichever direction you look from the three beautifully landscaped courses, each with eighteen holes. Because the sun is not putting in an appearance today, the temperature is around eighteen degrees, ideal golfing weather. Lots of people are walking around all the holes. Nothing but happy faces from the tourists, for whom it's fantastic to be able to practise their favourite sport during the winter months. It's also very busy on the clubhouse terrace, even if everyone has put on a distinguished pullover and the hot drinks are very popular. With more than eight hundred hectares of grasslands and pine trees, the enclosed domain exudes tranquillity. Players can fully concentrate on their game. The chirping of birds or the sound of planes landing at Faro airport fifteen kilometres away are the only sources of distraction. Or else the self-propelled golf carts driving back and forth between the holes. They are mainly intended for less mobile players. Being electrically powered, they make a humming sound at most.

On the way to hole seven, located on a high cliff, one such golf cart is driving with two passengers in it. Hole seven is the favourite of many players because of the beautiful view it offers of the

Atlantic Ocean. The flag is not that far from the edge of the cliff, so your stroke must be perfect or you'll be in trouble. There is also a constant light breeze blowing, which needs to be taken into account when calculating the trajectory of the golf ball. Listen closely and you can even hear the waves lapping against the rocks, tens of metres below.

Meanwhile, a lively conversation ensues in the golf cart that has just left hole six.

'Shall we go straight to our hotel room afterwards?' asks André Gantois, grinning as he places a hand on the bare thigh of Laura, the woman sitting next to him.

'First golf, then we'll see,' she corrects him. Sixty years old and in his final years as a European Minister of Justice, Gantois does not give up. His index finger moves along his assistant's tanned leg, toward the hem of her elegant plaid golf skirt.

'André, didn't you hear what I said?' she says, with faked indignation. She pushes his hand away and fixes her gaze on the deep blue waters of the ocean. 'Have you told your wife yet?' she asks with her face turned away from him. She immediately feels his hand pulled away, and she has to swallow for a moment. She didn't really want to ask that question, not for the umpteenth time. Because she knows his answer by now.

'I'll tell her tomorrow. Right now I'm too busy with the problems in Europe.'

Procrastinating again and again. Sometimes she thinks he's never going to do it. That he wants to keep having it both ways. Her, the younger assistant, blond and slim, for sex. His wife, in her early sixties, brunette and sedate, good for his reputation as a politician. Sometimes Laura falls asleep crying because of the desolate situation she has been in for so long. But the next morning she wakes up in a beautiful room in a five-star hotel. When she then sits down to the extensive breakfast with her busy politician on the phone in front of her, she has forgotten her worries for a while.

The golf cart whizzes on and they're almost at hole seven. She knows that André always swears there because he keeps missing the ball, literally. Maybe she shouldn't have asked that question now, it wasn't the right time. She looks back at him and sees that he is staring straight ahead with his thick, hairy arms crossed on his voluminous stomach.

'André,' she says, placing a perfectly manicured hand on his arm, 'Sorry, I shouldn't have said that. Not now, let's talk about it later.'

Immediately his face brightens and for a moment she sees again that younger version of him she once fell in love with. That handsome, driven man, determined to climb the ranks as high as possible, and then kick all injustice out of the world. And once he had attained that coveted position as European minister, he had immediately started to do just that. In all the years she had been his mistress, she had seen him crack down on criminals and fraudsters, and gain great European fame. However, at public events, it was his wife who was allowed to attend. At first Laura didn't care. In those moments she was being pampered in an exclusive wellness centre or was out shopping with her lover's credit card. Gradually André started to specialize in the rapidly growing sector of criminal activities via the internet. She found that fascinating, it was a world she didn't know at all. She hung on his every word when he told her about it. But after yet another false promise that he would leave his wife, the gloss of her existence in the shadows had begun to dim. Even the most beautiful ring or the most elegant necklace could no longer appeal to her. And now here she was again, in that golf cart with him, while his wife was at home, knowing that he and his mistress were having a good time together.

She is torn from her musings as he presses a wet kiss to her mouth with his full lips.

'Honey, no problem. I promise you I will someday. But now I have to conquer hole number seven. Will you be my lucky charm?' he asks her in a very sweet tone.

She can't help but nod when she sees how happy he is. Who is she to take that from him?

The golf cart approaches the tee-off of the hole and they make ready to step out. To her surprise, however, the cart doesn't slow down. On the contrary, it even seems to be driving faster.

'André?' she asks uncertainly.

He seems as surprised as she is and she sees him pushing on a non-existent brake pedal. She feels the wind in her hair and hears the buzzing sound go crescendo.

'André' she repeats, grabbing his arm.

'Wait!' he replies gruffly.

She recognizes that tone and that frowning expression. She can see from this that he's under stress and in normal circumstances she knows that she should leave him alone. But this is a totally different situation. She is even more startled when the golf cart leaves the neatly raked gravel road and drives onto the lawn.

'Damn it!' he exclaims and she sees him looking around in a daze. There are two golfers at the tee-off and André starts to wave and shout at them. 'Help, I can't stop! Help!' he screams.

In all these years she has never seen him so panicked. Suddenly she realizes he's still wearing his seat belt. She herself never puts it on, she finds that exaggerated and even ridiculous, what can happen in a golf cart?

The golf cart, meanwhile, continues to drive tirelessly, bumping and colliding, only just dodging a sandbox. She tries to grab André's arm, but he immediately jerks free again. He does not look at her, his eyes are fixed on a point somewhere directly in front of them. She follows his gaze and breaks into a sweat. The golf cart is hurtling right up to the cliff next to hole number seven. 'André, we have to jump! Remove your seat belt! We have to jump!' she shouts in panic. Her brain calculates the time she has left before they drive off the cliff at lightning speed. A matter of a few tens of seconds. Next to her, the man of her life, the top politician, the lover, has gone very quiet. He seems completely stiff and when she touches him, she hastily withdraws her hand. His arm feels icy cold! Determined to get him out of his lethargy, she shakes him up and in a hoarse voice calls out his name.

'André! André! We have to jump now!' she screams.

But nothing seems to get through to him. So there's only one thing to do: free him from his seat belt, push him out of the hurtling golf cart, and then jump herself. The abyss approaches very quickly and she tries to unfasten the buckle on his seat belt. But it doesn't give an inch. She tries with all her might to open it and then André seems to wake up. They both yank his buckle like mad, but in vain. She has a hunch, grabs his belt, which is stretched taut over his big belly, and pushes against his torso with both arms to get him out. But her lover is way too heavy, and she can't budge him. He looks at her with fear but also resignation in his eyes. That look would haunt her later in her dreams. From the corner of her eye, she sees that they're only a few feet away from the cliff edge. If she wants to jump, she has to do it now. She makes one last frantic attempt to open his buckle, but it doesn't work.

'Jump,' he stammers. When she hears that, she starts to cry profusely and takes his face in her hands. 'Jump,' he says softly again, 'it's okay.' Crying, she takes one last look at the man who gave her a rich life but who was never ready to marry her. She pushes off against the dashboard and lands rolling on the soft grass. When she comes to a stop on her back, she sees the golf cart driving towards the cliff as if driven by the devil himself. A moment later, it thunders with its passenger from the high rock and is gone. She puts her hands on her ears crying so as not to hear the blow as it smashes onto the rocks tens of metres below. The last thing she sees before passing out is a hand placed on her shoulder, and she realizes that it will never be André's hand again that she feels.

NATO Headquarters, Evere, Brussels

Lara and Frank have returned to NATO and are sitting opposite each other in a small conference room. Frank is so close to her that he thinks he can smell her perfume. She sits frowning, with both elbows on the table, in a pose that reminds him of an aggrieved little schoolgirl. Would she have sat at the table like this with her parents when she was young and they had forbidden her to do something? The only thing missing is a pout.

Suddenly he realizes he's staring at her again even though she's already commented on his doing this. 'A penny for your thoughts?' he asks quickly.

Her gaze seems to go through him as she answers him. 'What's the motive? Everything starts from there.'

'Why did the attacks take place, you mean? Yes, if we knew that, the case would be almost solved.'

Her gaze changes and her eyes bore into his. 'I know you're only responsible for communication, but you could think along with me, couldn't you?'

Startled by her fierce reaction, he nods. 'Yes, of course, I'm not an inspector like you, but I do want to be a sounding board for you. Do you have any suspicions already?'

She gets up and starts walking around. 'We're dealing with two different attacks. The first was aimed at one person, the second at a large group of people.'

He listens attentively and tries not to look too much at her long legs.

'It often happens that a whole group is attacked when in reality only one person is the target.'

He has his reservations about that scenario and expresses that too. 'Then the perpetrators of the attack can never be sure that that person will be killed, can they? The chance of success is much higher if they go about it on an individual basis. Isn't that a rather amateurish approach?'

She shakes her head firmly. 'No, not necessarily. Remotely blowing up the heating system of a conference hall is not exactly amateurism.'

She says this casually, but he suddenly feels very stupid because of his comment. She's right, of course. To commit such an attack, a great deal of knowledge of hacking is required. 'We need to go through the list of everyone attending that conference and check everyone's past. Let's get going with that.'

She sits down again and asks for the list of attendees she has received earlier. Hundreds of names appear on the virtual screen on the wall. They are arranged alphabetically and a company name is always listed after each name and first name.

'They're mostly security experts,' she says more to herself than to Frank. 'But there were also company directors present, journalists, marketing people, and so on.'

He sees all that data passing before his eyes and wonders how they are to handle it. 'Doesn't NATO have software where you can enter those names and it will give the desired result?' She gives him a disdainful look and there's that cute frown again. 'What sort of result do you want? Their demographics? Their criminal records? For twenty years there's been talk of merging all databases into one large, overarching database. We're still nowhere on that front. And then I'm not talking yet of harmonization across all European member states, that's even further away.'

He feels the frustration bubbling up in her, it probably won't be the first time she's been confronted with this. 'But... suppose you did have that large database available to you. It's still like looking for a needle in a haystack, isn't it? Then you still don't know why someone on that list had to be killed, if that was the intention?'

'Not one hundred percent, no, but it could provide a lead. Moreover, we could then use our own software with artificial intelligence to look for connections between all that data.' She sighs. 'I'll now forward the list to my second-line analysts. Hopefully they can identify potential targets.'

After sending the file, she calls up the Dome's website on the big screen, specifically the announcement of the RSA Virus Bulletin Conference.

'Second scenario now. Now suppose the attack was not aimed at an individual. Then why precisely this congress?'

'I'm not well versed in this yet,' he says hesitantly, 'but isn't the motive obvious?'

She looks at him and voices his own thoughts. 'You think the attack was intended to kill as many antivirus experts as possible?'

He nods.

'I find that a bit naive. There are certainly many, many more security experts than were present at that conference. Just think of all those specialists at NATO.'

'Rather a signal then to those experts?' Frank asks, trying to think along as best he can. He likes this conversation, it's like he's actually cooperating with the investigation.

'Do you mean this attack is a warning? That all those people have to stop their work and that otherwise they take a big risk?'

At first glance, her question appears to be an ordinary request for clarification. But not for the first time she makes him doubt himself. She even called him naive just now. 'Yes, that's what I mean,' he says uncertainly. 'Maybe because they're up to something and don't want to be thwarted?'

She gets up and starts pacing up and down. 'The RSA Virus Bulletin Conference is the showpiece of the security industry. So if they wanted to give a signal, they certainly chose the right platform.' She walks through the projected image and her contours appear on the wall. She joins him and leans forward on the table. 'Since NATO has controlled the global internet, nothing has gone wrong except for the incident a year ago. Is that now past tense?'

He realizes she doesn't expect an answer from him, that she's reasoning out loud.

'That would mean more attacks to come.'

He is shocked by that conclusion. If she's right, other innocent people could die. Men and women just doing their jobs, just like Lara and himself.

'We must absolutely avoid that. Are more such conferences planned?'

She doesn't wait for an answer and requests all planned conferences via the web. A chronological overview appears neatly on the screen. Two more major events are planned for the coming month, and three smaller ones.

'Save', Lara says and the contents of the screen are saved. 'I'll suggest to Anthony in a moment to postpone those conferences for a while.'

Frank notices she says 'Anthony'. Does she know NATO's head of security so well that she calls him by his first name?

'If he decides to do that, can you handle the communication?' Frank nods, he takes that for granted.

'If our assumption is correct, we urgently need to find out what they're up to. Number of virus attacks 2034', she says, and they both turn their eyes back to the white wall of the conference room. Statistics and graphs in green colour pop up and give the requested overview. 'This many?' she says startled. 'There are more than I thought.'

Frank, however, is not shocked. When he joined NATO last year, he began to delve into all things concerning viruses and security. His father Eddy was delighted that his son was finally showing an interest in what had fascinated him for four decades.

The wall is literally full of tables, numbers and arrows that indicate a growth or a decline. Lara moves close to the projection. 'Look here, an increase of fifty-seven percent, that's huge. We're already at 900 virus attacks per minute!'

The horror on her face is clearly visible in the light of the projector.

'Attacks, as in attacks on companies?'

'Not only on companies, but also on private individuals. But what's the link between those attacks and the terror attacks?'

While they're thinking about it, Lara gets a call. Frank sees the corners of her mouth drop as she hears more.

'What's up?' he asks anxiously when the call is finished.

European Justice Minister André Gantois has died. Thundered off the cliffs in Portugal in a self-propelled golf cart. According to witnesses, the cart seemed to have run amok.' She casts a bewildered look at the wall. 'This can't be a coincidence.'

Cyberspace

'Hey.'
'Yes?'
'I have another assignment. To free someone from prison. Taking remote control for a few minutes and then a little extra.'
'It's doable, but it'll cost. Five thousand crypto, half of it in advance.'
'Money's no problem.'
'Okay. Who's to be freed?' ' 'Me.'
Connection ended.

NATO Headquarters, Evere, Brussels

'Why do you think this is also a terror attack?' Frank asks intrigued.

'Frank, you're in the communications sector, do you remember the publicity when all the European member states switched to self-driving cars?'

Of course he remembers that. His communication agency belonged to the chosen group of advertising agencies brought in to put together and implement the international campaign.

'Remember how strongly it was emphasized that self-driving cars couldn't be hacked?'

That was indeed an important element in getting the hesitant Member States over the line. All countries immediately saw the benefit of the great turnaround. But all of them were very concerned about the security of the infrastructure.

'Well, I think that despite that advanced security, a hacking has already been successful for the second time. And just like the explosions at the conference, this can also be a signal to certain people or sectors.' Lara turns away from him and says: 'Wiki André Gantois.'

The complicated tables and graphs disappear and are replaced by the extensive Wikipedia page about the deceased minister.

'It's no coincidence that it's this man. He was a staunch supporter of a comprehensive European cybercrime unit and worked closely with NATO. A worthy opponent of all cyberspace criminals.'

'That's a heavy blow in the fight against those criminals, but it's also bad for his family,' Frank comments.

'Yes, of course,' she says, somewhat briskly. 'It's a drama for them, I know that. But we need to focus now on why he was killed.'

He is surprised at the harsh tone with which she makes her point, but can only agree with her.

'There's another reason we know it's not an accident,' she continues. 'Someone was in the golf cart with him.'

'A friend or his wife?'

'No, his mistress. We need to question her and we're going to do it right now.'

She dashes out of the door and Frank looks after her in surprise. There she goes again and as he gives chase, he thinks of the deceased minister's family. Would his wife be aware that he was playing golf with his mistress in Portugal? And why was Lara so angry when he brought up the man's family?

Lara turns the corner and he runs to keep up with her. It's evident that her physical condition is better than his. Fortunately, she is held up at a guard post like so many between the various NATO departments. They are forced to pass through a narrow corridor with large metal screens on both sides. These vet everything and everyone. When they're past that, Lara briskly steps into a room without knocking. Before Frank steps in, he glances left and right into the corridor. If she leaves him here later, he'll never find his way back, that's for certain. What a labyrinth this building is. Not more than normal when you know how many people work here. Not only the delegations of the twenty-eight Member States and the liaison officers, but also the diplomatic missions of nineteen partner countries, each with its own administration.

He closes the door behind him and ends up in a room divided into ten compartments. Each compartment is sealed from the others with soundproof panels. Lara takes a seat in one of them and he hears her say: 'Europol, Portugal.' A message appears on the screen in front of her that the connection is being established. Immediately afterwards, a man comes into view.

Frank has meanwhile realized which room they are in now. This infrastructure was hastily set up during the lengthy corona crises of years ago. At that time, due to the multiple pandemics, it was impossible to have physical contact with other people owing to the high risk of contamination. All personal and professional contacts were therefore forced to take place remotely, i.e. via the internet. This type of space was designed to meet the need for one-on-one conversations with NATO colleagues or with external security agencies. Because the Internet connections in NATO staff members' homes were not deemed to be 100 percent secure, this space was very popular at the time.

Today, however, Lara and Frank are all alone here. Frank sits down next to Lara and thinks about the enormous advances that have come about in technology since 2029. That was the year in which the current internet satellites were introduced, the successors to those Elon Musk had sent into space in 2020. A large number of them have been circling high above the earth for a long time and together they provide strong, global internet connections. On the vast savannas in Africa, in the depths of the Amazon rainforest, even in Antarctica — every earthling has enjoyed access to the internet ever since. This has also caused a shock effect in Frank's field of business communication and has given him many more opportunities to do business.

'Hello João, are you okay?' he hears Lara say in English and turns his attention to the man on the screen. The image is ultra-sharp, as if he were sitting in the room with them. Frank can literally count the hairs on the man's luscious moustache. The audio too is perfect, noise or delays are a thing of the past and to all intents and purposes no longer occur.

'Hello Lara, all is well. With you too?' João replies with a funny accent.

She nods and points to Frank. She introduces him as a 'communication worker' and Frank is back on the ground as a result. He was already seeing himself as a full member of the investigation team, but she has now almost carelessly dashed that hope to the ground.

'Is she there with you?' Lara asks the man, clearly not wanting to lose any time.

'Sure, next door, I'll have her brought here. Do we have to keep her here after the conversation?'

She shrugs her shoulders. 'That depends on what will be said. We'll talk some more afterwards.'

As her colleague disappears from view, she turns to Frank. 'It's best if she doesn't see you, then it's easier for me to forge a bond of trust.'

Frank moves his chair out of camera range. After a minute a woman appears. Her eyes are swollen and there is no trace of make-up, probably wiped away by the tears.

'Are you Laura Guldix?' Lara asks. 'Yes that's me.'

'I know you've already told your story to the Portuguese police, but I have to ask you to tell it to me too.'

'Is… is this confidential? I mean, do you know what my relationship was with André?'

'Yes, I know,' Lara replies, and Frank thinks he hears that snappy tone from just now. 'This conversation is being recorded, but the investigation is secret. So go ahead.'

Frank takes a quick look at Lara. What's up with her?

'Okay, I… we were at the golf club, what's it called again, Quinta do Lago. Everything went well, we had already completed six holes and we were on our way to hole seven. André loved golf, that was a safety valve for him. He was always so busy. I can't believe he's gone.' She sobs.

'You were in a self-driving golf cart. Did you notice anything strange beforehand? A problem with the steering, stalling, something else?'

'No not at all. We also drove it between the other holes, and it went smoothly. Do you know what happened? Was there a defect?'

'That's under further investigation, madam, and for that it's important you give us as much information as possible. How was that golf cart controlled?'

The woman takes out a handkerchief and wipes away a few tears. 'It was very simple, on a screen there were buttons showing the numbers of the holes. You just had to hit the hole you wanted to go to and the cart would go off on its own.'

'Did you push the button for hole seven yourself?' Lara asks.

For a moment the answer is not forthcoming, and the woman looks open-mouthed at Lara. 'Why do you ask that? You think I'm involved?' she asks indignantly.

'Did you hit that button, yes or no?' Lara insists, and Frank considers that when it comes to building trust, he'd go about it differently.

'No, André always did that', he hears the woman say sullenly.

'What happened after he pressed that button?'

The woman averts her gaze. She seems to be reminiscing about what she has gone through as the mistress of one of the leading European politicians of the decade.

'The golf cart started moving, just like it always did. Not faster or slower, but as usual.'

'So it didn't speed up, at any point?' Lara insists.

'Yes, I think, at the end, but I'm not sure.'

'Did you try to take over the controls?' Lara asks.

Strange question, Frank thinks, that option doesn't exist on vehicles like golf carts, only on regular cars and trucks. 'Well, no, I didn't see André try that. Is that possible?' the woman asks surprised.

Lara dodges the question. 'You didn't see him try, okay. But why didn't he jump off like you?'

Laura Guldix, who has held up so far, now starts to cry uncontrollably as the incident unfolds before her eyes again. 'He was still wearing his seat belt,' she says, sobbing. 'We didn't get it off in time.'

Frank takes pity on the woman. What she has been through must be terrible. That powerlessness, the frustration, horrible to have to endure that.

'Was there a problem with that belt?' Lara asks.

'I don't know, we both yanked hard, but it was absolutely stuck.'

'And yours?'

'I never wear it in a golf cart. André always did that, I laughed at him several times for that, poor thing.'

'Are there any witnesses who can confirm that?'

'Confirm? What do you mean, confirm he was wearing his seat belt? Of course not!'

'Did other golfers see you riding in that cart?' Lara continues.

From his position diagonally to the screen Frank sees that the woman is gradually becoming despondent. She won't be able to endure that interrogation for much longer, he suspects.

'I guess so, I don't remember. Anyway, at hole seven there were some golfers at the tee, I remember that now.'

'Okay, we'll be able to identify them, maybe they've already been interrogated by the local police. What did you do when you couldn't unfasten his seat belt?' Lara continues unabated.

Frank feels something of vicarious shame, because he feels Lara is showing little empathy for that woman right now. She has lost the man she may have had a romantic relationship with for years. The fact that they were lovers is irrelevant. Grief knows no formal boundaries.

The woman starts to cry again and it takes a while before she continues her story, which is difficult to understand. 'I... I had to make a decision. I couldn't free André, so I had to choose. If I didn't do anything, I'd fall over that cliff too. When he said 'Jump!' to me, I didn't believe my ears. When he repeated it and I saw the look in his eyes, something snapped in my head and I jumped out with my mind at zero.' She stares straight ahead, now that her thoughts are on the man she has adored all these years and who is now gone out of her life for good.

'Thank you, madam, I understand this is difficult for you. One last question, did you hear Mr Gantois talk recently about certain criminals or things he was involved in?'

'He seldom talked about his work,' the woman states with downcast eyes. 'When we first came together, he made that clear to me right away. 'Worry and fun don't mix,' he said. And we were together to have fun, to enjoy life. Together, until death do us part.'

The umpteenth cry of pain now also makes it clear to Lara that the conversation had better stop. 'Thank you, Mrs Guldix. You can go now, my colleague will direct you further.'

When João reappears, he asks if they should still keep the woman at the police station.

'No, João, she's not under suspicion, just let her go. Tell her to remain available for any further contacts.' Lara finishes the call and the screen goes black.

'So what do you think?' Frank questions her. 'If you ask my opinion, I personally don't think she has anything to do with it. She's very moved by what happened.'

'That's right, I'm afraid this is the third case of hacking, and the second of a self-driving vehicle. We need to inform Anthony and action needs to be taken that goes beyond postponing a few conferences.'

Frank isn't the fastest thinker in the room, but he quickly realizes what Lara is referring to. If two self-driving vehicles can be hacked, they can all be hacked. And to avoid that, there is only one thing to do: to shut down global car traffic with self-driving cars.

NATO Headquarters, Evere, Brussels, Grand Auditorium, one day later, 16 February 2034

Members States' top politicians gradually file into the large auditorium of the NATO building. They proceed to the tables with signs on which their countries' names are written in large letters. Along the way, they nod politely to those who cross their path, but all hurry to their familiar places. The days when the men and women — especially those from the southern countries — greeted each other with a handshake or even with a kiss or a hug, are definitely over. Ever since the corona virus spread wildly in the 2020s and several international politicians succumbed to it, international summit consultations have taken place in a much more distant manner, certainly at NATO. Literally, even. In the first years after the crisis, many member states flatly refused to send their government leaders to the headquarters in Belgium for fear of contagion, even though a highly effective vaccine had long since been developed by the scientists. In the end it took five years before ministers reluctantly returned to Brussels and meetings were held with fewer holograms or video screens.

Anthony Dice now also enters the auditorium and steps straight to the podium. He takes the four steps with two hasty strides and immediately takes his seat. It does not bother him that, with his small stature, he almost completely disappears behind the lectern. The image the cameras make of him is projected on a large screen behind him, giving everyone a good view of him.

'Start,' he says softly, and behind him the image splits in two. The Anthony Dice on the screen shrinks by half and an agenda appears on the other half. A special agenda, because unlike other meetings, there is now only one agenda item.

'Ladies and gentlemen, welcome to this hastily organized meeting. The Secretary-General, who is unfortunately unable to attend, and I, thank all Member States for their flexibility and for their presence here in Brussels.'

Despite the fact that Dice is speaking English, he notices that several leaders, especially from the Eastern bloc countries, put their mini-simultaneous translators into their ears. Yet English is the language of communication at such conferences, and has always been the case. When he casts his gaze over those present, he understands why not everyone is fluent in that language today. He sees many unknown faces.

All the presidents and kings he's met have mastered the English language. Did they have to send subordinates because things had to go so fast? Or because some Member States were underestimating this problem?

'I've called this meeting because of a major and imminent problem. On 13 February, a self-driving car was hacked and yesterday the same thing happened to a self-driving golf cart.'

His words are not yet cold when there is a commotion in the auditorium. A dozen green lights flash on the screen, each representing a country. So all those government leaders are already asking for the floor.

Dice holds up both hands with palms out. 'I'll let you speak in a moment, but first let me explain further.'

Behind him on the screen appears a report on attempts at hacking self-driving cars over the years. There have been thousands of such attempts, but none of them successful. Each time, NATO has managed to nip them in the bud.

'You see here, NATO has always successfully guarded this mechanism. Our experts are facing a mystery as to how this could have happened.'

Dice tries not to watch the green lights multiply and blink for his attention. He clicks on 'next slide', and behind him appears a photo of Jan Goethals, the driver of the hijacked Tesla.

'This man was in the car of which the remote controls were taken over. Jan Goethals, a Dutch computer security expert.'

He clicks again and now a picture of a smiling André Gantois appears.

'Of course you know this man, the much-regretted European Minister of Justice André Gantois. He died yesterday after the golf cart he was in was also hacked. Our sympathies go with both families in these sad times.'

He pauses for a moment and doesn't let the flashing lights bother him.

'We immediately started the investigation and commissioned our best experts and inspectors to find the perpetrators.'

Dice notices that government leaders are starting to talk among themselves and realizes it's time to let a few of them speak. There is no doubt in his mind whom he will let speak first. He is pressing the key assigned to the country that has made the largest financial contribution since NATO was founded.

'Why don't we know about this and why wasn't the FBI called in?' shouts the American vice-president in a heavy Texan accent.

Dice, himself the son of an American father and a Belgian mother, shows understanding for this reaction. 'Today the status of the investigation is being shared with the FBI and an update will follow every day, that has already been arranged. I would point out that it is the Europol special department EC3 that will be tracking down the perpetrators of these attacks. They have a wealth of experience in that area and I am confident that we shall achieve results quickly.'

He presses the button for the Netherlands, prompted by the fact that the first victim came from that country.

The Prime Minister, a tall, staid man with a drawling voice, and normally very friendly, now speaks. 'How could this happen?' he exclaims. 'Not only do I demand a very thorough investigation, but I also want NATO's assurance that this will not happen again. Can you give me that guarantee?'

Dice, who has faced hotter fires in his career, remains calm and tries to calm the clearly afflicted man. 'Prime Minister, that investigation is already under way and we will not rest until the perpetrators are found and brought to justice. You will be the first to be informed.'

France is there clucking for the floor, so Dice presses the corresponding key.

'Mr Dice, my apologies, but you have not answered my colleague minister's question. Therefore, I repeat the question: can you give a guarantee that this will not happen again? In other words, what have you done since 13 February to prevent that?' 'Within an hour of the incident, Europol was already investigating the cause,' Dice replies confidently, fully aware that what he is about to say will hit like a bomb.

'We do not rule out the possibility of a computer virus.'

The noise in the auditorium becomes even louder and everyone starts talking at once.

'Ladies and gentlemen, please, if you'll allow me I'll give you some further explanation. If that turns out to be the case, our people will be working day and night to create an antivirus as soon as possible that will neutralize this threat.'

Seeing the British Prime Minister spring up and wave his arms angrily, he decides to give him the floor.

'We have to shut everything down!' the Brit roars and to emphasize his words he hits the table with his fist, so hard that the sign with the name of his homeland falls to the ground. 'I demand that all self-driving traffic be stopped until we are sure that no more cars can be hijacked,' he shouts.

Dice watches with sorrow as several leaders nod in agreement. They don't realize what they're saying, he thinks. The consequences of stopping self-driving traffic would be incalculable. The risk of accidents, finally reduced to almost zero, would rise enormously again. Because for most drivers it has been years since they have had control of a vehicle themselves. And the youngest drivers have never even really driven a car in their lives.

'I understand what you're saying,' he replies thoughtfully, 'but that's a decision that could have many adverse consequences. Just think of accidents, deaths, traffic jams on the highways, delays in transportation. Because if we abolish self-driving passenger cars, we have to do the same with self-driving trucks, buses and trains.'

He notices that his words nevertheless impress certain government leaders. Like him, they see the far-reaching impact of such a decision. The lady president of Russia, a distant relative of the previous president, apparently does not belong to that group, because she also stands up and urgently asks to speak. Although Russia is not a NATO member, it is invariably invited to important meetings. After Dice presses the correct key, she addresses him directly.

'Mr. Dice, my country has the best and most comprehensive knowledge of computer viruses and antiviruses in the world. I urge you to let us carry out the investigation.'

Dice isn't surprised by this, as it isn't the first time Russia has posed as a lifesaver. That country still considers itself the big, strong bear it once was. When in reality it has become a clay-footed giant, weakened by an idiosyncratic, self-centred policy pursued for years by a megalomaniac president. Moreover, the strong suspicion has already arisen several times among the other member states that they are being spied on by Russia, making it very unlikely that this demand will be met by the other states.

'As you well know, I can't decide that,' Dice replies. He tries to catch the eye of the stately Russian lady, but unfortunately she is too far from him. With her pronounced cheekbones and steel-blue eyes, she makes a deep impression on him every time he meets her. Besides the fact that he finds her beautiful, her acumen and great intelligence make her the ideal woman in his eyes. Too bad she has beliefs that he absolutely does not share. 'If you submit this as a proposal, I'll put it to a vote.'

The Russian lady president sits down and Dice watches her submit a proposal via voice control. He decides to give the floor to two more major powers, Germany and Italy.

The German Chancellor is the first to speak and surprises Dice with his politely asked question. 'Is there a connection between the two hacks and the explosions at the antivirus conference in Brussels?'

Dice had not planned to discuss that topic, as they are still uncertain about that. He therefore decides to keep it short. 'For the time being, there is no reason to believe that this is linked to the other two events. But that investigation is also in full swing and we shall keep all member states as informed as possible.'

The mutual conversations start up again and Dice lets go for a while. Some government leaders have made contact with their home countries, he sees them busy talking to their watches.

'Last question, and then we'll vote,' Dice announces. In the meantime, two proposals have been submitted: that of Russia, to transfer the investigation to them. And one from the United Kingdom, to shut down all self-driving traffic in the world.

Italy comes last and its question is also a difficult one. 'Why isn't the Chinese envoy here today? Do they have anything to do with this?'

Dice sighs as he sees the other leaders, especially from the West, nod. It's not the first time China has taken on the role of global scapegoat. The People's Republic of China has always steered a separate course, reluctantly joining NATO for a very limited number of powers. Internet surveillance is the most important element for them, given their dominance in the field of online sales. However, the fact that no one from China was delegated to this exceptional summit does not mean there will be no response. Dice has no doubt that a message from the Chinese president is waiting for him. No doubt he will want to speak to him and the secretary-general privately.

'Today there is no indication that China or any other country, let alone a NATO member state, was involved in what happened. I propose that we now proceed to the vote on the two proposals that have been submitted.'

He forwards the two questions to everyone present via the communication system and waits quietly. Soon the result for Russia's proposal appears on the big screen behind him: four in favour, thirty against. Just as he expected, only the communist countries have voted in favour. After a minute, the result of the second count of votes also appears: fifteen in favour, nineteen against. That was close, he thinks.

'Ladies and gentlemen, the investigation continues and we shall keep you informed. This closes the meeting. Thank you for your presence and your concern.'

Dice steps away from the podium and hurries down the stairs. He does not want to be bothered for a moment by the representatives of the smaller Member States, who, as usual, did not speak. He also prefers not to exchange views with the other heads of government, because he knows very well that he's nowhere yet with the investigation. However, when he sees Irena Damatova, the graceful Russian president, beckoning him, he quickly changes his mind. He slows down, sticks out his chest and puts on his sweetest smile.

NATO Headquarters, Evere, Brussels

Two hours later, Lara and Frank are sitting in Anthony Dice's lavishly furnished office. While Dice answers another call, Frank looks at the bookcase behind Dice. He's impressed by the number of books neatly arranged in a row. He estimates there are at least five hundred. Without exception, they are all non-fiction books, including many biographies and historical reference works.

Dice ends the call and sets off. 'There was an extraordinary meeting between NATO member states this morning. During the vote it was decided not to shut down self-driving traffic. I know that you, like some Member States, believe that this should be done. But the economic impact would be too great, and luckily the majority of the countries were aware of that.' Frank still has his doubts. Driving off a cliff, as happened to that minister, is not possible in this part of the world. But what if the car he's in is hijacked and then driven off a bridge?

'There's a downside to that decision,' Dice continues. 'We absolutely must avoid a third vehicle being hacked. I've cancelled all leave for our experts and shut down all other projects. This is the number one priority for everyone working at NATO and in Europol's cybercrime department. We urgently need to find an antivirus that can block these attacks. But for that we first have to find a clue that will lead us to that virus.'

Lara and Frank nod.

'We could use everyone for that, and that's why I thought of your father, Frank. Would he be willing to cooperate? And not just him, but those two others as well?'

Frank is surprised by that request. 'Yes, I think so,' he says hesitantly. 'I'll give him a call right away if you want.'

'Do that and tell him to contact these persons.' Dice turns his screen towards them and Frank sees that there are pictures of four children.

'Photo Peter Black', Dice says, and the photos make way for one large photo of a man in his forties. At first glance it looks like a Scandinavian type: light blond hair, clear eyes and a pale complexion. 'He's coordinating the search for the antivirus for NATO and Europol. Peter is a respected researcher and a true leader. He heads two NATO laboratories and has consistently achieved excellent results. For your information, he doesn't do it for the money. After starting up and selling a few small specialized companies, he has been a millionaire for years. I'll send you his details.'

Dice turns the screen back toward him, enters the instruction, then addresses them again.

'And then, what about you? What are the next steps in the investigation into the attack on the conference?'

'My intention was to find the criminals based on the email address with which the virus was sent,' Lara answers. 'Unfortunately, I was informed this morning that this appears to be impossible,' she adds, disappointed.

Frank looks up surprised. This is new information to him, although they had already discussed the matter this morning.

'The IP addresses of the sender of the e-mail changed constantly. So far we haven't been able to trace anyone. Frankly, there is very little hope that we can ever do that. The team will keep trying.'

'What about the virus that came with the email?'

Lara shakes her head. 'Negative. Not a trace of it. It may have destroyed itself, there are viruses that can be programmed that way.'

'I want the NATO team to look at it too. And those three experts too, as soon as possible.'

'That's possible, but if we haven't found anything, then...'

However, Dice won't let her finish. 'As soon as possible, Lara, is that clear?'

Frank sees Lara cringe. 'Got it,' she says briefly.

'We must try to fish out whether the three attacks were committed by the same perpetrators. And that's only possible if we identify the virus used in the three cases', Dice concludes. 'How far is Europol with the investigation of the car and golf cart that ran amok?'

'All we know is that control of the individual Butlers in the two vehicles was taken over by someone or something. Today, however, there is no indication that this could happen simultaneously in all autonomously driving cars,' Lara says.

'But there's no indication that it can't either, is there?' asks Dice, who is shifting in his chair.

'Hmm, no,' she confesses.

'Have all updates been made to the system that controls the self-driving traffic?'

'Yes, that was checked immediately after the first crash, that was not the problem.'

Dice gets up and goes to his window. 'So our defence mechanism just isn't strong enough to stop that virus?'

'I fear not, Anthony,' Lara answers softly.

Dice gives her an angry look and then looks out the window again. His gaze has not escaped Frank's attention.

'How far are we in developing the antivirus at Europol?' Dice asks.

'It's not ready yet, but I expect we'll have it in two days.'

'Two days,' Dice says thoughtfully. 'That's a long time. Isn't it true that an antivirus is sometimes developed within an hour?'

'That's right, but then it's usually about protecting oneself against simpler viruses, usually mutations of other viruses from the past. Here we're dealing with something completely new and much more complex.'

Dice thinks for a moment and then comes to a decision. 'Involve the entire security industry, everyone has to help. I want that virus faster than two days. Frank, you make sure all those companies don't communicate about this under any circumstances. Don't let me catch a single report on social media, understood?'

'Okay, I'll take care of it,' he says. 'But may I suggest something? Why don't we apply the 80-20 rule?' Lara and Dice look at him uncomprehendingly and he explains it to them. 'Today, eighty percent of antiviruses are produced by twenty percent of companies. I think it would be safer for the confidentiality of this investigation if we just ask those big firms. They have the greatest know-how and I think they'll be immediately willing to participate in this.' 'Because of the potential commercial added value that would result later, you have a point there,' confirms Dice. 'Okay, we'll follow you there, put them to work. One more thing, do you know who sent the warning about the explosions through those access badges?'

'We haven't been able to investigate that yet. NATO has those badges in its possession and nothing has been shared with Europol about them yet,' replies Lara.

'Okay, I'll ask Peter to get you involved in this. To work now. Lara, will you stay a moment?'

Frank gets up and leaves the office. He pauses in the corridor. What might they be discussing in there? Could it be about him? Perhaps Dice is now asking Lara what she thinks of her partner, whether his contribution to the study is up to expectations.

Just as he's about to call his father, Lara comes out red-faced and slams the door behind her. As expected, she hurries away and Frank can only follow.

'Lara, is something wrong?'

'No, we just have to hurry, that's all.' But Frank is convinced that this is not all.

Federal prison, Haren, Brussels, same time

'Man, you're seriously emaciated,' the guard says mockingly to Larry Lane, who is standing bare-chested behind the bars. 'Maybe you don't like our food?'

Larry Lane, incarcerated for over a year and with ten years to go, gives the jailer a disdainful look.

'How do you do that, eat so little?' the jailer continues to tease him. 'You should share your secret with me.' He points with a grin to his own belly, which hangs right over his belt.

Larry Lane takes a few slow steps forward and gestures for the man to come closer. The guard steps forward cautiously and puts his hand on his baton, ready to respond if Lane should try anything. He doesn't trust that sly fox one bit. He's seen often enough in movies how a prisoner grabs a jailer through the bars and forces him to open the door. Lane now has his face against the bars, still gesturing for him to come closer.

'That's close enough,' the guard says sternly. 'Say what you have to say.'

An evil grin slides across Lane's face, making the long scar on his jaw seem to move for a moment. The warden remembers very well how that ugly scar came about. When Lane was only a few days in prison, he already came into conflict with his cellmate. Before the guards could intervene, the two had seriously injured each other.

At first it was a mystery to the jailers how they both got hold of the two sharp shards of glass. It later turned out that they came from the drinking glasses from the cafeteria, which had been deliberately broken to make weapons. This was possible because a fellow prisoner, responsible for the management of the canteen, was involved in the conspiracy. Since that incident, Larry Lane has been alone in a cell.

'I've lost so much weight because I want to be in good shape. There's nothing wrong with that, is there?' says Lane with mock friendliness.

The guard says nothing and shrugs.

'I want to be fit to take your wife and daughter several times once I'm out of here,' Lane adds with a wicked grin.

When he hears him say that, the warden rages, grabs his baton and lunges at Lane. A fraction of a second earlier, however, Lane has already pulled away from the bars and the baton hits the metal with a hard blow.

'Bastard,' the jailer hisses. 'If you say that one more time, I'll knock all your teeth out.'

Lane pulls the corners of his mouth apart with both hands and reveals a row of amazingly white teeth. 'Come on, try,' he says defiantly.

The warden furiously takes his badge from his shirt pocket, which he uses to open the doors, but just manages to contain himself. Realizing he's about to do something stupid, he puts the badge and his baton away again. He decides not to waste words with such a figure and steps away from the cell. To his frustration he hears Lane behind him roar with laughter. His anger flares up again and he clenches his fists. To avoid changing his mind and thoroughly working that ugly face with his baton, he hurries down the corridor towards the courtyard, gasping for a cigarette.

NATO Headquarters, Evere, Brussels

On his way to their office with Lara, Frank calls his father. He notices that Lara is also making a call.

'Hi son', he hears his father say.

'Hello Dad, I've news for you. Anthony Dice asks if you want to cooperate in the investigation into those two hacks. Great, isn't it?' Frank says enthusiastically.

'Aha,' replies Eddy Willems, 'I'll have a look at my diary.'

Frank doesn't believe his ears. 'Father, you don't mean that, do you? This is about NATO and...'

'Son, that was a joke, of course I want to participate. But what can an old rascal like me teach all those young foals at NATO?'

'Your experience, of course. And not only NATO, but also EC3 are involved.

'Hm,' Frank hears him say admiringly. 'All the clever heads put together. It seems the whole world is in danger.'

'It does look a bit like that,' Frank replies. 'As I hear Dice, it's a very smart virus. By the way, he asks if your two friends will also cooperate.'

'Righard and Luis? Okay, I'll call them right away. They're certain to agree. How much does it pay?'

Frank laughs. 'Hm, I'm afraid it's pro bono.' 'No problem, how do we meet?'

They've now arrived at their office and Lara looks at him impatiently. He understands it's time to wrap up the conversation.

'You're to call a man named Peter Black, I'll send you his phone number.'

'Peter Black? Don't know that one. Send it through, your father will still save the world. .'

Frank hangs up with a smile and quickly forwards the number.

'Okay, how do we get started?' he says to Lara, who's still scowling at him.

'We set up a video conference with the bosses of the major security firms and we instruct them, that's all.'

'Okay, who's doing what?' Frank asks.

'I've already asked my colleague at EC3 to organize it,' Lara replies. 'That way we have our hands free to continue the investigation.'

'Neat. It's better if I'm present at the video conference so I can remind everyone of the confidentiality of this assignment.'

Lara nods. 'I'll shortly be questioning some known hackers. Perhaps one of them is involved in everything that's happened in the last few days. Or maybe they've heard or seen something. It's a world in which everyone pretty much knows everyone.'

'Can I come with you?' Frank asks and he feels like a child asking if he can join the adults on a trip.

'Why not? But first I want to talk to this Peter Black about the Dome badges. Will you give him a call with a picture?' she asks.

Frank sits down and activates one of the screens hanging on the wall. He dictates the number and they hear the line ring. After a long wait, the call is answered and the man appears whose photo they've seen while in Dice's office.

'Let me guess, you're calling me on behalf of Anthony Dice. Right?'

Lara stands behind Frank and introduces them both.

'Yes, we want to investigate the Dome access badges,' Lara replies straight to the point.

Black looks away from the camera for a moment, then shrugs his shoulders. 'That's possible. But I'd be surprised if you find anything.'

'Why not?' Lara wants to know.

'Because they're very simple badges. They do indeed have a limited messaging function. But my team has established that neither received nor sent messages are stored on the microchip inside it. Sorry about that.'

'Send them anyway,' Lara insists.

Black shrugs for a second time and looks at them with a tired look. 'Okay, I'll have them delivered to Dice. We're not going to waste any more time on it. There are more important things to do. Anything else?'

'Yes', Frank intervenes. 'My father is going to contact you; he'll also be cooperating with this investigation.'

'The more souls, the more joy,' comes the ironic reply. 'Are you going after the hackers?'

'Yes, how do you know?' Lara asks in surprise.

'Logical step, I'd do the same thing. Cyber, know that bunch? I think they have something to do with this.'

'Yes, I know them,' Lara says. 'But why do you think they're behind those attacks?'

'Who else? Larry Lane? He's behind walls. China or North Korea? They don't have the technology for it. I think it's those filthy anarchists. Good luck with your investigation.'

The screen goes blank.

Federal prison, Haren, Brussels

Fifteen minutes have passed since the jailer left, and all this time Larry Lane has been crouched in his cell. Every five minutes he moves forward a bit in that position. If a warden came just that moment, he would undoubtedly laugh at him squarely in the face. But that practice is absolutely necessary for what he intends to do. And losing weight is also part of that. The warden had seen right, he has indeed lost more than ten kilos. That weight goes quickly if you just skip a few meals.

He feels his leg muscles tighten and decides that enough is enough. He doesn't want to risk tearing his Achilles tendon now that it's almost time to act. He glances at the virtual clock on the wall of his austerely furnished cell. To his delight, he establishes that his last six minutes in this cell have arrived. He feels the muscles in his legs slowly relax, glad they've finally been freed from that bent position. He stretches and proudly looks at his tight stomach. He's so glad he's never been overweight like that jailer. What a shame it is, what must his wife and children think of it?

Lane notices there's one minute to go. He takes off his shoes and socks and stands quietly in front of his cell door. Now he's waiting for the liberating click of the lock in his door. To open that lock remotely, he had no choice but to call in outside help. Against his will, he has had to give up his plan, knowing that that person could take it to the police. From his earphones come the strains of 'Help' by The Beatles, a group he's been an unconditional fan of since childhood. The song he's now playing on the small music player he's been given by the prison was not chosen by chance. The chorus plays through his head. 'Help! I need somebody. Help! Not just anybody.' He can only hope the reward he has promised his helper is high enough.

He banishes the negative thoughts from his head and concentrates on the lock of the door. He knows that when he senses the click, he has only a few seconds to slip out and close the door again. If the power cut lasts just a second, there's a good chance it won't be noticed by the guards sitting in front of their screens. If they are indeed sitting in front of their screens. And if they do see it, hopefully they'll consider it a false alarm. He understands this is a weak point in his plan, and unfortunately, it's not the only one.

Lane puts his hand on the door, ready to push it open. In the corridor he hears the hum of the service robot, which has finished delivering the meals and is on its way back to its charging station. You can always count on robots, he thinks with satisfaction, they're never late.

And there's the long-awaited click that releases the lock. As if stung by a wasp, he pushes the door open a little, just enough for his thin body to squeeze through. In one fluid movement, he closes the door with his other hand and squats behind the robot, which slowly drives past. Successful! Lane follows the robot in the crouching position he's practised countless times. In this way he escapes the eye of the camera trained on this corridor. He pricks up his ears, but so far no sound of any alarm. At the same time, he counts in his head the seconds since the moment he escaped from the cell. That's important for the second phase of his escape. The robot approaches the locked door leading to another section, and gradually slows down. When he is a few centimetres from the door, a hatch opens in the front part of the robot and a sensor becomes visible. This is recognized by the door mechanism, which slides open silently. Lane closely follows the robot as it accelerates and drives through the doorway. Once Lane is through, he quickly jumps to the side and presses against the wall next to the doorway. The first hurdle has been cleared. He glances up and sees another camera hovering above him. This is aimed at the second corridor he has to pass through. Unfortunately, to put that camera out of service temporarily, he has had to rely on outside help a second time. He knows that if the guards see a grey screen, they'll immediately realize that something is wrong in the corridor. Lane will have to run fast to get to the other side in time, because it's there he wants to surprise them. He realizes there is a very good chance that his escape attempt will fail here. But he has no alternative.

He's still counting, and when he's over a hundred, he'll be on the starting blocks, as it were. They've agreed the camera will be shut down exactly two minutes after he gets out of his cell.

Hundred and eighteen, hundred nineteen, hundred and twenty, now! Lane shoots off the starting blocks and can only hope the camera is off. Like a true athlete, he sprints down the corridor barefoot. He watches the position of his arms and takes very large steps. In addition, he raises his knees as high as possible, just as he's seen professional sprinters do on the track. While running, he still keeps counting the seconds. Time remains a very important element. After a few seconds that seem like minutes, he comes to the end of the corridor, panting, and quickly presses himself against the wall next to the door. It's still closed. But he realizes it could be slung open any minute now by a bunch of guards alarmed at the camera's malfunction.

Lane takes a few deep breaths and tries to calm his body with his mind. He is still working at it when he hears noises behind the locked door. He pulls something out of his back pocket and braces himself for what's to come.

A1 Motorway, direction the Netherlands

After a short consultation with Anthony Dice, who thought Peter Black's idea far from stupid, Lara and Frank hurriedly left for Utrecht, where Cyber's hackers have their home base.

'Are these criminal hackers we're visiting?' he asks as they drive silently down the highway. He's curious how this will turn out. He's heard a lot about hackers, but he's never seen one in person.

'The majority stick to the rules, luckily,' she replies. 'And that's why I think there's little chance that it's them who caused the cars to crash. The attack on the Dome is certainly not their work. They count themselves among the ethical hackers, because they say they help big companies protect their data. They search until they find a hole in the company's security system and then they get in touch. If it stays that way, it's fine indeed. But usually they try to sell their achievements and such things still make the news.'

'Now that you mention it, there was a hacker trial last year, wasn't there?'

Lara looks at him in surprise. 'Yes, an Italian. You have a good memory. A multinational had promised him large sums of money if he could break into their biggest competitor and steal some business secrets.'

'Yes, that was it,' he recalls. 'Didn't he steal the secret recipe of some world-famous cookie?'

'You're right. Very stupid of that guy, incomprehensible really, because he was at the top of his hacker collective. With that crime, he lost all his credibility and was completely excluded by all the other hackers.'

He glances at the Butler on the dashboard. It has now been proven several times that it can be hijacked, and that's not a comforting thought. He looks outside and notices that they are driving across the border. When they've passed the sign telling them they are entering the Netherlands, he uses it to change the subject. 'Were you born in the Netherlands?' he asks as informally as he can.

'I can't hide that, can I?' she replies.

'You mean your accent?'

'Yes, what else?' She looks at him quizzically.

'No, just your accent, yes. Do you like the Netherlands?'

She grins. 'My ideal country is a combination of Belgium and the Netherlands, with the climate of southern Spain. And I mean a real southern climate, no three heat waves a year due to global warming and grey weather and rain in between.'

'There's something in that,' he confesses. 'The bourgeois lifestyle of the Belgians...'

'... combined with the assertiveness from above the Moerdijk. Absolutely.'

He's glad they're talking about something other than the investigation, and tries to keep the conversation going. 'Where were you born, if I may ask?'

'That's not a state secret, Frank, my cradle was in De Bilt, a part of Utrecht.'

'So we're driving to your home country now?'

'Yes, but you know, I'm long gone. Since… I mean, because of my job I'm either at Europol HQ in The Hague, or somewhere on the road in Europe. With the close cooperation with NATO on cybercrimes, I've been spending a lot of time in your small country lately.'

Her brief hesitation in the beginning has not escaped Frank's attention. It's as if she first wanted to mention another reason that prevented her from spending so much time in her native region. He feels he'd do better not to ask about it, so he doesn't revert to the subject. 'So you like Belgium?' he asks.

'Yes, Frank, despite your flaws, I like being there.'

'Our flaws? What flaws?' he reacts mock innocently.

'Well, you're not too bad. But most Belgians are so closed up. It's not necessary at all, is it?'

'No, I understand what you're saying, but we are indeed quite on our own. There are sociologists who claim to have found an explanation for this behaviour. They say it's due to the fact that Belgium has been occupied by so many different countries over the years that we've built a kind of wall of mistrust around ourselves.'

She bursts out laughing and Frank briefly sees another Lara, a young woman who is herself for a moment, not the serious Europol inspector, focused on her case. 'It reminds me of that little Gallic village that's the only one to resist the Romans, behind a high wall.'

'You mean in the Asterix comics?' She nods. 'I have them all,' she says proudly.

'I could never have imagined that you like comics.'

'Don't think in clichés, my dear Frank, never.'

'You're right. Personally, I prefer Hergé's drawings. But Asterix is nice too.'

There's a moment's silence and Frank hesitates a little too long to ask any more personal questions.

'Who do you actually think the perpetrators are?' Lara asks, looking at him curiously.

'Not a clue,' he says honestly. 'I can only go by the stories my father sometimes tells me. And the Larry Lane incident that I was involved in myself.'

'Then what does your father talk about?'

'About the black economy, among other things. I don't have to tell you how much is offered and sold via the dark web.'

'No that's right. Some people even claim that it equals or even exceeds the normal above-ground economy.'

'Yes, it's unbelievable what goes on in the dark recesses of the internet. Ordinary citizens have no idea at all. My father tells me that everything on the dark web is for sale, from passwords to weapons, to assassins, and so on.'

'Indeed,' Lara confirms. 'It's much worse than the practices of the mafia or the Colombian drug cartels. A major problem is also that it's difficult for governments to get a grip on the situation because you need special browsers to access those web sites. All government agencies break their teeth here.' She sighs. 'They've let it go too far, and in the meantime a whole proliferation of black entrepreneurs has arisen. Take one website down, there's another one minutes later. It's like fighting a rising tide.'

'But I don't think those dark web traders are behind these attacks. They like nothing better than for everyone to quietly let them do the business that shouldn't see the light of day. So they certainly won't do anything that could draw attention to them.'

'Do you think Cyber's hackers could play a role?'

'Maybe. It's mainly because Peter Black mentioned them and talked to Anthony about them, that we're on our way there now. The hackers in Belgium could also have given us the information just as well.' The Butler signals that they are about to leave the motorway and Frank glances outside. After taking the exit, they drive on a road that could just as well be in Belgium. The branches of the large retail chains along the road also resemble those in

Belgium. Here and there the colour or name differs, but the appearance is almost identical. The naming of the municipalities and districts, on the other hand, always surprises him when he's in the Netherlands. He sees 'Overvecht' and 'Haarzuilens' on place name signs, not exactly names you'll find in Belgium. The car slows down and drives smoothly into a side street, after which they arrive at a kind of annex parking square. The Butler reports they have reached their destination and Frank is very happy that nothing has happened along the way. He gets out of the car and stretches his arms and legs. In the front garden of a terrace house overlooking the park, a group of young people is seated around a table. He estimates their average age at twenty-five and he immediately notices that the girls are in the majority. Could these be the hackers? His question is answered immediately.

'Come on,' Lara says, 'let's go.'

They quietly walk towards the group, but suddenly several of the young people get up and enter the house. Two remain, a girl with long dreadlocks and an inconspicuous boy who would pass you by on the street without your noticing him. When they are within a few metres, the girl lights a cigarette with languid movements. The wind carries the smoke in their direction and Frank has to correct himself. This is clearly no ordinary cigarette; the sweet smell indicates something completely different. He's curious to see how this conversation will turn out.

Federal prison, Haren, Brussels

William, the obese warder who wanted to knock out all Larry Lane's teeth, and Liam, the warder in training, rush out of their guard post. In the corridor there's no one to be seen. It's the quietest time of the day, just after the robots have distributed lunch.

Prisoners and guards are all eating now, except for both of them, who are on duty.

'Damn,' William curses as he walks. 'I knew, I told you, that interruption was not normal.'

His younger colleague opens his mouth to say something, but decides to remain silent to keep the peace. His mentor never said that that brief interruption wasn't normal. On the contrary, he hadn't even noticed it. Liam had pointed it out to him, after which his older colleague dismissed it as a common malfunction. There was no denying it, however, when the image from the camera in corridor B disappeared. Two incidents in a row, that can't be a coincidence.

Liam, who is only on his second day as a jailer, follows in the wake of the man who's task it is to train him, although he could easily catch up. His gaze falls on his colleague's heaving backside and quickly looks away. He never wants to get that fat. They have only been running for a few seconds and he can already hear his colleague puffing and moaning. The baton and can of pepper spray dangling from his belt slap back and forth rhythmically against his way too wide hips. Liam jogs after him, wondering if the man is capable of doing his job properly. What if that camera isn't just broken, but someone has sabotaged it? And that it comes to a fight? He fears it would soon be over. He himself has never fought in his entire life and he has no intention of starting now. To be on the safe side, without slowing down, he removes the pepper spray from the holder on his own belt and holds it out in front of him.

They've almost reached the door to the corridor where the possibly faulty camera hangs. His fellow jailer grabs his baton and slows his run. Liam hears that he's completely out of breath and thinks about the theory lessons he'd taken the day before, his first day in prison. Didn't the instructor say, even three times, that colleagues should always be warned before intervening?

'William,' he says, placing a hand on the shoulder of the panting man in front of him. But he's too late. William stands in front of the iris scanner, he's recognized and the door slides open.

Federal prison, Haren, Brussels

The door is not yet fully open when Lane springs up and with a targeted kick he relieves the warder of this and immediately afterwards puts his left arm around his throat. Out of the corner of his eye he sees a second guard, so he pulls the heavy man between himself and the other guard. With his right hand he holds a thin object to the throat of the man who recently came to bully him.

'Do nothing or I'll slit his throat,' Lane hisses between his teeth. 'Move back!'

The young guard immediately recoils with his hands in the air. Great, Lane thinks, he doesn't seem to intend to resist immediately. But he mustn't give him time to think.

'Drop that pepper spray,' he orders, holding his hostage well.

The young man obeys and the can of pepper spray falls to the stone floor and rolls a few metres further.

'And now that baton.'

The baton is also thrown to the ground.

'Back to the guard post,' Lane says, starting to move himself. The door, still open, could set off an alarm, so it needs to be closed quickly.

The young guard steps back and continues to stare at him wide-eyed. Lane pushes his fat colleague through the doorway and the door slides shut behind them both.

'Advance', he says. Because he has the heavy man in a headlock, he cannot walk quickly himself. On the contrary, it's pretty difficult. Hopefully that young jailer won't run.

Lane realizes he's lost count by now and curses under his breath. How much time has passed already? There is nothing for it but to take a well-reasoned gamble. He takes a number in his head and continues counting.

'Faster,' he urges the jailer, because ever since they've gone through that door, they've been filmed by the camera here at the end of the hall. At any moment, a guard could return from his lunch break or a supervisor could come and check the guard post.

They arrive at the entrance of the guardroom and he gestures to the young guard to enter. Lane looks around and sees at once what he needs. 'Unplug that cord and come here, quick,' he orders the young guard, still standing with his hands in the air. He hesitates for a moment, then ducks under the desk, unplugs the cord from the power outlet and the computer, then stands in front of him. 'Billy Bunter, now it's up to you,' he whispers into the fat jailer's ear. 'Now tie up your young friend.'

The profusely sweating jailer, terrified by the pressure of the sharp object on his throat, doesn't dare move.

'Junior, give the cable to Billie here and turn your back to him,' he orders the other guard.

A minute later, the young guard's hands are tied behind his back and Lane needs one more thing before he can continue. He puts his hand into the pocket of the man he's holding tight, takes out a large cloth handkerchief and stuffs it unceremoniously into the handcuffed guard's mouth. It makes him gag a lot, but that's not Lane's problem.

'On the floor,' he says in a calm, undercooled voice. 'If you don't want anything to happen to your colleague here, lie here quietly until your colleagues come to free you. If you warn them and they try to stop me, I'll slit his throat. Understood?'

Lane is pleased when the boy lies down meekly on the floor. He pushes his hostage out of the guard post and makes his way to the last door separating him from the courtyard, his ultimate goal. With the guard's badge, he opens that door and a cold blast of air hits him. The timing he has set in advance, namely the lunch break, has proved to be a good choice so far. The only downside of that time of day is coming now.

He roughly forces the guard to step out into the courtyard and immediately both are the centre of attention. Dozens of inmates smoking or exercising stop and look at Lane in bewilderment. Lane, who for a second time has forgotten to keep time, realizes he must hurry. As agreed, he must be in the centre of the square when exactly six minutes have passed since his escape from his cell.

'Hey Lane, what are you doing, man?' asks a dark man covered in tattoos.

Lane grins and pushes the jailer further into the centre.

'Lane, where are you going with that pig? Going to slaughter it?' shouts someone in the crowd.

Loud laughter ensues and Lane notices several men approaching him.

'Can I have a piece?' asks a spindly older man who is missing some teeth.

Lane is still a few steps from his goal when he hears the sound. His grin turns into a smile and he looks up. Dozens of pairs of eyes follow his gaze and they too see the drone approaching.

Lane grabs the can of pepper spray still dangling from the guard's belt and pushes the guard to the ground. He falls backwards on his back on the hard stones. 'Here, this is for you, because you've cooperated so well,' Lane sneers, throwing the object he's been restraining him with onto his stomach.

The jailer takes it and to his surprise it's not a knife, but an ordinary comb.

Lane continues laughing, holding out the pepper spray with outstretched arm. 'Don't get any wrong ideas, guys. Unfortunately, I can't take any passengers; maybe next time.'

The drone now descends quickly and Lane stands just below it. When it hangs at a height of two metres, Lane jumps up to it and grabs the two handles attached to it. The drone takes off without any problems and Lane glances down at all those men watching him. Some are even applauding. He regrets not being able to enjoy a dash of music at that moment.

'Ticket to Ride' would have been very appropriate right now. The hardships were not in vain after all: he is free at last. The drone zooms unperturbed at a height of twenty metres and Lane enjoys the wind in his hair. Just a little while and he'll finally be able to take revenge on everyone who has got in his way. And that's just the beginning.

Utrecht, Netherlands

'Hello,' Lara greets the two youths, who are hanging more than sitting on their creaky chairs.

The girl looks at them dreamily and gestures for them to sit down. Lara sits across from her and when Frank drops onto another wooden chair, it creaks very loudly.

'Don't worry, those vintage chairs are very sturdy,' the boy says, noticing Frank's look. 'I'm Jonah and this is Saartje. Tell us, who are you?'

Lara and Frank introduce themselves and Jonah nods. 'I was already thinking: when are they coming?' he says with a smile.

'Really? And what made you think we'd be coming over?' Lara asks kindly.

'It would be strange if no one came by. Whenever something happens, whether it's a hacking or a ransomware attack, we're always in the top three potential suspects. But before we talk… would you like a beer?'

'No thanks,' Lara says, and Frank politely declines as well.

'Saartje, would you be so kind as to get something for the two of us, please?'

The girl nods, takes another pull on her joint again, then presents it to Lara. With a horrified face, she shakes her head, and the joint is then placed in the ashtray.

'Am I right?' Jonah asks. 'Do you think Cyber has something to do with the attacks on the Butler?'

'We're here because we're conducting an investigation and we hope you can help us do that. Or do you have something to do with it?' Lara asks the man.

'No,' the youth replies shortly, and Frank notices he's looking Lara straight in the eye as he says that. No dreamy look from him, and he quietly leaves the joint in the ashtray. This young man is probably the leader of this group. 'No. We don't busy ourselves with this. And if we decided to try to hack the Butler, and by extension the mechanics of self-driving cars, we certainly wouldn't kill those drivers.'

He seems to be telling the truth, Frank thinks. If these are truly peaceful hackers, their intention is never to kill people. But what if someone offers them a lot of money to abandon their principles? He can imagine they need expensive IT equipment for their hacking. So the temptation to accept such money could be large.

'Would you guys know how to hack the Butler?' Lara asks.

'Pff, that's a tough question. We are talking here about a system that's been in use for several years and was developed by the best minds in the security industry.'

The girl's dreadlocks jingle as she puts two bottles of beer onto the table. Then she grabs the joint and sits down uninterested in the grass a little further away.

'In theory everything can be hacked. But the conditions are always the same: you have to look for a weak point in the defence. Just like a football coach does when preparing for a match. On top of that you need a lot of time, a lot of money and skilled people.' The boy's gaze shifts briefly to the girl in the grass, who is looking the other way. 'I'm not going to deny that the Butler fascinates me. It would be weird if it didn't.'

'Who could have done it then?' Frank asks.

Jonah takes a sip of his beer and points to the house behind him. 'None of us, I'll put my hand in the fire for that. Do you know who our great heroes are? Anonymous. That says enough, doesn't it?'

When Frank hears that name pronounced, he remembers this group of hackers. They undertook various retaliatory actions against companies which made what were in their view wrong decisions. One 'victim' was Arcelor Mittal, which had put thousands of people onto the street by closing a factory. 'You know who was the only one who dared to stand up against IS about twenty years ago? Right, Anonymous.'

'Sorry, but we're digressing,' Lara says. 'Can you help us or not?'

'Not with information, because we've no idea who's doing it. But I'll ask the group to listen to their various contacts. The net has been buzzing with rumours since those two attacks.'

'Are any names being mentioned?'

'No, not until now. If I were in your shoes, I wouldn't waste time looking for the little shrimps. You have to start at the top, because whoever developed this virus is, in my view, no less than a genius.'

'That we'd already gathered,' Lara says sadly.

'Let me add one more thing,' Jonah says. 'All the hackers I know are very shocked by the murder of Minister Gantois. He was a great gentleman, who was always open to dialogue, including with us. We were once invited to his place to see how we could work together on a European level to take out the cowboys among the hackers.'

'Do you know if he had specific people or associations in mind at the time?'

'No sorry. That meeting dates back a long time and he didn't drop any names. He was too smart for that.'

'Okay, if you hear anything, call me right away,' Lara says and hands Jonah a card.

He accepts it in surprise and looks at it like a fossil that has just been excavated. 'A calling card, how old-school!' he exclaims.

'If you can't reach me, you can also contact Peter Black,' Lara adds.

Jonah almost lets the card slip out of his hand when he hears that name. 'Peter Black? Does he work for Europol?' he asks genuinely surprised.

'No, for NATO, but he's cooperating with the investigation. Do you know him?'

Jonah pulls himself together and nods. 'I've heard of him, yes. In another life. But I don't want to get into that right now. Okay, if I hear something, you'll hear it too.' He gets up and walks leisurely to the girl, who in the meantime is sprawled out on the little lawn and staring at the clouds in the sky with half-open eyes.

Lara and Frank walk to their car and exchange a knowing look. Words are superfluous. Both wonder what the relationship is or was between Cyber and Peter Black.

'I don't think Cyber has anything to do with it,' Lara says as they're back in the car.

Frank notices that, unlike the first time they drove together, she now invariably turns her seat toward him. He wonders whether he should take that as a sign that she appreciates him. 'To be honest,' he replies, 'it just seemed like some youngsters looking for a pastime and ended up hacking.'

'Hm, no, I wouldn't take it that far, don't underestimate them. They did pull off some stunts that went around the world. Some companies are lucky it was they who penetrated their networks and not real criminals.'

'Is it a dead end?'

'I'm afraid so. But what this Jonah said about the rumours circulating on the dark web intrigues me. I think we should go in that direction.'

He's not sure he understands her correctly. 'You mean we should start looking for information on the dark web? How do you do that?'

She fiddles with a small bracelet she has on her wrist. It's the first time he's noticed that. Before he can read the name on it, she pushes it under her sleeve. 'We can pretend to be someone else. Like shady businessmen who need something from the black market.'

'You mean incognito? Isn't that illegal?'

She looks at him like he's a choirboy. 'It's only illegal if we arrest someone on that basis. In that case, it would indeed be provocation', she says, irritated. 'But that's not what I want to do. I just want to get some information that will help us move forward with this investigation. We urgently need a lead to bring us to the developer of this computer virus.'

Frank finds it an exciting prospect in any case and feels the excitement increasing. It's like he's on a journey to an unknown destination with the added plus of doing so in the company of this beautiful lady. An almost inaudible beep announces an incoming call, and as Lara answers, Frank is already convinced of the assignment. Just the two of us at his or her home, glued to a screen for hours, maybe with a glass of wine. He certainly wouldn't mind that. However, his daydream falls to pieces when he hears what Lara tells him after making the call.

'Incredible! Larry Lane has escaped from prison.'

Cyberspace, same time

'Hey.'
'Did you find it?'
'The telephone? Yes!' 'Isolate yourself and call me.'
'Now?'
'Now.'
Connection ended.

Encrypted phone line, five minutes later

'Hello?'

'Yes. What do you think of the phone?'

'I'm impressed. I'd always assumed the Sectra Tiger was for NATO personnel only. How did you get your hands on it?'

'Doesn't matter. Most importantly, all our conversations are encrypted. Did you know the device can even withstand hacking with quantum computers?'

'Yes, and it's handy that all messages and conversations are destroyed immediately afterwards.'

'I have another assignment for you.' 'I'm quite busy.'

'I don't care. It's a house that must be razed to the ground. Must look like an accident.'

'Okay. What address?'

'Here it is.'

Larry Lane disconnects and leans back in his chair. He glances out of the small window of the apartment where he has temporarily moved in. With the grey sky outside and the grime on the windows, it looks like he's staring into nothingness. He wrinkles his nose in annoyance at the pungent smell lingering in this small flat. It's the smell of damp that got into the walls years ago and doesn't intend to come out again. Fortunately, he doesn't have to stay here long. If his plan succeeds, he'll soon be so rich that he can buy a castle in every country. He likes the idea and he cannot help but smile there all by himself. Until then, he will have to make do with these thirty square metres in Sint-Jans-Molenbeek.

He didn't choose this part of the city just like that. He's convinced this is the ideal place to go into hiding. The police don't turn up to register apartment residents and tenants. They've been avoiding the district for decades and arrive on the scene only when it's really necessary, and then it must already be a real disaster. Here Lane can move about easily and unnoticed, completely absorbed into the crowd. He did have to adjust his clothing style for it. Bespoke suits like the old days, when he was CEO of Bio Dynamics, are completely a thing of the past. Here he walks around in a grey T-shirt, sweater and bleached jeans, just like most men here. He hasn't shaved since he was in prison. He has changed the shape of the beard, which he could no longer do without, immediately after his escape. For the model, he looked closely at how the Muslims in his neighbourhood wore theirs.

Lane gets up, takes one of the two kitchen chairs in the flat, and stands on it. A neon lamp hangs from the ceiling in an elongated, transparent plastic box. At one time it would have been transparent, now there are large black spots on it and the plastic has acquired a pale yellow colour. He unclips the box and removes it. It's full of dead flies and their droppings. He turns the box upside down and the dirt all falls onto the dark brown carpet. Then he takes the precious telephone that he used for calling and places it into the box near a black spot. Then he clicks the box back onto the holder fixed onto the ceiling. He gets off the chair and looks up. You can't see the phone. Satisfied, he puts the chair back in the small kitchen. He doesn't have to be afraid of missing a call, because this type of phone only works between two predetermined phone numbers. And if someone were to find the device, which would surprise him greatly, he would also have to know the password, which must always be entered for every call or message.

Lane reaches for the bottle of gin on the kitchen table that he went to buy at a night shop. Using a glass is one step too far for him. He doesn't dare open the kitchen cupboards for fear of what he will find there. Ditto for the refrigerator. When he was negotiating the rent with the landlord, he had learned that the previous tenant had died. Shot down a hundred yards from here. The landlord said Lane could use everything that was still there, after all the man didn't need it any more. And he had no family in Belgium.

Lane puts the bottle to his mouth and lets the alcohol run down his throat. Gin has always been his favourite spirit and he plans to stock up on the best brands later on. The drink plunges into his stomach like a block of concrete, reminding him he hasn't eaten yet. He decides to go get something, but not before taking precautions not to be recognized. For this he's purchased a few indispensable accessories, which now lie on the table. He puts the two wads of cotton wool into his mouth. This is not a pleasant sensation, but the end justifies the means, which is to make his cheeks appear fatter. Then he puts on the special, thicker lenses he bought on the black market, and finally thick glasses. All this should ensure that any facial recognition cameras do not identify him on the street.

His thoughts turn to the computer virus he has in his possession. A computer virus the likes of which the world has never seen before, against which all previous versions pale.

One with so much strength and intelligence that nothing and no one will be able to stop it. It will be his revenge for his defeat a year ago, when a handful of ignoramuses unexpectedly placed spokes in his wheels. This time they won't succeed. If his plan works, they'll be watching open-mouthed.

In anticipation of that moment of glory, Lane leaves the flat where he is temporarily hiding, and heads for the takeaway shop. In his ears is another song by his idols from Liverpool, England.

'Nowhere man, please listen. You don't know what you're missing. Nowhere man, the world is at your command.'

Just a little bit more patience, he thinks, just a little longer, and then the world will look completely different.

A27 Motorway towards Belgium

'What?' Frank exclaims in astonishment, and that creep's mean features come right back to his mind.

'That was Anthony, and he wants us to not only find the virus, but also find and handcuff Lane. He was very clear. Those two things go together and have the highest priority. He agreed that with my boss.'

There goes the cosy get-together, Frank thinks disappointedly. 'How could he have escaped?', he says. 'If I'm not mistaken, he was in Haren federal prison? That's the newest prison in the country, ten years old at most, isn't it?'

'That's right,' Lara agrees. 'Equipped with all the high-tech gadgets you can imagine. But very likely, Lane didn't do it alone. There's no way he could have done it without outside help. An international search warrant has been issued, everyone is helping in the search.'

Lara quickly calls out the prison's address and passes it on to the Butler as their new destination. On the large display they see the map renew itself and the arrival time adjusted. There is not much time difference, as the prison is in Haren, which is not that far from NATO.

Frank is thinking about what this new event means for their investigation. Is there a link between the two? It can't be a coincidence that right now Larry Lane is back on the loose, can it?

Lara apparently thinks the same. 'This was planned like that,' she says thoughtfully. 'The man or woman behind the attacks also freed Lane. Perhaps to help him with what he's up to next.'

'What could that be? Do you have any idea about that yet?'

'It must be something he can't accomplish without Lane's help. I'll take his file with me.'

She asks the Butler for access to Europol's database and leans forward to allow the facial recognition to do its job. Once logged in, she calls up the file and a millisecond later it appears on the windshield. Frank tries not to look at the photo, because each time he's annoyed by the arrogance this man radiates.

'Quite impressive. Doctor of Applied Computer Science. Postgraduate in Information & Cyber Security. That last one is ironic.'

'Yes, imagine Lane as a well-behaved security expert.'

'Hm, judging by the comments in his file, that was never his intention. His name is mentioned several times in major scams over the Internet. Look right here, he was supposedly even involved in Russia's influencing the European elections in 2019.'

'But he was never convicted, am I seeing that right?'

'Indeed, he must have always been smart enough to cover his tracks.'

'Or to have known the right people?' Frank suggests.

'That too is possible. Now let's focus on the added value of Larry Lane for someone who has big plans and who doesn't shy away from killing people to achieve his goal.'

'The added value? What do you think of the development of the computer virus?'

She shrugs her shoulders. 'Maybe. He has the scientific background. In theory he should be able to do it. And if he created the virus, he probably worked on it day and night when he was CEO of Bio Dynamics. Because until the incident a year ago, there was not a single entry in his file during that period.'

'And is it that virus he used a year ago?'

'That, my dear Frank, is the million-dollar question. No trace of it has ever been found, on any server or in any email. It had completely gone up in smoke, it even seemed as if it had never existed'

'Or it was set on inactive and well hidden somewhere waiting to be activated again.'

'Not a stupid comment. If so, things don't look good for NATO and by extension for the whole world. And then there is only one man who can tell us how to disable that virus. Because it has definitely become active again. Are we going to get a quick sandwich at a petrol station before we drive to jail?'

'Good idea,' says Frank, whose stomach has been growling for a while.

Their sandwich has just been finished when Lara's car stops in front of an electric gate that closes off the prison entrance. This is where their search for Larry Lane begins. Frank is both excited and terrified of what's to come. But he resolves never to show the latter. And certainly not to Lara.

Federal prison, Haren, Brussels

Lara and Frank arrive at Belgium's largest prison, built to replace the three oldest prisons in the country. Once they are identified, the gate opens. Frank is amazed at how the prison is constructed. It doesn't look like he imagined it, as a large, grey, old building. What he sees now looks more like a village. They drive on to a long, low block that is probably the main building. He has never seen the inside of a prison before and his eyes are everywhere. He really needs to adapt his former image of a prison. Flowerbeds, lawns, hedges and trees, not at all what he expected. As they get out, he glances at the high wall that surrounds the site. That at least is there. But there are no rolls of barbed wire on the top. Nor dog patrols either. Frank follows Lara, who steps towards the entrance, and looks amused at a large black robotic lawnmower that is clipping the lawn and sowing grass at the same time. Soon they'll no longer need gardeners. But wouldn't that be a nice job for the inmates? After logging in at a video screen, the door opens and they step into an office space. The gruff receptionist shows them a compact device on the counter, where they have to leave their fingerprints. Then they follow her down a corridor with similar screens to NATO's, scanning everyone who passes. They arrive at a frosted glass door with a screen with the single word 'Director' on it. The receptionist, who hasn't said a word, knocks and they hear a female voice calling for them to come in. As they step into the room, a tall woman of about sixty steps out from behind her desk and greets them warmly.

'Ah, the people from Europol. Sit down, please. I'm Helena, the director of this prison.' She sits down again and points to the door. 'You may have noticed it says 'Director' and not 'Directress'. I'll tell you right away how that happened. Dimitry Keuleers is, or rather was, director until a few hours ago. Larry Lane's escape, which is why we're sitting here together, has caused quite a bit of commotion. The pressure on Dimitry was enormous. He was being asked from all quarters how such a dangerous criminal could escape from a state-of-the-art prison, in which politicians had invested tens of millions. Initially he tried to defend himself by pointing to the recent cutbacks and the shortage of personnel. But half an hour ago he threw in the towel and resigned.' She narrates this with a look that betrays her fondness for the former director. 'I don't know whether that was under gentle coercion. But the chances are high.'

'And you're replacing him?' Lara asks.

'Right. I was second in rank, so that's only normal.'

'Can you tell us in detail how Larry Lane managed to escape?'

The imposing woman, formally dressed in a dark blue blazer and skirt, sighs deeply. 'Let me first mention that this is the first successful escape in ten years. Our institution scores best in terms of security and the satisfaction of our detainees. We have even won several international prizes, including the prize for the best social infrastructure.'

Frank is surprised to learn that satisfaction surveys are being conducted among inmates. That's interesting information for his communications agency and he makes a mental note to be sure to learn more about it later.

'I can also assure you that this escape could never have happened without outside help.'

'In what way?' Lara asks, turning on the recording function on her watch and alerting the director.

'No problem. It has to be that someone has broken into our network and helped Lane to flee.'

'Do you know who?'

'No, of course not. But frankly, we're counting on Europol for that. We don't have enough knowledge in-house to check that.'

'Okay, that's indeed our responsibility. I need your network's log files from twenty-four hours before the break-in to now. If it turns out that we don't find anything there, I'll have to request a longer period.'

The director plays with an old-fashioned and expensive-looking fountain pen and nods. 'Obviously. You can count on my full cooperation.'

'How did Lane get away?'

'The lock of his cell was opened remotely and two cameras were temporarily disabled. It clearly looks like everything was planned. That's an important element that I think should be investigated.'

'Do you mean how he could have contact from your prison with his helper?'

'Exactly,' the lady replies. 'How could he know where and when those cameras would be turned off? And when his cell would be opened? They must have communicated about this.'

'A watch that was smuggled in? A jailer who was bribed?' Lara asks.

The director spreads her arms. 'I don't know. All I know is that Dimitry took his job as director very seriously and that he always closely followed the procedures. Smuggling in a watch, I don't think this could happen. All visitors are thoroughly scanned and searched, both on entering and leaving.'

'A jailer then?'

'Dimitry had a lot of confidence in our staff, and so do I. But I can't rule out that someone accepted money in exchange for passing on a message to the outside world.'

'Didn't he have the right to call anyone outside the prison?' Frank asks in surprise.

'No, that right was temporarily withdrawn. Dimitry was planning to change this after another six months.'

'Did anyone get hurt in his escape?'

'No, fortunately not. It all happened without bloodshed.'

'And what was your impression of Lane during his stay here?'

'His stay? You make it sound like he was sitting here in a hotel. Right from the start, Lane was at odds with both inmates and prison staff. To give you an example, he harassed the staff by constantly playing very loud music. And always the same, always one particular Beatles song, 'Penny Lane'. We'd take his speaker away for a while, but since we're legally obliged to hand it back, the game always started over again. That's why he's also spent a lot of time in isolation. But it was clear that the man didn't care. Special type of person, you know.'

'Yes, that's right. How did he finally escape? My boss said something about a hostage.'

The director puts down her fountain pen and looks at them with a slightly guilty look. 'That's true. He threatened William, one of our warders, with a weapon and forced him to go with him. In the guard post, he left another guard handcuffed and then went into the courtyard. A drone picked him up there and he literally and figuratively flew off.'

Lara and Frank are both amazed.

'A drone? That must have been a big one', Lara says.

'It was. Lane is not fat, on the contrary, but it was a powerful model, the kind used by mail order companies for delivering the largest sized parcels. We have a picture of it, I'll get it to you.'

'But this is not the first time this has happened, is it?' Lara says thoughtfully. 'A helicopter even landed once in a prison yard, I seem to recall.'

The director says nothing and bites her lip.

'Didn't this result in a directive that nets should be stretched over the places where the prisoners exercise outdoors?' The director looks at them guiltily. 'That's right, and we had one too. But the day before, one of the inmates had set it on fire and it had to be replaced. Tomorrow, in normal circumstances, it will be delivered.'

'That's quite coincidental,' Lara says sarcastically.

'Part of the plan', Frank agrees. 'Did Lane have any visitors during his, hmm, captivity?'

'I'll have to check that, just a moment, please.'

Lara and Frank silently exchange a look of understanding. Both fear that they will leave here without a trace to follow.

Until they hear the names of the only two visitors Lane has ever received.

NATO base, Zemst

The driveway gravel protests with a crunching noise as Righard's heavy Polestar drives slowly up to the old house.

'I have to charge the battery soon,' Righard tells them, looking at the battery status.

'Yes, and I don't think you can do that here,' Luis says, looking at the detached house.

'Are you sure it's here?' Eddy asks from the backseat.

Because Righard likes to sit in the front and Luis firmly believes that where he is sitting is safest, Eddy is sentenced to the back seat. But he doesn't care, because now he has three places all to himself.

'According to the Butler, yes,' Righard says.

'Do you still have faith in that stuff?' Luis mocks.

'Come on, guys, if we start like this, we'll get paranoid. That can't be the intention.'

The three get out and walk to the house.

'I still think it's crazy that NATO has set up a research centre here. In terms of security, you're better off in Evere, aren't you?'

Eddy thinks otherwise. 'I think this is sort of a plan B for if something were to happen in HQ. Then you still have a second, fall-back base. I'd bet my bottom dollar that they have a separate network here that can continue to function independently of the servers in Evere. In other words, they learned their lesson after Lane's coup last year.'

Righard laughs and squeeze's Eddy's shoulder. 'Eddy, always thinking logically. How complementary we are.'

'What about me?' Luis asks. 'Don't I think logically?'

'Calm down, Luis,' Righard soothes him. 'Your brain is just wired differently. One day it'll turn out that you have a talent too.'

'What?' Luis shouts, giving Righard a shove in the back.

Laughing, the three men stop in front of the apparently abandoned house.

'There's no intercom,' Eddy notes. 'Just an iris scanner.' 'Are we in their database?' Luis asks.

'Yes, since last year, don't you remember?'

All three take turns standing in front of the scanner and when a green light comes on, the door opens and they step inside.

'Did anyone notice there was also a fingerprint sensor on the door handle?' Righard asks.

His two colleagues answer in the negative.

'A double protection, which apparently can be deactivated manually, as just happened.'

A moment later they are crammed together in the small lift that slowly starts moving.

'Like a Brussels tram', Luis jokes.

'Just imagine if this lift breaks down now,' Righard says.

Fortunately, this does not happen. The doors open again and they hasten out. Before this, they had been discussing what that underground laboratory might look like. They were very curious and were not disappointed. It was even bigger than they had imagined.

'Welcome gentlemen,' they hear a voice behind them. They turn and in front of them is a man as large as Righard, which is not an everyday occurrence.

'Ah, finally someone of my calibre,' Righard crows. 'I'm Righard Zwienenberg, pleased to meet you.

'Black, Peter Black,' their host replies with a smile.

Luis and Eddy literally have to look up at the man and introduce themselves.

'Good day Luis, good day Eddy. Eddy, you were the man of the moment a year ago, I understand?'

'No, it was teamwork', he replies modestly.

'Can I ask you something? Is it true that people call you the Three Amigos?' The three older men look at each other and nod.

'It is, and I don't really know who started it,' Luis says.

'Nice, such a nickname,' Black remarks. 'I wonder what they call me here.'

After those words, he steps on and gestures for them to follow him. The introductory round is apparently over, because his tone is now very business-like.

'I suggest we get started. Anthony has asked me to brief you fully about the situation.'

He leads them past one room after another in which small groups of people are sitting at screens.

'Is everyone here busy with the virus that got into the Butler?' Eddy asks.

'No, we're facing a lot more threats than that, you've no idea.'

Eddy looks at the tall man in surprise, but decides to be silent. He sees that Righard wants to respond, catches his eye and shakes his head. Righard holds back, despite being visibly outraged. Together they have built up so much experience and expertise, how can that man think they have no idea about all the threats on the internet?

Eddy takes comfort in the thought that Black might be someone who likes to tease others. Or he's jealous, that's also possible.

'So, here we are,' Black says. 'This room is your headquarters.' He steps in, activates one of the screens and calls up a list of three usernames and long, complicated passwords. 'Those are for you. And via this link you'll find the servers of the Brussels conference hall where the virus penetrated. We're working on the assumption that the virus in the Butler is the same as the one in the Dome. So far we have not found any trace of it. Hopefully you'll find something. Anthony is already very confident. Are you that good?'

'Immensely,' Righard replies without flinching.

Black returns his gaze and the two tallest men in the room stand in silence eyeing each other for a second. The atmosphere is tense, until Black starts laughing and the rest breathe a sigh of relief. 'Those Dutchmen, so self-assured. I'm curious. If you need anything else, just let me know.' And he's gone, leaving the door to the hallway open.

'What a nasty guy,' Righard says gruffly.

Eddy closes the door and shrugs. 'Look, there's no choice but to work with him. The head of NATO's Security Council personally appointed him to avert the greatest threat in years. So he must be capable.'

'That doesn't mean he should take us for newbies,' Luis joins in the conversation.

'Look, guys,' says Eddy, 'I think we should be thankful for this opportunity. Imagine we identify the virus and that there is an antivirus thanks to us. I can already see the press articles: 'Three Amigos save the world''

Righard and Luis laugh and the atmosphere is good again. 'Come on, let's get started,' Luis says and takes a seat at one of the screens.

His two old comrades do likewise and a moment later it's completely silent in the room. They're searching for a computer virus that has so far been able to hide successfully and seems to have no intention of being found.

NATO base, Zemst

An hour has flown by and they've checked all the log files from the various servers to no avail.

'Nothing to see. So there's no one who's taken over control with administrator authority. The control of the central heating must therefore have been hacked in some other way', Luis concludes.

'I'll call that Europol inspector and ask her to send us that e-mail with the attachment that contained the virus,' Righard announces.

Moments later he has her on the line. 'Hello Inspector, we're here at the NATO base...'

'Stop,' Lara interrupts. 'This is not a secure line. I'll call you right back.'

Righard is startled and quickly hangs up. The other two notice his reaction and look at him quizzically.

'She'll call me right back on a secure line. I feel like a spy.'

Eddy and Luis laugh and Righard looks at them timidly.

'It's all right, you know,' he says gruffly.

And there's Lara again. Righard picks up and chooses his words carefully. 'So, we need the e-mail, you know, to check something.'

'No problem, I'll forward it immediately. Found anything yet?'

'No, unfortunately not. We now want to focus on what was in that attachment.'

'You know that two departments have already searched that attachment and found nothing?'

Righard glances surreptitiously at his mates and nods. 'No, I didn't know. But we'd also like to take a peep.'

'No problem, the e-mail is already on its way. Something else, I've news for you. Larry Lane has escaped from prison.'

'What?' Righard exclaims so loudly that Eddy and Luis nearly fall off their chairs.

'Yes, he escaped and was helped by someone from outside. Can you try to identify that outsider? I'll send the necessary information shortly.'

'Of course,' says Righard, surprised. 'Are we the first to do that?'

'Yes, apart from the prison computer department. But they don't have the skills you have.'

At least someone who appreciates our experience, Righard thinks. 'Okay, send it on: we'll split up the tasks here.'

Righard hangs up and turns to his two colleagues. 'Larry Lane is at large,' he informs them. 'He escaped from jail and Europol wants us to find out how he did it and with whose help.'

Eddy and Luis are as stunned as Righard was just now. Lane was no longer in their minds. And now he's back on the scene.

'I'm assuming some form of hacking was involved? Otherwise, she wouldn't ask us,' Eddy says.

'She's forwarding everything: aha, here it is already. What are we doing guys? Luis, you Lane's escape? Eddy, you the attack on the Dome, and me the virus in the self-driving vehicles?'

Everyone agrees and Righard forwards the data from the prison to Luis. Then the three friends go silently back to work.

NATO Headquarters, Evere, Brussels

Lara and Frank have meanwhile completed the short drive between Haren and Evere and are walking in the NATO parking lot.

'Do you miss your Europol colleagues?' Frank asks casually.

'Yes, very much,' Lara admits to his surprise. 'It's funny you ask, because I've just received an invitation from three of them to join them in town tonight.'

'That's a coincidence indeed,' he says, feeling a twinge of jealousy. He'd love to come along; he doesn't feel like spending another evening alone in his flat and falling asleep in front of the TV.

They pass the security post and enter the familiar building.

'But before that, I want to start the search for Lane and take a quick look at the dark web. If it's true there are rumours circulating there about a new kind of virus, then I absolutely need to know about it. I'll call now my colleague inspector to ask him to start the protocol for the missing person's notice in my place. He owes me a favour, so we'll be even again.'

She stops and out of courtesy Frank steps away. While she is phoning, he ponders the press release he has to make at Meredith Weston's request. Although he's always liked his craft, he has to admit that what he's doing now with Lara fascinates him much more. It's more varied and there's also more thrill in it. He routinely speaks in a few standard sentences in the usual pattern of a press release. They say that journalists are customarily lazy, which is why it's important that you deliver the information ready-made and always with the same structure. Once you've created one press release, it's a breeze to whip up the next one in next to no time.

Lara comes to him smiling. 'He's doing it. Come on, the dark web is waiting for us.'

She leads him to the room where they also interrogated Minister Gantois' mistress. They sit down and Lara immediately starts typing furiously. Frank can only watch her slender fingers hover over the keyboard.

'Do you have a special web browser that provides access to the dark web?' he asks.

'Have you forgotten which department I work in? Of course we have. Look, I'm almost logged in.'

A long text appears on the screen. Frank scans it briefly, and notices that it's a kind of warning for the users of the web browser. It states that certain websites on this part of the Internet offer illegal goods, products or services and that their purchase and use are punishable by law.

'That text is one of the realizations of the murdered Minister of Justice. Before that text was in place, the court could not convict the customers of those rogue companies, they had nothing to hold on to. The customers were apparently not aware that buying there was a criminal offence.'

She clicks 'agree and continue' and a page opens that is no different from the home page of a normal search engine such as Google or Bing. Frank had imagined it differently.

She looks to the side and smiles. 'Did you think this would be a morbid black screen, with ominous red letters and diabolical names?'

'No, I didn't, but there's absolutely no difference with a regular web browser.'

'No, and that's intentional. The traders here want the exact same thing as their legal counterparts, which is to create turnover and make a profit. So why make it difficult for the customer?' She types in a name and clicks 'search'. 'First I'll look at the top three of the largest websites: maybe I'll find an announcement of a new computer virus there. They are usually clucking there like chickens when something new's just been launched.' She skims through the pages, but moments later she slides her chair back. 'No, nothing found. Time for plan B.'

She cracks her fingers and moves closer to the screen again. She types in a few commands and Frank now sees a black page pop up, on which Lara enters one instruction after another. The program reminds him of the old MS-DOS operating system from ages back. Perhaps a deliberate choice was made to give it this format, out of nostalgia for computer prehistory.

After a few more minutes' strumming, Lara is ready. 'So, the Wanderer has left. Now we can only wait.'

'Who or what is the Wanderer?' Frank asks curiously as he sees rows of data rolling across the screen at high speed.

'The Wanderer is software that we've developed at Europol. That is, we've basically applied the same technique as the cyber criminals. They use malware that roams the web and constantly looks for weaknesses in websites. When it finds such a breach in the defences, it tries to break in to steal sensitive data or to commit other crimes. At Europol we've also created such malware, called Wanderer, and we use it to do the exact same thing with the websites on the dark web.'

'In other words, Europol is using a virus?' responds Frank.

'Let me rephrase it, it's a matter of equal weapons, equal battle. It's not the time to play morality knight, Frank.'

'Okay, I understand, all means are good to deal with criminals. What exactly are you looking for with that Wanderer?'

'I want to find usernames and passwords with which to log into Internet forums on the dark web. Because that's where we have the best chance of finding news. I'll keep our impersonation as buyers on hand for a while.'

They sit quietly next to each other for a moment and just as Frank wants to ask where she's going tonight with her colleagues, Lara starts strumming the virtual keyboard again. 'While we wait, I'm going to call up the login details for websites that we've taken down. That way I can also try to get onto the forums.'

Frank watches sadly and understands this may take a while. He then decides to concentrate on his own work and logs in on the screen next to it. For half an hour they each work focused on their terrain, until Lara breaks the silence.

'Yes!' she exclaims. 'I've got a bite, four times, no less! Now let's hope I can get something out of it.'

Frank is curious and rolls his chair closer to her again. She selects the first of four lines on her screen and then enters various commands. Obviously, it's not the first time she's done this.

After a few seconds, she curses. 'That won't work,' she says and selects the second line. But she quickly gives up on that one too. 'Too heavily secured, this is going to take too long.' She tries the third of four and that seems to go more smoothly. She pokes Frank with her elbow. 'I'm in,' she says very quietly, as if the website owner could hear her. 'I'm now in the software he used to build the website.'

Frank grins. 'I hope you never take the wrong path.'

'Even if I wanted to, I still have a lot to learn. What I just did only works with smaller traders. They usually set up their own websites and are not particularly expert. With the bigger players it takes much longer.'

Doggedly, she searches her way through what seems to Frank to be a maze of data, search fields and links to other pages. She bites her lips in utter concentration and finally stops typing. She leans back with a triumphant look.

'Voilà, or how do you say that in Belgium? Username and password, ready to use!'

NATO base, Zemst

'Sometimes I feel like Davy Crockett,' Luis says to no one in particular. Righard looks at Eddy, uncomprehending, and shrugs his shoulder.

'Who?' Righard asks.

'Davy Crockett, don't you know him?'

'From the *Miami Vice* TV show?'

That gets him an indignant look from Luis. 'Not at all, that was Sonny Crockett, played by Don Johnson! Know your classics, man.'

'What do you mean, Luis?'

'Davy Crockett was a frontiersman and a tracker. Well, sometimes I feel like a tracker too.'

Righard sighs. 'I don't think it's that adventurous here, you know.'

'No, unfortunately not. And it frustrates me that I still haven't achieved a result. The man or woman who helped Larry Lane managed to cover his tracks well.'

'Have you been able to get the facts on the hacking?' Eddy asks.

'Yes, it was in fact very short. There were only two actions: opening the cell door and turning off a camera. That's all.'

'How could it have happened?'

'With the prison director's user data. They probably used a password finder. Since the username was easy to guess — it was just his name — the password wouldn't have been too difficult either.'

Eddy shakes his head. 'They'll never learn. Can't believe how easy they make it for the thieves.'

'If it's any comfort, Luis, I haven't found anything yet,' Righard says. 'I've been browsing here for quite some time now in the NATO servers, where the self-driving traffic is controlled. It all looks very normal. No data added or removed unexpectedly, no programs that don't belong there.'

'You could almost admire the perpetrator,' Luis muses out aloud.

'Yes, it takes near-genius to design something that can get past that electronic defence wall.'

'Or...' Eddy says.

'Or what?' Righard asks.

'Or it's someone from NATO itself.'

There's a moment of silence as Luis and Righard think about it.

'Even then,' Luis says. 'They work with strict classifications here. Each staff member is given a specific authorization depending on his position. In this way, everyone has only a partial view of the various applications.'

'So that person already has to be stealing an authorization from someone else to get started.'

'I leave things like that to others to figure out,' Luis says.

'Yes, to that attractive female inspector, for example. I saw you looking, Luis, she's your type, isn't she?'

'Oh man, she could be my granddaughter.'

'She seems quite a tough cookie if you ask me', Eddy remarks. 'Okay, something else now: since I haven't found anything yet, I'm off to the Dome now to continue my search on the infected PC.'

'Good idea, Eddy, I hope you find something. Take my car', Righard suggests spontaneously and gives him access to his car.

Twenty minutes later, Eddy steps into the Dome and is welcomed by the same supervisor who accompanied Lara and Frank. Five minutes later he's sitting at the desk of the administrative assistant whose PC was infected by the computer virus. Eddy takes a sip of the hot chocolate offered to him by the friendly supervisor and sets to work. He boots the PC via a USB stick, specially made to perform a secure analysis. The infection seems at first to be gone, but he doesn't stop there. The first thing he wants to investigate is the PC's so-called cache memory, where temporary files and documents are stored. However, that's completely empty. It's probably set to erase everything regularly. Or did the virus do that? Sure enough, so he can forget about that part. He then just opens the internal memory, which corresponds to the hard disk of olden days, and is presented with a lengthy list of files. Eddy lets out a deep sigh. He had hoped beforehand that this would not be the case. But this is apparently an employee who, against her better judgement, always saves documents on her internal memory. There's nothing for it but to go through it. First, he sorts everything by size, with the heaviest files at the top. He subjects the top ten to a close examination. He checks the properties of each file, the date of creation and the dates of any changes. He doesn't notice anything abnormal. It then sorts everything by date, with the most recent first. He patiently checks everything one by one, up to one month back. Again nothing abnormal. Last chance, sort by file type. He ignores the Word and Excel documents, they're not what he's looking for. He's hoping in particular to find an .exe file. To his delight, there are three in the list with that extension. However, it is legal software found on almost every PC in the world.

So Eddy continues looking and starts to comb through all the folders. When he gets to the 'Applications' folder, he sits up in his chair. It's here he has the best chance of encountering a virus. The problem is that there are also many applications here, ranging from antivirus software — which didn't do its job well, by the way — to printers and photo software. He patiently checks folder after folder, until he comes to one which immediately intrigues him by the meaningless name it bears.

Eddy senses he's on to something. He smiles and thinks of Luis, who was just talking about tracking. He'd be quite jealous of him if he discovered something now. He takes a mouse and carefully right-clicks on the file to call up its properties. It's neither big nor small, the creation date is six months ago and no changes have been made. Could this be the computer virus they're looking for? But it's odd that he found it so quickly. Most viruses destroy themselves or leave almost no traces. If this is really the virus, it says a lot about its creator, because then he was really sloppy. However, since this is Larry Lane, he shouldn't take any chances. Eddy doesn't wait and calls Lara.

NATO Headquarters, Evere, Brussels

Frank moves his chair a little closer to the screen to follow what Lara is typing. She is trying to log into a forum on the dark web, using the name and password she has captured via the Wanderer. She gains access without any problem and starts searching the web page, which looks very normal and recognizable to him. There are all kinds of conversations between traders and so-called consumers, neatly classified by category. She searches through some, but finds nothing interesting. She quickly switches to another forum, which at first sight seems promising owing to its beautiful design and orderly structure. She types in the word 'virus' in the search field at the top, and that is far from fruitless. She skims the search results until she stops at one.

'Here, look,' she says.

Frank bends over to read the dialogue. It's a conversation between some traders with crazy names like Hacking Tom and Cyrus The Virus.

'Did you hear? They say White Penny is busy with something big.'

'Something big? 'What do you mean?'

'Huge. Never shown.'

'Can you give more details?'

'No, and you know why.'

Frank reads a little further, but unfortunately the two change the subject.

'White Penny? Do you know that firm?' he asks.

Lara shakes her head and is already typing the name into the dark web. There are all kinds of variations on the name, but there is no exact representation. 'Could you check the normal web, Frank?'

'Of course'. He slides his chair to the right, so that he is also sitting in front of a screen. But he can't find any reference to that name on the regular internet either. 'Could this be the rumour that Dutch hacker was talking about?'

'I think so. We'll give him a call.' Before she can do that, a call comes in.

'Lara Hartman.' She listens for a moment, then raises her thumb to Frank. 'Forward it directly to Black. I'll warn Anthony Dice.'

She disconnects and is clearly very happy. 'I'll have to change my mind about the Three Amigos. Your father claims to have found something on the hard drive of a computer in the Dome. That could be a breakthrough.'

'For real? Awesome!' says Frank, feeling proud of his father. 'And now?'

'The laboratory will analyse the file in several steps and thus be in a position to conclude whether it's a virus or not. An antivirus can then be made, based on these findings.'

Just like a vaccine is concocted against viruses that cause a disease, Frank thinks.

Meanwhile, Lara calls Dice and is disappointed to land on his answering machine. She leaves a message and a second later she's on the phone again. This time she does get someone on the line. 'Can I speak to Jonah, please? Lara Hartman, Europol.' As she waits, she raises her eyebrows. 'Guessing from that hoarse smoker's voice, it's the girl with the dreadlocks. Perhaps due for her umpteenth joint', she says disapprovingly.

Minutes later, the hacker still hasn't answered the phone and Frank notices that she's getting agitated. Just when she's about to give up, she is answered.

'Jonah,' she says, crossly, 'you may want to give your secretary a lesson in efficiency. I've a question for you. Does the name White Penny mean anything to you?'

Frank is curious about Jonah's answer and hopes he can help them further. But when Lara hangs her lip, that sadly turns out not to be the case.

'Okay, thanks, Jonah. If you hear anything else, please call me.' She looks at Frank and shakes her head. 'It means nothing to him. Just check the Europol databases, you never know.'

But this control is also fruitless. While she is doing that, Frank is thinking about what was on that forum.

'Lara, what those two were talking about, "something big": would that be about the attack on the Dome? What was the date of their conversation?'

'Good question.' She calls back the dialogue and points to the date. '14 February: That's the date of the attack. But there's no time indication. So in principle it could be, because the attack took place in the afternoon.'

'But is that "big" enough?' he wonders aloud. 'What's bigger than an attack that destroys an entire conference hall?'

'Something global perhaps?' She gives him a piercing look and he sees a moment's hesitation in her eyes. But then she grins. 'Let's wait first for news from Black's lab. We must now concentrate fully on locating Larry Lane. And for that, we're going to start by interrogating the only two visitors he's ever received in prison: Peter Black and Anthony Dice.'

NATO Headquarters, Evere, Brussels

Lara first sets up an online meeting with Peter Black. Fortunately, he's available and soon comes onto the screen. 'Hi, Peter. Are you already analysing what Eddy Willems sent you?'

'Of course, why should we wait? It's too early to say anything, though.'

'Yes, I understand,' Lara responds. 'Actually I called you for something else. FYI, this conversation is being recorded.'

'Yes, I saw that already,' Black replies with a grin.

Lara goes straight to the point. 'Why did you go and visit Larry Lane in prison?'

Frank, who is sitting next to her off screen, is no longer shocked by her approach, he is already used to it. He can't see Black, but the calmness with which the latter answers with a counter question doesn't shock him either.

'Is that relevant to your investigation?' Black asks, deadpan.

'A criminal being visited in jail by a senior NATO official, I do consider that relevant, yes', Lara states bluntly.

Frank hears Black sigh excessively.

'Okay, if you think this might help. At least know that I don't regret visiting him at all. I'll explain to you why I did so. Look behind me, Inspector.'

Frustrated at not joining the conversation, Frank is curious to see what Lara sees next.

'Books,' she says, 'all books.'

'Not just any books,' Black replies indignantly. 'Without exception they deal with one specific theme, namely the brains of criminals. My interest is purely scientific. Everyone has a hobby, Inspector, you too, I suppose. You have to know that I studied psychology in addition to computer science. My passion is trying to fathom the minds of criminals. More specifically, criminals working in my sector. Criminals who design viruses to achieve their goals of money or power. Or both, because they usually go together, don't they?'

Lara doesn't answer and Black continues.

'Larry Lane was and is an interesting phenomenon. He first caught my attention when he was CEO of Bio Dynamics. He delivered some serious punches, the pinnacle of which was, of course, the hijacking of NATO's systems. Listen, Inspector, it's purely out of scientific interest that I went to see him, that's all. Your boss, Anthony Dice, is aware of this, by the way. Feel free to ask him.'

'What did you talk to Lane about?' Lara questions him.

'I especially wanted to know how he came up with his ideas. How that process works in his head? My intention was to find a certain pattern in that and then compare it with the process in other criminal geniuses.'

'Did you record that conversation?'

Frank hears Black laugh, but it's a fake laugh. 'Inspector, I didn't have the opportunity to do that. I had to hand in all the electronics at the entrance to the building.'

'Did he say anything about the plans he had if he were released?'

'Yes. It'll come as no surprise that his great dream is world domination. He's quite a megalomaniac, but that you already knew.'

'Did he give details about that, how he would go about it?'

'No, not that. He's too smart for that. You know, with Lane we lost a great scientist. He could have done a lot of good for our planet. Unfortunately, somewhere along the way, he chose the wrong path and now he's permanently lost to humanity.'

'How can we find him? Did he say anything about his dream destination? Or about accomplices?'

'He never talked about running. I don't think that crossed his mind. The only person he mentioned briefly was the manager he appointed at Bio Dynamics for operational matters. He spoke highly of him, but his name escapes me now.'

'Not Blair by any chance? Leslie Blair?'

'Yes that's him. So you know him?'

'Blair disappeared without a trace after we rounded up Lane. We haven't heard from him for a year.'

'Aha. Lane told me then he was convinced others would take his part now that he was behind bars for a long time.'

'Did he insinuate that Blair would?' Lara wants to know.

'No, not in those words. But I remember he said that a man can trust no more than one person outside of himself. And in his case that was Leslie Blair, as he confirmed at the time.'

'Anything else?' Lara asks impatiently.

'No. My conclusion was very simple: Larry Lane is a genius. And, unfortunately, also a psychopath.'

Lara thanks Black, ends the call, and turns to Frank, who pulls up his chair.

'Do you believe that?' she asks. 'That he went to see Lane out of scientific interest?'

'It could be, he wouldn't be the first with such interests.'

'It's a pity that the conversations between prisoners and visitors are not recorded.'

'That's absolutely forbidden,' Frank says, shocked. 'That's an invasion of privacy.'

She dismisses that argument. 'Lane is and remains a dangerous, convicted felon. I don't think he ever stopped planning.'

'I can buy into that, but would Black have anything to do with that, do you think?'

'I don't trust him,' she says, staring straight ahead. 'On the other hand, Anthony seems to trust him. And very much so, because he has given him an important role in NATO.'

She leans back in her chair and closes her eyes. Her face is completely relaxed and the frown that is so typical of her is now nowhere to be seen. She thinks for a moment and then takes a decision. 'I'm going to call Anthony about his visit to Lane and then ask his honest opinion about Black. Are you moving out of the picture again?'

Frank pushes his chair a bit to the side and keeps still. He's not frustrated at having to do this, after all, he's not an inspector. Rather, he's flattered that she doesn't ask him to leave the room.

A minute later he hears Dice's voice. 'Lara, quick, because I don't have much time.'

'Hi, Anthony, can I ask you something? Why did you visit Larry Lane when he was in prison in Haren?'

'Why do you want to know, Lara?' Dice replies curtly. Even her boss no longer seems surprised by her straightforward approach.

'Well, I thought, *hoped* he might have said something to you that might help me track him down.'

'Larry Lane? That man's too cunning for that. No, I put him on the grill to find out his motives. But all he did was look at me with that mocking smile of his.'

'Did he talk about Leslie Blair, his second-in-command from those days?'

'No, why?'

'Because he did mention it to Black.'

'Oh yes, that's true, Peter went to visit him too. He returned as empty-handed as I did. So you haven't tracked down Lane yet?'

'No, but his description is spread all over Europe. All facial recognition cameras in Belgium have been updated so that they are now actively searching for him. The privacy committee has given its approval for this.'

'That's good, but it won't be enough to catch Lane. Dig deeper, Lara, I'm counting on you to find him as soon as possible.'

Frank hears nothing more and understands that the conversation is over. Lara looks a bit non-plussed and for the first time, he gains a glimpse of her vulnerability. 'We'll find Lane,' he tries to encourage her. But his words of encouragement fail to register and he just keeps quiet. He doesn't believe them himself anyway.

Elewijt, same time

The municipality of Elewijt lies a few kilometres away from the secret NATO base in Zemst. This village was a real battlefield during the First World War one hundred and twenty years ago. Hundreds of Belgian soldiers lost their lives in the unequal struggle against the disciplined German troops. Today the village is very quiet, especially in the dead-end street that leads to the illustrious Tervuursesteenweg, where battles to the death took place all those years ago. In that quiet street, where car traffic consists solely of the residents commuting to and fro, the houses are all set back from the street. As a result, they all have fairly large front gardens with — depending on who lives there — seas of flowers or easy-to-maintain lawn. On almost every home, a small appliance just below the gutter bears the name of the company that provides security to the house in question.

On a neat house, just beyond a bend, there are even two such devices, in an unobtrusive grey colour. The fully automatic shutters have been raised to let in as much daylight as possible. The Google Assistant, in the form of a slender speaker, has nothing to do and has placed itself in sleep mode. That's because Eddy Willems is the only one who eagerly uses it, while his wife Nadine has never really been a fan. This ex-policewoman with a busy social life is currently busy in the kitchen preparing a cake for her elderly neighbour. As she puts the round pastry into the oven, she happily hums along to a song she hears on the Internet radio. She sets the baking time and then, smiling, settles into her cosy sofa with her e-reader to devour the latest book by her favourite author.

After a few minutes a click is heard in the kitchen and the light in a second oven comes on. The small screen above the oven window, with the blue numbers for the temperature display, also lights up at the same time. Then the numbers climb at lightning speed, without stopping when even the maximum temperature is reached. This creates a destructive heat inside the oven. After thirty minutes at full power, the first crack appears in the glass of the oven window, followed immediately by another. The top layer of the wooden cabinet into which the oven is built starts to peel off due to the impact of the heat. The inner wall of the oven itself is now red hot. Everything within a metre of that intense heat source is now subject to the radiant heat.

Gradually the oven turns into a bomb and it is too late to do anything about it. With a deafening blow, the oven explodes and shards of glass and razor-sharp pieces of wood shear into everything within reach.

The Dome, Brussels

Immediately after the phone call with the Europol inspector, Eddy forwards the potential virus to Peter Black's laboratory. After that he does further research for an hour, but unfortunately finds nothing else relevant. Tired, he leaves the Dome and heads to the parking lot to pick up Righard's car. He plans to drive back to Zemst to help his two colleagues with their search. The euphoria from just now, when he discovered the virus on the computer, has already disappeared. He's not sure this virus is also responsible for the crash of those two vehicles. If the laboratory analysis shows it to be a very complex and powerful virus, then he will have to change his mind. But his gut feeling tells him this will not be the case. He resolves not to discuss this immediately, certainly not with Righard, who has a tendency to bang on. Eddy realizes he doesn't have a leg to stand on. But his experience teaches him that this is not always necessary in order to be right.

Just as he is about to get into the car, his smartwatch starts beeping loudly. He is startled, because he does not recognize the shrill sound, which is completely different from the normal ringing tone he hears when he is called. He looks curiously at the screen and his heart skips a beat. It spins in front of his eyes for a moment. Is what he sees there really what he thinks it is?

He brings the watch closer to his eyes and the monotonous sound penetrates deep into his head.

Fire alarm kitchen. Fire alarm kitchen.

These two words keep running through the display, where he normally only sees names and phone numbers. A shiver runs down his spine. Is his house on fire? The first thing that comes to mind is his wife Nadine. Is she at home? With a dry mouth he says: 'Call Nadine', and the connection is made.

The three words, meanwhile, go on and on, and while he waits, they hypnotize him. To his dismay, Nadine doesn't answer. Her answering machine starts and Eddy disconnects.

Oh God, let nothing serious be wrong.

'Hey amigo!' he says to activate his Google Assistant. His voice trembles as loudly as when he proposed to Nadine years ago in Italy.

'Hi, Eddy', he hears. He's happy that the assistant answers, because he has no idea as to the situation in his own house.

'Show camera images.'

The instruction is immediately followed and every few seconds he is shown a different part of his home. Eddy made some serious investments in security some time ago. He had every reason to do so as one wave of break-ins followed another. 'Come on,' he hisses between his teeth. He realizes he is now confronted with a design flaw in the system he had not foreseen. He has to wait until he gets to the images of the kitchen, he cannot summon them first. When they finally appear, he shouts in panic: 'Stop... Oh no,' he moans. The screen shows that where his oven used to be, a large, gaping hole has now appeared. The cabinet that housed the oven has been largely torn to pieces and parts of it are completely in flames. He deduces that something must have exploded. 'Sprinklers!' Eddy yells way too loud, attracting the attention of some businessmen walking to their car a little further away on the parking lot.

His relief is great when he sees the jets of water coming down from the ceiling. Although he still has no idea what the hell has happened, he hopes that this will at least quell the disaster. But where's Nadine?

'Show camera images,' he says again. He wants to make sure she's not in the house and there's no fire in the other rooms. There, however, everything seems normal and when he comes back to the images of the kitchen, he sees that the flames have practically gone out.

The tension in his shoulders eases and when he sees no more flames, he says: 'Stop sprinklers', thinking of the water damage. He remains focused on the screen. Could Nadine have been present at the time of the blast? Is she maybe hurt or worse? Is she lying there somewhere, out of camera range? Eddy feels his heart racing in his chest and takes a deep breath. He's pleased to see that the fire seems to have been extinguished, but where is the fire brigade? In theory, they should have been warned simultaneously by the alarm system. He immediately gets the answer to that question when his watch rings, and now it's the everyday ringtone.

'Mr Willems? Vilvoorde fire brigade here. We've arrived at your house, will you open the door, please?'

Eddy switches to Google Assistant and instructs it to unlock the front door. To his surprise, this instruction is not understood by the device and so he's asked to repeat it. Eddy curses and gives the instruction again. Not recognized again! He realizes he's losing precious time and can't bear to think that his wife is in there, injured or… Then he suddenly remembers he changed the door opening instruction some time ago. He did this for security reasons, in case someone succeeded in communicating remotely with his Google Assistant. After pronouncing the new instruction, he receives confirmation that the door is open. Quickly he switches back to the fire brigade. 'The door is open. Is my house on fire? Can you see my wife?' he asks anxiously.

'No, there's no visible fire. I'm going in now.' After a minute's silence, the firefighter returns. 'At first sight, no one inside. We'll keep you informed.'

The fireman disconnects and Eddy drops his wrist. It dawns on him what just happened, and his legs suddenly go limp. He opens the car door and slumps into the driver's seat. Staring straight ahead, he hears the regular ringing tone again and immediately picks up.

'Eddy, has something happened!' he hears Nadine say in a hoarse voice and it's like a hundred-pound block of concrete falls from his shoulders.

'Nadine, I'm so glad to hear you. Where are you? You didn't answer when I called.'

'At the neighbour's. I went to take her a cake and I was walking outside when I heard the bang, and my smartwatch is still inside because I was just doing the dishes at Ria's. Eddy, it's horrible. Something exploded in our house,' she replies.

'Yes I know. I received a fire alarm message and could extinguish the fire using the Assistant. Are you okay?'

'Yes. But Eddy, it was really close. If I hadn't made that cake for Ria then…'

There's a moment's silence as they both think the unthinkable. 'Nadine, stay there, I'll be over right away.'

'Eddy, wait, what actually happened? What exploded?' 'An oven, I think.'

'An oven? But I just used it to bake a cake. And I'm sure I turned it off, there's no other way.'

'Nadine? It's not your fault. This needs further investigation.'

There is a moment of silence and Eddy knows what his wife is going to say next.

That it's enough now. That he must stop fighting the virus developers and all those criminals circulating around them. And that the fire is not an accident, but malicious intent. After their conversation, which went exactly as he had predicted, Eddy thinks about it for a moment.

If he is very honest, he has to admit she's right in saying that a line has now been crossed. First there was the attack on the conference, now there is an attack on their house. He's not a police officer who is being threatened with the aim of stopping an investigation. He's an expert in security, in computer crime. A very well-known one indeed, but so far he has only given advice to anyone who wanted it. Is it because he is now helping NATO? That's the only reason he can think of. But how does the perpetrator of this attack know he's cooperating with NATO? There's been no communication about this. He must find out who tipped off the perpetrator of this attack about his helping them find what could be the virus of the decade.

Sint-Jans-Molenbeek, same time

Larry Lane opens his ultra-thin laptop and types in some instructions. He repeats this a few times, but to his frustration he is then blocked by the website security. So he has to start over again. Like an accomplished 1960s secretary, he quickly types commands on the virtual keyboard. To circumvent the unexpectedly smart security, he uses a few techniques that he has developed himself. While waiting to access the website that will hopefully provide him with interesting information, he opens a bottle of water. The nasi goreng he's just eaten from the Chinese takeaway dances around in his stomach and intestines. He drinks the bottle dry in one gulp and grins on seeing that he has entered the website.

Lane remembers what a fun moment it was when he hacked into a website for the first time, as a 12-year-old. It was all euphoria then. Now he feels only a hint of the excitement he experienced in those early years with every successful hacking or scam. Unfortunately, that feeling has faded more and more into the background as the years have gone by. That's why he raised the bar higher and higher, just like an athlete keeps pushing his limits. It's time for him to come to the fore again, and for the débâcle of a year ago to be erased for good.

Unashamedly letting a harsh burp reverberate in his shabby flat, he exhorts himself to calm down. It's important to do this step by step. And the first step is to make sure no one can find him. That's why he's very interested in the website he now has on screen. On that site, the data from the active face recognition cameras is stored and modified. Curious, he goes in search of the parameters that have been set for the cameras. After finding them, he changes some data, and moments later claps his laptop shut again. That was a breeze.

NATO Headquarters, Evere, Brussels

In the evening, Eddy has returned to the NATO base in Evere. He's sitting there with Righard and Luis at the table in the immense canteen. They can speak freely, as none of the staff are around at this time. His two colleagues are shocked when he tells them what has happened, and have a hard time believing it.

'Are you sure it wasn't an accident?' Luis asks again.

'Luis, an oven doesn't explode just like that. Certainly not a device that's only two years old. It was even still under warranty!'

'Luis, this is no coincidence,' Righard intervenes. 'Eddy discovers a virus and wham, there's an attack on his house.'

Eddy shakes his head. 'That would be very quick, Righard. One hour afterwards? Then, so to speak, there has to be a camera pointed at me to see what I'm doing.'

'But if not for that reason, then why?'

'Because someone's found out you're assisting NATO?' Luis asks in turn. 'We're helping them too, does this mean we're in danger too?'

'Shouldn't we first ask ourselves who knows we are here?' Righard adds.

Eddy points. 'There's someone who might be able to tell us.'

Lara and Frank enter the canteen and approach them.

'Nice,' Righard says. 'We're like a bunch of superheroes with the five of us.'

Frank is very happy to see his father in one piece and that nothing has happened to his mother.

'Sorry about the damage to your house, Eddy,' Lara says. 'I suppose you have a small server at home, when can we take a look at it? If your home network was hacked, we might find traces of it.'

'Anytime you want. All I need is a computer and an internet connection.'

'Okay, then let's go.' Lara gets up, but Righard stops her.

'Inspector, I'm sorry, but we want to know something first.' Lara crosses her arms over her chest and waits.

'Who knows about our collaboration?' Righard asks.

Lara doesn't seem surprised at that question. 'Except myself and Frank, there's only my boss, Anthony Dice, and the head of the engineering research team, Peter Black. The members of the lab in

Zemst have seen you too, but they don't know who you are. Your assignment there was not explained.'

'And no one else? Administrative assistants, assistants or someone like that?'

Lara shakes her head. 'We've deliberately kept the number of people limited. We feared that if other experts heard this, they would be asking why they weren't part of the team.'

'So not because you fear reprisals?' Luis asks. Lara can't hide a smile. 'With all due respect, you're not secret agents or spies. We enlisted your help as independent experts, that's all.'

'Inspector, so you don't think the fire at Eddy's house is in retaliation for his helping NATO?'

'That's why I want to check whether someone has penetrated his home network. If that's the case, we should indeed assume it.'

Eddy hasn't said anything for a long time, but now speaks. 'Inspector, can my colleagues get protection, please? I don't want the same thing to happen to them.'

Lara nods. 'I've just talked it over with my boss. While we're not thinking about that scenario, we're looking internally at how best to approach it. It's true there's little we can do against your system being hacked. A colleague of mine will contact you today, I've already sent him your details.'

'Thank you,' Righard and Luis say in unison.

'Now, as we're talking about it, I don't think this was a murder attempt,' Lara tells Eddy. 'For me it was a warning. There was no way the perpetrator could have known that you or your wife would be home at the time of the explosion.'

'Unless he's watching Eddy?' Luis suggests.

Lara has been very calm so far, but now she's agitated. 'Please, what did I just say? If someone really wants to thwart the search for an antivirus, he has something else to do than shadow Eddy. Then it would make much more sense for an attempt to be made to blow up the lab or something like that.'

Everyone at the table recognizes the reasonableness of this statement.

'Could it be Larry Lane?' Frank thinks out aloud.

Righard nods. 'Yes, out of revenge, you mean. Because it was your father who succeeded in wiping out the contamination of NATO's systems a year ago.'

'It could indeed be Lane, because he's now at large,' Frank states. 'On the other hand, I don't think he knows it was my father who gave the final blow to his beloved virus.'

It is Righard who now speaks. 'Supposing it's Larry Lane, which I think is very likely, how did he find out? And is he also responsible for the death of Jan Goethals, Minister Gantois and all our colleagues?'

'At that time he was still in prison, so that's impossible,' says Luis. 'Unless he ordered someone from outside the prison. In that case he has an accomplice.'

'You mean Lane planned all of the above and had someone else carry it out?' Righard asks. 'But then he had to be able to communicate with the outside world in some way, right? How did he do that?'

'Yes, good question,' Lara has to admit. 'This needs to be investigated urgently. But first your home network, Eddy, let's go?'

All five get up and walk to the exit. Frank goes last and watches Lara take the lead again. The older men have trouble keeping up with her. No, they are definitely not superheroes.

Stock Exchange, Brussels, 8 pm.

Frank is cold and pulls his coat collar a little higher. Lara, walking beside him, seems unbothered by the frosty temperature. The clouds that appear when they exhale are nevertheless proof that it's very cold in the streets of Brussels. Frank sees the Stock Exchange building looming at the end of the street, which is home to ten Thai restaurants. He still can't believe Lara has asked him out. True, not with her alone, but with her friends.

After their futile attempts to find traces of hacking in his father's network, she had unexpectedly asked him if he'd like to join them tonight. He had, of course, said yes immediately. They had said goodbye to the three older men and had driven straight from Evere to the centre of the capital. There Lara had left her car in an underground parking lot. He doesn't mind that he's dependent on Lara to get home again. In an emergency, he can always take an Uber, although he doesn't like those forced conversations with drivers who are total strangers. On the way they only talked about the virus, but he thinks that's okay. When all's said and done, he doesn't know her well enough to talk to her about other things. Which doesn't mean he wouldn't like to. Maybe later, in the restaurant where they will meet her colleagues.

'Do you know the Art Nouveau brasserie we're going to?' Lara asks.

'The Falstaff? Sure, that's a well-known name in Brussels. Has been around for a hundred years, I think.'

'Since 1903,' she corrects him.

'That's very precise. Did you look that up?'

'Yes, I always like to know the history of the places I go to. You Belgians should be proud of your capital, with its glorious history.'

Frank doesn't exactly share her opinion. He sees Brussels mainly as a tangle of grey streets and one big chaos, even now that the centre has been made completely traffic-free.

'I love those beautiful stained-glass windows, they're really unique', Lara continues.

With that he wholeheartedly agrees. 'Yes, they are wonderful. Almost a work of art.'

He went to eat there once and he was impressed. Nowadays you would have to search a long time for someone who can produce something like that.

They arrive at the old brasserie and through the windows he sees the warm glow of the burning fireplace. There are lots of people inside: all the tables seem to be occupied.

'Have you made a reservation?' Frank asks.

'Nick always takes care of that, he's the most organized of us all. Just remember one thing, they're not colleagues from the cybercrime department. That means they don't know anything about what we're doing right now,' she says, pushing open the heavy glass door and entering.

He follows her inside and a soothing warmth envelops him. At one of the tables someone waves at them and Lara waves back.

'There they are, come on,' she says eagerly.

Frank follows her through the history-soaked building and can't help but glance at the plates of the chattering people at the other tables. What he sees are without exception very popular dishes. Stew, mussels, filet américain, they are all there. The odours are delicious.

'Hi, colleagues', Lara greets two men and a woman who get up when they see them coming.

'Hi Lara, you look great!' replies the woman, who could be Lara's antitype. Not as tall as her, with short, almost shaved blond hair and with hips twice as broad as Lara's. The two women embrace each other warmly while Frank introduces himself to the two male colleagues.

'Hello, I'm Frank,' he says holding out his hand.

'Sorry man, we're not going to do that,' says one of them. Remember covid? I haven't shaken hands since. Nothing personal. I'm Nick, pleased to meet you.'

The other, a large man with a friendly face, does hold out his hand to Frank, who is still perplexed by the first man's reaction.

'Hi, I'm Steven', he says, giving Frank a firm handshake. 'Don't be angry and blame my friend here, he has no manners.'

In return, he gets a shove from Nick and they sit down laughing.

'Hello, I'm Nina,' says Lara's female colleague, who has come to stand next to Frank. She grabs him tightly by the shoulders and smacks a kiss on his cheek.

Lara sees this happen with a smile and gestures for him to sit next to her. 'Frank is helping me with my secret investigation,' she informs the others when everyone's seated at the table.

'What are you investigating again, Lara? Has another hotel chain been hacked and should we be concerned about our credit card details?'

Lara shakes her head. 'No. Come closer.'

Everyone leans towards her curiously. 'Frank and I are experimenting with an antivirus that can be inserted into the human body using a chip. And we're looking for guinea pigs for this. Will you join us?'

Amidst the hubbub in the Falstaff, their table becomes very quiet. Frank enjoys the consternation on the three faces. He sees confusion, disbelief and, in Nick, especially disgust.

Until Steven starts laughing loudly and points to Lara. 'For a moment, just a moment, I thought you meant it, Lara!'

Nick now also realizes that none of this is true, and relaxes his shoulders. He was probably already thinking about the best way to say he won't.

'Okay, we understand. So it's top secret', says Nina understandingly. Lara shrugs and nods apologetically.

'What are we going to eat?' Nick asks.

'Carbonades,' Lara, Steven, and Nina shout in unison.

Lara leans toward Frank. Our regular joke. We eat the same thing every time here and we can't get enough of it. What will you eat?'

'Haven't thought about it yet,' Frank says truthfully. 'Mussels maybe.'

'Shall we order?' Steven suggests, drumming on the table with the blade of his knife and his fork. 'Okay, but first a half-and-half?'

'Of course,' is the reply and Lara waves to a passing waiter.

Everyone orders and soon four large glasses are placed on the table. Frank, who doesn't know what a half-and-half is, ordered one anyway because he didn't want to spoil the atmosphere.

'Santé', they shout, and the glasses are clinked.

Frank carefully tastes the drink, which is apparently the Falstaff's house cocktail. He concludes that it's not the best cocktail he's ever drunk. 'What's in there?' he asks Lara.

'Beer and Sprite,' she replies mischievously. 'Nice, isn't it?'

He pouts like he's seen Lara do, and she gets the message. 'If you don't like it, feel free to order something else: we'll drink yours, you know.'

He shakes his head. 'No, it's okay.'

'Frank, tell us something about yourself?' Nina inquires.

Frank has seen that question coming, and has thought ahead about what he will answer. He has decided to

keep it superficial, which he does now, with a touch of humour.

'And isn't Lara having you running around everywhere?'

'No, rather after her, actually.'

This is received with a smile and Nina adds something puzzling. 'Then you're not the only one, Frank.'

There's a moment's silence and then Steven starts telling a joke. It's not a very good one and Frank laughs more out of courtesy than the joke. Before Steven can start another, they are saved by the waiter, who brings four carbonades flamandes and one dish of mussels. From his question 'Who are the carbonades for?' Frank deduces that the waiter has not yet gained much experience in the hospitality industry.

The food is eaten with pleasure and the conversations at the table remain interesting all evening, also for Frank. He's always part of the conversations, and he really appreciates that. Before he knows it, several hours have passed and the bill is asked for. It is neatly divided into five, a principle that everyone immediately agrees with. Once outside he and Lara say goodbye to the rest as they have to go in the other direction. It seems to have become even colder and they hurry to the underground garage. They chat for a while on the way.

'Did you like it?' Lara asks.

'Yes, nice people, your colleagues. I was surprised Nick wouldn't shake my hand.'

'Yes I know. But don't hold it against him. During the pandemic fourteen years ago, he lost his grandparents to covid. He's never really got over it. Sometimes I suspect he's contracted some kind of contamination fantasy.'

'I'm very sorry. Thanks, now I understand better.'

They enter the parking garage and Frank is happy to find himself in a warm environment again. 'I'll pay the parking,' he says and opens the payment app on his smartwatch.

'No way,' Lara replies, and with a wink: 'Business expenses, you know.'

Moments later they are in the car and Lara heads for Evere. When they arrive, Frank refastens his coat. He has to go and fetch his car from the NATO parking lot.

'Thanks for being there,' she says and before he can say anything back, she kisses him on the cheek. 'See you tomorrow?'

'Till tomorrow, and thanks for the invite and the lift,' he replies surprised. He gets out and as she drives off he waves at her.

Walking to his car, he remembers that tonight he got two kisses from two different women. But the latter was by far the better.

Grimbergen, 17 February 2034, 7:02 am

Frank is startled awake by the sound of his watch. Sleep-drunk he shouts 'Sleep!' to his smartwatch with the intention of snoozing his alarm clock. But the sound repeats itself And then again. He shouts again, but in vain. With half-closed eyes, he grabs for it with the intention of switching off the alarm manually. But then he sees that it's not his alarm clock at all. It's three messages in a row and they're from Lara.

He is immediately wide awake and sits up in bed. Why does Lara send him three messages so early in the morning? He rubs the sleep from his eyes and reads the first message. 'Antivirus OK. Takes effect today.' The second message is even shorter. 'Make press release!' And finally, the third message he reads as an invitation. '9:00 am, meeting at Anthony's.' She didn't dress it up at all. No 'Good morning, Frank', no smileys, no avatars. He now stows away any illusions he might have been under after yesterday's evening out, and that goodnight kiss.

He throws off the sheets and goes to the bathroom. An hour later he's in the car and arrives at NATO in plenty of time. Along the way, he's already figured out what the press release ought to look like, hopefully Weston will agree. He thinks she will; so far she has not interfered with the communication, but of course there's not been much communication. Today they can finally bring good news to the outside world. That will be good for everyone involved in this case. He still finds it amazing that an antivirus can be developed so quickly. Perhaps they worked double shifts in the laboratories, but it's still impressive. Hopefully that antivirus works as it should and they will be spared from new attacks.

After passing through the guard post and following his escort, he arrives at the conference room where he first met Lara. He steps inside and notices that everyone is already there, including his father and the two other experts.

'Now we're all here, we can start', Dice announces and dims the windows of the room.

Frank closes the door behind him and quickly sits down.

'First the good news. Peter Black's team has completely analysed the virus and was able to identify it. It's very similar to another virus that we already had in our archive and for which we have an antivirus. They worked through the night to make a modified version of it and they've succeeded.' He points to Frank. 'Now it's up to you. Prepare a press release and send it to Meredith Weston. It must be sent out into the world as soon as possible. Then have it translated from English into all Member State languages.'

Frank nods and is happy to feel again the excitement he feels when a tight deadline is imposed on him. Others may be stressed by this, but it only energizes him. He wonders if he should leave the meeting now, but Dice doesn't say anything, so he just sits there. He's curious as to what they will learn next.

'Peter is ensuring that the antivirus is installed as quickly as possible on the servers where the Butlers are managed centrally. He'll also make it publicly available and urge the biggest companies to activate it today. Frank, you also have to write a text for that. So much for the good news.'

Frank knows what's coming next.

'Larry Lane is still at large. How is that possible, Lara?' Dice gives her an angry look, but Lara doesn't lower her eyes. 'It's true. We haven't found him yet. But a lot of work has already been done that allows us to rule out all kinds of things. For example, the company from which the phishing email was sent has nothing to do with it, my team has investigated this. The golfers who witnessed Minister Gantois' death have been questioned. They have stated that they saw how the female passenger tried everything to get the driver out of the golf cart. In this way we can rule out that she had anything to do with his death, especially since she had no motive to kill him. We have checked that. She has no legal claim to any part of his money or property, because there is no record of it anywhere.'

She pauses for a moment and Frank notices that Dice is still glaring at her.

'The payment made by the slain security expert in crypto currency is also a dead end. Before we could identify the account holder, the money had already been transferred to other accounts and split into different amounts. The amounts were all collected in cash.'

'Lara, there must be something we can continue with, right?' Dice asks, disappointed.

'Yes, we have something. Just before this meeting I received a message from my colleagues at EC3 who have been examining the access badges to the Dome. It's via these badges that these three gentlemen here were warned about the explosions.'

'Yes, and?' Dice urges her on.

'My team has traced the sender of the two messages to within a few hundred yards.'

She glances at everyone around the table and then throws it out. 'They are 100 percent sure that the messages were sent from the territory of the municipality of Zemst.'

NATO Headquarters, Evere, Brussels

Zemst? That's where our laboratory is!' exclaims Dice, looking at Lara in disbelief.

'I've checked personally, Anthony, the data they've shown me is spot on.'

'So Lane has an accomplice in Peter's lab?' Dice thinks out aloud.

'Looks like it, yes,' Lara says. 'In Zemst there's no other base than ours, so...'

'May I say something?' Eddy asks.

Dice, whose anger has turned to disbelief, nods.

'First, those messages saved our lives and the lives of many others. So maybe the sender is not the same as the perpetrator of the attack. Second, it takes a lot of skill and guts to penetrate the Dome's network and hack into the messaging functionality there. Not just anyone can do that.'

'Could it have happened via the virus?'

Righard explains: 'In principle, yes. It's a type of virus that takes control of an operating system, in this case the control of the central heating. It can equally well have taken control of the messaging module in the badges. Lara, can your team pinpoint the location more precisely? Can they say which lab computer was used to send the messages?'

'No, I asked them directly. Sorry.'

'Good, then I'm going to have Peter screen the history of all computers in the lab in Zemst. That's the only way to find out. Perhaps Peter even has an inkling as to who might have done it.'

Frank notices that Lara is hesitant to say something. Dice has also seen it. 'Yes, Lara?'

'Anthony, with all due respect, it could be Peter himself.'

Dice thinks about that for a moment and then nods. 'Yes, in theory. But I don't believe it. I've known him too long for that and he has too good a track record for NATO.'

Lara falls silent and looks at the floor.

'Frank, are you starting the press releases?' Dice asks gruffly.

Frank is startled and jumps up. 'Yes, I'm starting now,' he says, and he steps to the door.

Apparently the meeting is over, because everyone follows suit. Frank sees Lara storm off in her typical style. He would like to consult with her, but he really has no time for that right now. Further on he finds an empty room, where he throws himself into composing the texts.

An hour and a half later he's done and forwards everything to Weston and Dice. Immediately afterwards he thinks of Lara. She didn't seem to agree with what Dice said. Her comment that Peter Black could be the culprit intrigues him. Is that the logic used by all inspectors, i.e. not excluding anyone in advance? Or does she have a concrete reason to suspect that man?

Frank is curious about her train of thought and goes looking for her. He soon finds her in the room where they questioned the woman in the golf cart the day before. She's on the phone and Frank tries to make as little noise as possible as he settles down at the desk next to her.

'What do you mean?' Can you give more details?' he hears her say. There's a moment's silence and then she presses for more information. 'What was he busy with at the time? Why can't you tell me?' Apparently the person on the other end of the line doesn't want to reveal anything more. 'Okay then. If you change your mind, call me, okay?' she says grumpily. She hangs up and sighs. 'He won't say what he was doing,' she says disappointedly.

'Who?'

'Black. That was Jonah, the Dutch hacker, you remember? I want to find out where he knows Black from.'

Frank remembers indeed that the hacker had said something about it.

'Well, he did give a hint and I appreciate that.'

Frank can't follow. 'What do you mean?'

'After I asked him a dozen times, he finally said: 'Black hasn't stolen his name.'

He looks at her and she observes that he fails to get her meaning. 'For me he means that Black was a *black hat hacker*. A hacker who does not work ethically and sometimes dares to take illegal paths.' 'You really think that man has something to do with it, don't you?'

'Yes, I do,' she confesses. 'I wouldn't be surprised if he's the one working with Larry Lane.'

'Could Black have committed those attacks?'

'Why not? Maybe he did it at Lane's behest, maybe he's even his partner and they've hatched a grand plan together.'

For Frank, she's jumping to very big conclusions. 'To what purpose? To sabotage self-driving traffic. What good does it do them?'

'Creating chaos in the world. And benefiting from it, in one way or another.'

They're interrupted by a ringtone. It's Lara's watch. She answers, listens carefully, and just before hanging up, thanks the caller with a straight face. Then she looks at Frank.

That was Anthony. The screening of the computers came back negative, just as I expected. Are you coming?'

'Where to?' Frank asks in surprise.

'You'll see. Come on, are you my partner or not?' she asks, smiling.

He has no reply to that and without knowing where they're going, he follows her outside.

When Lara gives the address in Zemst to the car's Butler, Frank knows where they are heading.

'What are you up to, Lara?' he asks when they've left.

'I want to find proof that Black's the man we're looking for. Or proof that he isn't.'

'Are you going to interrogate him?'

'No, I've already done that, it wouldn't work. We have to approach it differently.'

'Then what are you going to do?'

'No, what are we going to do', she corrects him. 'Because I need your help. Sorry, I know what I'm about to ask you has nothing to do with your assignment for NATO, but I can't ask anyone else. Are you willing to help me?'

'Yes, of course, but what do you expect from me?'

She looks at him quizzically. 'Simply come with me and keep a lookout.'

He studies her face and sees that she's serious. A lookout? That sounds like she's about to do something she shouldn't. And he'll be involved in that.

'Listen carefully, this is the plan,' she says, and when they arrive at the remote house where the lab is located, Frank knows exactly what he's about to be involved in. And he's not happy about it.

Eddy's home, Elewijt

After the meeting at NATO, the Three Amigos leave together for Elewijt. Eddy has invited his two companions to his home for a drink and to talk things through. On entering and seeing the damage to the kitchen, Righard and Luis are very impressed.

'That oven really exploded,' Righard says. 'Just like the heating installation in the Dome. Here, too, they took over the remote control.'

'Yes, and my home network is well secured anyway. I'd be angry with myself if that were not so.'

'The most important thing is that nothing happened to you or your wife,' Luis says.

Eddy agrees. 'That's right. But I'm still not convinced. If the perpetrator knows I'm helping NATO fight the virus, he'll also know that I survived.'

'Or this was just a warning, as that Europol inspector said.'

'That's possible. Anyway, whoever it is, he or she is capable of a lot. But let's have a drink first.'

'Drink? It's only eleven o'clock!'

Righard laughs. 'It's already aperitif time in New York. Have you got any of that good whisky left, Eddy?'

'Of course,' Eddy says, and steps to his bar cabinet.

A little later, the three men are sitting in the drawing room, each holding in front of him a glass half filled with the golden liquor.

'What do you think of the whole business? Will NATO be able to solve this?' Luis asks.

'If you ask me, I think they came up with an antivirus very quickly,' says Righard.

Eddy concords. 'Yes I agree. That worked in the past, but in this case I would have expected it to take much longer.

It's like the antivirus was ready waiting in a cupboard and all they had to do was take it out.'

Then Luis, who was just drinking, chokes and puts down his glass. 'Luis, are you okay? Otherwise I'll drink it,' Righard jokes.

'Lads,' Luis says to his colleagues, even though they are both over sixty, 'I've an idea. Now suppose that inspector's right and that the perpetrator is to be looked for in the NATO laboratory.'

'Yes and then?'

'What if he already had an antivirus ready? That could explain why one was found so quickly.'

The two others look at Luis uncomprehendingly. 'What advantage would he gain from doing that?' Righard asks. Luis shrugs his shoulders. 'I hadn't got that far yet.'

There is a moment of silence in the house as the three men work their grey cells.

'The only reason anyone would do that is to be considered a lifesaver.'

'And to please the bosses.'

'Right, but I don't think that's enough. He must have some other advantage.'

What if that antivirus doesn't work at all? If that's the case, then we can expect other attacks soon.'

Eddy shakes his head. 'No, he wouldn't get away with that. Before it's put into production, it goes through a whole series of checks. The perpetrator has no control over that.' He jumps up without a word and hurries over to the two gigantic computer monitors sitting in the corner on a desk. He sits down and starts typing instructions.

'Eddy, what's up?'

'I have an idea, but before I tell you, I need to look up something,' he says, turning his back to them.

The other two sit on the edge of their chairs trying to see what's on the screens.

'Eddy, now you're making us very curious. What do you have on your mind? Eddy turns his desk chair towards them and raises his index finger. 'We just said 'what if' a few times. I'm now going to do that once again. What if the virus didn't come alone?'

'Do you mean two viruses?' Luis asks pensively.

'Yes, but not two the same. What if the task of that first virus was not only to cause the explosion, but also to smuggle a second virus into the network?'

Righard silently puts down his glass and Luis is also speechless. 'Damn it, Eddy, I hope you're not right. Because then we're in serious trouble.'

'I know. It's what I wanted to look up. A coup like that has been committed several times, with varying degrees of success.'

'That would mean there's another virus floating around the Dome's network. But why? What do they want to achieve with that?'

'Like Luis before, I must confess I hadn't got that far.' 'Wait a minute,' Righard says, 'and the Butler then? Was a second virus also dropped there? That would be a real disaster.

'We can't rule that out. But I don't understand the connection between the Butler and the Dome. One has nothing to do with the other, does it?'

'Maybe the Dome was a test?'

'A test? That was a direct attack!' Luis counters indignantly. 'On the other hand, they did warn us to enable us to evacuate. Then he shakes his head gruffly. 'No, I can't get my mind round this. It was a nasty attack, period. If we can figure out why a second virus was dropped in the Dome, we'd be a lot further. Let's brainstorm that for a while.'

'Okay, but when I'm thirsty, it doesn't work very well,' Righard says with a grin.

Eddy takes the hint and a moment later the glasses are filled and the three men are busy discussing again.

'Hey Eddy, maybe there's a second virus hidden in your home network,' Luis says.

Eddy's mouth drops open, he steps to his server cabinet and unhesitatingly pulls out all the plugs. 'Thank you, Luis, I hadn't thought of that. I'll restart the server shortly and will perform a thorough scan.'

There's a moment's silence when the three men realize that, despite their years of experience, they are puzzled. If there is indeed a second virus hidden somewhere, where is it? And what is that virus there to do?

Eddy's thoughts go back to 1989, when the world was much simpler and when it all started for him.

Antwerp, 1989

'Here, Eddy, see if you can do something with this.' These were the instructions from his boss at the insurance company where he was then employed. Eddy examined the diskette that had landed on his desk and curiously inserted it into his computer. It turned out to be a survey that examined if you had a good chance of contracting the then common disease AIDS. After filling it out, he was disappointed and the diskette soon disappeared from his mind. But the next morning at the office, he unexpectedly couldn't get his computer to work. On his screen was a text asking him to send a sum of money to an address in Panama, after which the computer would be released again. Eddy had fallen victim to

one of the first ransomware attacks in history. But he didn't give up. He began to unravel what had changed on his computer, and after a while he actually found the solution. He didn't make much of it until watching the TV news that night. There had been a wave of puzzling ransomware attacks, for which no cure had yet been found. Eddy saw his opportunity and called the VTM channel to say that he knew the solution. VTM didn't hesitate, came to interview him and the ball started rolling. At that point, his career as a security expert had begun and continues to this day.

NATO base, Zemst

Lara and Frank have passed all the control points in the laboratory in Zemst, and step out of the small lift into the laboratory. Lara has asked him to act relaxed, as if they were there for tea. Frank tries his best, but he fears all the time that someone will see on his face what they're up to. They walk down the corridor between groups of employees who are so busy that they don't look back at them. Most are mesmerized by what's on their screens.

At the end of the hallway, they see Peter Black's office, the only one on this floor with a door. He hears Lara growl and understands why. The door is closed, so that probably means Black is in there. Lara turns into a side entrance, moves a little further on, then sits down at an unmanned desk. Frank takes a seat at the next one and has to admit that she chose the spot well. From where they are, they have a side view of Black's office door, which will allow them to see immediately when he goes out. At least if he goes out. He could just as well stay in there all day and they would waste their precious time here.

But they are in luck. A few minutes later, the door opens. Frank has to suppress the urge to duck under the desk. But Black doesn't even look in their direction. Frank assumes Lara has prepared a good explanation in case Black or anyone else asks them what they're doing here.

Black has not yet made it all the way down the corridor when Lara already jumps up. They go straight to his office, the door of which is now open. Before entering, they look back again, but no one seems to be paying attention to them. Lara rushes in and Frank follows closely behind. As he closes the door behind him and turns off the light, a weight lifts from his shoulders. Imagine if they were caught. He sees a projection of a landscape on the wall opposite the entrance door. It reminds him of Finland, the land of a thousand lakes. He had just noticed more such projections as he walked down the aisle. The images compensate for the lack of windows and help the people working here forget that they are metres underground.

Lara turns off the image and the office gets much darker. Then she takes a small, rod-shaped object from her pocket, presses a button, and a beam of blue light appears. While Frank watches everything through the narrow window in the door, Lara walks around, letting the light beam fall on various objects.

'Bingo,' he hears her say softly.

He looks back and sees that she has aimed the beam at a glass of water. Another object appears from her pocket, a small black box. She takes out a wafer-thin white strip of foil and sticks it on the blue-lit glass. She pushes it in firmly for half a minute, then gently pulls it off. Frank takes up his lookout position again. From where he stands, he has a good view of the main corridor running between the desks. There's not much movement, so it's a good time to leave the office.

'I'm done,' she says.

Frank takes another quick look through the window, then opens the door and they both quickly step outside. He suppresses his excitement and tries to behave as normally as possible. Lara walks remarkably slowly down the hall, and he therefore does exactly the same. He follows her into another section of the lab, and as they pass through a large dividing door, he breathes a sigh of relief.

'That was exciting,' he says.

'It worked again.'

From this he understands that she must have done more such things in the past. He follows her down a main corridor identical to the one in Black's department and they come to a little locked office, far from everything, in the far corner of the floor. Lara knocks and identifies herself. 'Gerard, it's me, Lara Hartman.'

From behind the closed door, Frank hears a moving of furniture and someone saying something in a high-pitched, but unintelligible voice. Then he hears footsteps, followed by the unlocking of the door.

When it swings open, Lara magics up a smile. 'Hello Gerard, how are you? This is Frank.' She gestures to Frank to follow her. They step into the office and in front of them is a short, fat man with a round head and a few wisps of grey hair around his ears.

'Hello Lara,' he says and timidly extends his hand to her. 'Come on, Gerard, don't be silly. Come on, give me a kiss.'

She hugs the lab technician in his white smock and as they chat small talk, Frank looks around the office. It bears no comparison with that of Peter Black. There it was expensive furniture, a nice library full of books, and everything neat and tidy. Frank stands agape at the muddle on the cupboards and tables. There's no space left, even on the floor are creations made out of what seems to be some kind of plastic. For the most part, they're mini versions of well-known buildings. There's are mini versions of the Eiffel Tower, the Taj Mahal and the Golden Gate Bridge. On another table are replicas of expensive sports cars of all kinds of exclusive brands. Frank takes a step closer and notices that those models are finished to perfection. Someone has worked here with great precision and patience. The Eiffel Tower in particular fascinates him and he hovers over it to admire the details.

'Hey there, don't touch!' comes a panic-stricken voice.

He could have sworn it was a woman calling. But it is Gerard who is looking at him very angrily.

Frank raises his hands, palms facing out. 'I'm not touching anything, just admiring,' he says truthfully.

The angry expression doesn't disappear from Gerard's face. Frank takes a step back to put more distance between him and the miniature world.

'Did you make all that?' he asks out of interest and to break the ice.

'Yes, with that.' The technician points to a huge 3D printer in the corner.

Frank has never yet seen such a large specimen. Despite the seemingly endless possibilities that these types of printers offer, they've never really made a breakthrough in the business world. 'What is it used for besides those models?' he wants to know.

Gerard shrugs and looks up at Lara, who is a head taller than he is. 'For many different things. I've already made computer worms and Trojan horses. That was for a student event, to shape the types of viruses. I also made the model of a new NATO annex. That building is now really standing and hardly deviates from my model.'

He says this with pride. Frank notices that the man is constantly looking at Lara and doesn't give him a glance. A blush has appeared on his plump cheeks, reminding Frank of a shy little boy standing in front of the prettiest girl in class, not daring to say anything to her. Could he be in love with Lara? Get in line, he thinks.

'They haven't called on me much lately,' Gerard says sadly. That probably explains those creative excesses, Frank thinks. Fortunately for him the NATO member states don't know that their contributions are being used for such hobbies.

Lara puts a hand on Gerard's shoulder and that makes his cheeks seem to get a little redder. 'Gerard, can you do me a favour? Can you print this, please?' She takes the box from her pocket, opens it and shows the foil she has pressed on the glass.

Gerard looks up at her with a loving look and carefully takes the foil out of the box. He takes it to the 3D printer and immediately sets to work.

Lara looks back at Frank and winks. So she is clearly not afraid to use her feminine charms. While the technician is busy, Frank walks around the office. This has to be a loner. He doesn't have much work and may not get many visits from other colleagues unless they feel like making fun of him. Yet he has an undeniable talent. Only now does Frank also see a miniature version of the world-famous temples of Angkor Wat in Cambodia. He was able to see them with his own eyes during an adventure trip some time ago. At the time, he was blown away by that unique temple complex. And what he sees now is the perfect image of it, only about a thousand times smaller. 'Ready!' he hears. Little Gerard walks proudly towards Lara and extends his hand to her.

Lara takes the white object resting in his palm and examines it closely. A smile soon appears on her face and to Frank's surprise she takes Gerard's head in both hands and gives him a smacking kiss on his big forehead. For a moment Frank thinks Gerard has passed out and he'll have to pick him off the floor. But he staggers back, blinks and manages to pull himself together in time.

'Thanks, Gerard, thank you very much,' Lara says, and Frank hears that she really means it.

In an even lighter voice than before, Gerard mutters something that sounds like: 'You're welcome, Lara.'

Lara gestures to Frank for them to hurry, and they leave the office together. As he exits, Frank nods politely to Gerard, who is rubbing his forehead with a blissful smile.

Sint-Jans-Molenbeek

The loud knocking on the wall has been going on for several minutes, but Larry Lane doesn't hear it. Nor does he hear the neighbour shouting in a foreign language for him to reduce the noise. Lane is in a trance. Not only because of what he's sniffed from the broken mirror lying on the counter, but also because of the music blaring out of the loudspeaker on the messy table. The volume is set to maximum and the loudspeaker vibrates so violently at times that it slides a few millimetres further towards the edge of the table. The Beatles' 'Can't Buy Me Love' plays and Lane is proving otherwise. He's in bed with a prostitute whom he's approached on the street and who has willingly come with him. The price she asked was much too low in his eyes, but of course he didn't say anything about it. He's on his back while he lets the whore do her job. He's staring at the ceiling, but can't see it. Instead, above his head is a starry sky on a clear night. With lots and lots of stars, way more than he's ever seen. Suddenly the stars change shape. The stardust disappears and gives way to shiny metal. He now also notices that they are in constant motion, as if in orbit around the Earth. Lane blinks and it's as if the stars are slowly coming closer. In the end he has to close his eyes because the glare is too strong and blinds him. He still feels nothing of what the prostitute is doing to him. His mind has turned off all bodily sensations. He's floating like water among all those stars, and tears come to his eyes when he realizes that he has finally become one of them. His big dream has now been realized, and an intense blissful feeling overwhelms him to the depths of his body.

However, that feeling immediately disappears when he receives a hard blow to the jaw. From one second to the next he wakes up from his daze and is back in the small flat. The stars have been replaced by the peeling paint ceiling. He lies on his back on his bed and he feels the weight of the whore sitting on him.

'Hey man, you okay?' he hears her ask from somewhere far away.

He looks at her, and the sound of her voice is out of sync with the movements of her mouth. The music that still fills the room — he had put the song on repeat — drowns out her other words. He looks at the woman languidly and feels the anger bubbling up inside him for her having taken him out of his dream. As if in slow motion, he sees her raise her arm to slap him again. Her palm falls and he sees the lines in her hand, every detail of her phalanges as if he were examining them from a millimetre away. Then he sees his own arm rise involuntarily. His hand grabs her arm before she can strike, and clasps her wrist. A second later his other arm rises and his fist touches the woman's cheek. He sees her startled eyes and her open mouth. He feels himself slipping out of her, then sees her fall sideways, out of bed. Without looking at her or listening to her, he knows she's scrambling to her feet crying and cursing him. Her hand reappears, but now it remains calm. He knows that this time it is not to hit him. He knows what she's going to do next. The money is snatched from the bedside table and she steps away cursing. Moments later, she slams the door hard behind her and Lane is alone again.

He closes his eyes to evoke that blissful intoxication again. After a few minutes he realizes it won't work. He's now wide awake. Lane sits on the edge of his bed, pulls up his trousers, and stands up on unsteady legs. He glances at his laptop, then shakes his head. No, it's too early. But is it really? He turns off the music and takes a sip from the bottle on the table. Why wait? Then he remembers a phrase he once heard. 'The desire for pleasure provides more pleasure than the ultimate pleasure.' Bullshit.

It's time. Lane opens his laptop, calls up the program he needs, then sits back. He closes his eyes, tries to imagine what the starry sky looked like in his dream, and pronounces the instruction that will turn the world upside down.

Peter Black's office, NATO Base, Zemst

Lara and Frank have slipped back into Black's office undetected. Frank is on the lookout as before and behind him Lara has dropped into the soft leather office chair. Glancing behind him, he notices she has activated Black's iPad and that the device is now requesting a login code or a fingerprint. Lara takes the object she has manufactured with the 3D printer. It looks like drops of water on a human finger. Admittedly a very white finger, and therefore rather morbid. Frank looks outside again and is shocked to notice a technician heading towards them down the aisle.

'Lara,' he whispers. 'Someone's coming here. What are we doing?'

She jumps up, turns the iPad over, and moves out of sight of the window. She puts her index finger to her lips and urges him to step aside as well. A second later, someone knocks twice on the door. Frank feels uncomfortably hot at the thought of that man stepping in. Perhaps he has his boss's permission to do so. But the door remains closed for now. There is another knock, this time a little more forceful. They both stand motionless in the darkness, and a moment later, to their relief, they hear footsteps receding. Lara gives him a thumbs up.

As Frank resumes his position at the window, he wonders what explanation she would have given for the fact that the projection is off and the lights are off. That they are a couple and wanted some privacy? Could be, but it's not certain that the man would have fallen for it. After all, they are NATO employees.

'Come on,' he hears her say softly.

When he looks back, he sees Lara pushing the fake finger onto the screen. A second later, her face lights up as the screen reads 'Welcome Peter'. With smiling eyes she looks at Frank and immediately sets to work. Hopefully it won't take too long. Of course she knows where to look. Hopefully it will soon become clear whether the head of this department is corrupt or not.

'I knew it,' Lara says quietly a moment later. With her watch she takes photo after photo of what she sees on the screen.

'Has he anything to do with it?' he asks curiously.

'To say the least, yes. I don't think he's an accomplice, but in fact the main perpetrator of the first two attacks.'

So her intuition turned out to be right. But what now? It's not for Lara to arrest him, is it? Perhaps she'll pass everything on to Dice.

'I have enough to prove his involvement,' she says agitated. 'What a bastard, he's got all those deaths on his conscience.' She puts the iPad down, changes her mind, and picks it up again. She presses the finger again and starts looking for something again.

'Lara, what are you going to do? I don't see anyone walking around, I think we better go now', Frank tries to convince her.

'I want to know if Black was in contact with Larry Lane while he was in prison. That can provide us with interesting information.'

She's right, Frank thinks. On the other hand, the longer they stay in this office, the greater the chance that they'll be caught. He checks the time, they've been here for fifteen minutes now. He gets short of breath and hopes she'll soon find what she's looking for. Then he hears footsteps approaching outside.

'Lara,' he whispers, 'someone's coming.'

Lara doesn't hear him or she ignores him. It's one of the two, because she just keeps working concentrated. Just like before, Frank steps aside to get out of sight of the window. He decides to leave it entirely to Lara to explain their presence here. His gaze remains on the door. It could swing open in his mind at any moment, after which someone from the security service would storm in to handcuff them. But that doesn't happen.

'Look,' Lara says. She shows him the iPad, which shows an exchange of messages. From where he's standing, he can't read any names. But looking at her face, he knows it must be a dialogue between Black and Lane. She also takes a few photos and puts the iPad down on the desk for a second time. Frank hopes she won't change her mind: they really have to get out of here now.

He's happy when she quickly checks that everything is as it was when they first came in. Then she finally gestures for him to open the door. After a hurried glance through the side window onto the deserted aisle, he turns the light back on, opens the door, and steps aside to let Lara through. She doesn't move and looks outside with tight-pressed lips. Frank follows her eyes and his heart almost jumps out of his throat when he sees an enraged Peter Black standing in the doorway.

Genetics headquarters, Brussels

On the top floor of the building belonging to the fast-growing company Genetics, CEO Ronald Vandenbussche looks through the window. It's not the first time he's enjoying the view. He's very pleased they've set up offices here, just a stone's throw from the Brussels-North office district, in one of Brussels' best-known green areas. What more could you want? As a history graduate, he loves this place. The Botanical Gardens, just a few hundred metres away, is a historically important location. Not many people know that extensive scientific research was carried out there starting in the nineteenth century. That's why for him it's a pity that it now functions only as the venue *par excellence* for concerts and exhibitions. The beautiful Orangery of the Botanical Gardens and the view of the lower city still inspire him.

A modest knock on his door snaps him out of his reverie. 'Come in,' he shouts, annoyed. With fresh reluctance he turns his back on the panorama. It's Sandra, his management assistant, a title his personnel manager says sounds better than 'secretary'. 'Yes?'

'Sir, Dirk from the computer department wishes to see you urgently.'

Oh no, that boring creep is crawling out of his hole. 'He doesn't have an appointment, does he?'

'No, but…'

'Yes, it's urgent, you already said that. Send him in.' Sandra makes her escape, slowed down by her high heels. Vandenbussche sighs. A waste of time, he already knows that. He appointed that man to head the IT department with the message that it's his job to sort out everything himself. That side of the company doesn't interest him. Sales are the most important thing, everything else must be second to that.

There is a knock, and a timid, middle-aged man pokes his head through the half-open door.

'Come in, Dirk. What's up? I don't have much time.'

'Mr Vandenbussche, sorry to disturb you, but we have a problem.'

'Problems are there to be solved, Dirk. What's up?

'Something's blocked.'

Vandenbussche looks at his employee as if he's telling him there's a pigeon in the gutter.

'Blocked? Unblock it then, man, do you need me for that?'

'No, but…'

The IT man hesitates and the CEO only now really looks at him. He's startled by the look on his face. The fear is written all over it. This could be serious.

'Dirk, come here, take a seat. What's up? What's blocked?'

'Everything,' the other says softly as they sit down. ' And it's not just blocked. There are other things happening in the background that are beyond our control.'

Vandenbussche thinks he's not hearing right. 'What are you saying? Did you say everything's blocked?'

Only then does he notice that his employee is holding a piece of paper. It shakes with his hand. 'What's on that paper, Dirk? Let me have it.'

Dirk, who looks as white as a sheet, doesn't dare look at his boss. He puts the sheet on the desk and pushes it towards the big boss. 'I don't know how it happened. But... suddenly there it was.'

Vandenbussche has become very curious about what exactly has happened. He's also starting to worry. Hopefully this will not impact the sales activities. His hand darts forward, grabs the sheet and reads what's on it. It's a print of a photo. The photo shows a computer screen. On the screen is a short text, in white letters on a black background.

The sheet of paper falls out of his hand when he realizes what he's just read and what the consequences are. The primal cry he lets out is so loud that Sandra cringes at her desk and reaches for a box of tissues that is invariably close to her.

NATO base, Zemst

Frank expected Black to berate them for entering his office without permission. Or at least ask them what they are doing there. But he says nothing and looks at Lara, or at something behind Lara. What is he looking at? Did they forget something? The iPad is back in place and the glass of water has not been moved. Lara took care of that, he saw her do it. Then it hits him. The projection! They forgot to turn the landscape projection back on. Frank doesn't understand how they could have overlooked that. There's no time to ponder this. Everything is moving at a rapid-fire pace. Fast as a cat, Black grabs the door handle and slams the door shut. Lara jumps forward to open the door again, but then they both hear a short beep.

'Damn,' she shouts, 'he's locked the door!'

Frank feels the handle and indeed it's stuck solid. Lara wastes no time and is already on the phone. As she waits to connect, Frank examines the metal door. Kicking it in is certainly not an option, he would only injure himself. He glances at the side window in the door, but smashing it in isn't a solution either, because it's much too narrow to crawl through. Through the window he sees Black turn left at the end of the corridor, in the direction of the lift.

'Anthony', he hears Lara scream almost hysterically when she finally gets Dice on the phone. 'It's Peter Black, it's him, I've found the evidence in his iPad! But he caught us and has locked us in his office. You have to help us get out of here. If we can't go after him now, he'll escape.'

There is a moment of silence and then Lara nods.

'Yes I understand. I'll take full responsibility if he turns out to be innocent afterwards. But he isn't, Anthony, now please believe me.'

After a few seconds of listening, she thanks him and hangs up.

'Doesn't he believe you?' Frank asks.

'No, but he's going to help us. I'll send him the data now so he can see for himself.'

Frank opens his mouth to say something, but then closes it. He quickly dismisses the thought that Dice could also be corrupt.

After Lara sends everything, they wait impatiently. 'What's Dice going to do? Can that door be opened remotely?'

'That, or he asks someone to open it. Anthony has a man everywhere who keeps an eye on things, and that will probably be the case here too.'

'Unless that little man here was Black,' says Frank gloomily.

Two minutes pass, but they seem more like ten minutes. That's how long they feel it takes before they hear that beep sound again and the door is unlocked. None other than the creative loner Gerard is standing in front of them when Lara yanks the door open with a fierce jerk.

'Out of the way now, Gerard!' Lara shouts. Gerard steps aside in fear on seeing that fury coming towards him. 'Thanks,' she calls to him as she walks past him.

Frank does the same and they sprint down the aisle. They don't care about the surprised looks from the people at their desks.

'Europol!' shouts Lara, perhaps to prevent anyone from playing the hero and trying to stop them.

They turn left just like Black did a few minutes ago and enter the corridor, where the only lift is located. Above the closed door is the number zero. So Black is already above ground and has a serious lead over them. Lara positions herself in front of the iris scanner and the green light turns on. They hear the lift start to move. Frank is relieved. He was afraid Black might have blocked it somehow.

Excruciatingly slowly the lift descends until finally the number three appears and the door gradually opens. They almost collide jumping into the lift at the same time. Lara immediately stands in front of the iris scanner in the lift. The light turns green there too and the door slides shut. Frank feels his heart beating in his throat and tries to calm down. This isn't really for him, chasing a criminal. He thinks back to Lara's words when she said she couldn't ask anyone else for help. Isn't this case big enough to assign her a partner, a real one, someone from Europol? He should ask her that when this is over.

The lift door slides open, frustratingly slowly, when they're upstairs. It's not yet fully open when Lara squeezes through and darts forward. The door under the stairs behind which the lift is hidden is still open, and they run through. Black must not have closed it in his haste. They come into the open air through the also open front door and Frank takes a deep breath. They come to an abrupt halt in the gravel-covered clearing outside the house. Only Lara's car is there, everything else is deserted. No one is to be seen in the long driveway either. Could Black have fled on foot?

The answer to that question comes sooner than he thought. To the side of the old house, a gate creaks open. Frank is surprised, because the wrought iron gate is completely covered with climbing plants and therefore seemed more like a hedge.

'Staff parking lot,' Lara shouts, running towards the widening gap in the fence.

Frank halts hesitantly, prompted by common sense. He's not trained for these things, let alone carrying a gun. How can he best help Lara without endangering or hindering her? Then he gets an idea. Black must be planning to escape this way in his car. Frank may be able to prevent that by closing the gate again. But then he has to find the gate operating mechanism. Maybe there's an emergency button or something hidden somewhere. As Lara runs into the parking lot and disappears behind the gate, Frank begins to search frantically for a large knob or lever. On the side of the fence he pulls aside a lot of plants, but in vain.

'Frank, watch out', he hears. It's Lara yelling at him, and that can only mean that Black is closing in on him.

Frank does not give up his attempts and continues to search. When he removes one last branch with dense foliage, a sensor embedded in the fence becomes visible. He can't do anything with it, because you need a badge for that. Then there is only one thing left: manually prevent the gate from opening any further. Frank hurries to the gate, which is already three-quarters open, braces himself and pushes in the other direction. To his satisfaction it is not as unyielding as he had feared and it yields quite a bit. With all his might he pushes it back with both hands. When he has pushed the gate back about a metre, he hears the hum of a car. He realizes that if he doesn't pull over now, he'll get hit. Reluctantly, he lets go of the gate and jumps. Just in time, because an electric Porsche Taycan approaches like a whirlwind. It narrowly avoids the moving gate and continues on his way at high speed. The car flies over the crunching gravel toward the road, turns right and is gone in an instant.

Lara walks up from the parking lot and runs straight to her car. She opens the door and glances at him. 'What will it be, Frank? You can stay here if you want, you know.'

Her words are not yet cold when Frank has already walked around the car, opened the other door and got in. He doesn't want to miss this for anything in the world.

Mechelen

Lara starts the engine, switches off the Butler and gives full throttle. They dart down the driveway and, just like the Porsche, and turn right onto the N1, the old road connecting Brussels to Antwerp.

'And you know how to drive without a Butler?' Frank asks in surprise.

'Yes. I even learned it at Europol. In the cybercrime department it's not very often that you have to chase a car. But our boss thought it advisable anyway, and look, it comes in handy.'

He notices that she is now driving at the legal speed limit. She suddenly sees a gap in the traffic, puts her foot down even harder and overtakes the car in front. He's impressed by the acceleration every time she pushes the accelerator and his back presses against his car seat. 'Is this a special version of this model?'

'Yes, great isn't it?' she replies elated.

She really enjoys it, he thinks. It's very obvious that she prefers action to questioning witnesses or suspects.

'Where could Black be driving to?' he asks.

'I'm guessing the motorway, it's not far from here.' 'And after that?'

'He'll try to shake us off, and if he succeeds, he might go into hiding. I've no doubt he has a base somewhere. He won't be so stupid as to drive to his own house. I need to report this, Frank.'

She calls Europol and reports what happened. She then informs her colleagues that she has given chase. Finally, she provides the licence plate number and a description of the sports car Black has fled in. 'Can you send a drone?' Frank hears her ask. 'No? Can you have the cameras along the E19 search for a Porsche with that licence plate? Okay thanks.'

She disconnects and, without looking back, takes a right turn at a speed Frank didn't think possible. They now end up on a regional road, where the speed limit is only fifty kilometres per hour, but she overtakes one driver after the other at a crazy speed. They are all driving neatly at the regulatory speed and with the same distance between them, centrally controlled by the Butler. The road twists and turns, and even without a clear view of what's around the next bend, Lara continues to overtake other cars.

'Over there!' she shouts.

After the last corner they come to a straight section and in the distance Frank sees that there's an incline coming. That'll be the bridge over the motorway. At the top of that incline, they see the Porsche fly past everyone and then disappear behind its brow.

'He's driving onto the E19, just like I thought,' she says with satisfaction.

He doesn't understand that she can be satisfied with that. 'I don't get it. His car is much faster than ours, isn't it? We'll never see him again.'

'Once the car has been spotted, the description is passed on to all types of cameras, so that they actively start searching based on its registration number. It'll be fine,' she says confidently. They have also arrived on the incline, just as the traffic light turns red. Lara flatly ignores it and continues on her way, to the accompaniment of loud hooting. She nonchalantly raises her hand to apologize, pulls onto the motorway, then pushes the accelerator hard down. They're still on the slip road when over 160 kilometres per hour is already posted on the windscreen. Frank shifts in his seat and tightens his seatbelt, knowing full well it won't change anything.

A call comes in and Lara turns on the loudspeaker. 'Vehicle spotted. Driving towards Mechelen and Antwerp. Speed one hundred and eighty an hour.'

'Don't you have a flashing light to put on your roof?' Frank asks half seriously.

At this Lara laughs heartily. 'No, unfortunately not. But next time I see Anthony, I'll ask him. Maybe NATO will give me one.' She increases the speed to one hundred and eighty and slaloms through the rows of self-driving cars. Fortunately, she does not have to take into account unexpected manoeuvres by reckless drivers, because that's one of the great advantages of self-driving cars. However, despite her best efforts, they still cannot see the car they are chasing.

A second call comes in. 'Suspect has taken the Mechelen-Noord exit. And then driven to the business complex.'

'What could he be looking for there?' Frank wonders. 'Many of those buildings are empty since almost all employees are working from home, aren't they?' 'We'll see,' she says grimly as she overtakes one last car and then also takes the exit to Mechelen.

Practically without slowing down, they leave the motorway and come to a junction with a major road. The light is green, so Lara speeds ahead, crosses the road and turns right a few hundred metres further on. Frank sees an old traffic sign flash by with the image of a black factory. They are now driving on an elevated road and Frank glances at the street below. To his surprise, he sees the Porsche driving there.

'Lara, I've seen him! He's driving down there.' 'Okay, which direction?'

'The other direction, so not the way we're driving.'

After a long corner, which she takes quickly but in complete control, they come to a small roundabout.

'To the right here, then?'

'Yes', says Frank and, just to be sure, he also points to that side. He's been through enough misunderstandings about right and left.

They cross a bridge over the E19 and then arrive at an intersection where three streets converge. They look in all directions, but there's no trace of the Porsche.

'What now? Take a gamble?' Frank suggests.

'Gamble,' Lara replies, turning her steering wheel to the right.

After following that street for a few minutes, they come to another intersection.

'Damn,' Lara swears in frustration, slapping her steering wheel. 'We've lost him.'

Angry, she turns around, drives back to the first crossroads and then takes another road. After a slight bend, they notice that they're driving parallel to the motorway. A garage looms to their left.

'Look, that's also a coincidence, a Porsche garage.'

Lara slows down and the two of them admire the beautiful sports cars in the parking lot.

'Hey, wait a minute, this is the perfect place to hide if you're driving a Porsche,' she mutters more to herself than to her passenger.

'Do you think he put himself in there as some kind of camouflage? That's a good idea', Frank must admit.

At a snail's pace Lara drives into the parking lot and checks all the cars standing there. Frank does the same on his side. He searches for the licence plate he heard Lara spell on the phone. They draw a blank in the first two rows, so Lara turns into the second row of parked cars. They're less than ten metres away when one of the parked cars backs out very fast and screeches away.

'That's him,' Lara yells, and she hits the gas.

Before they leave the parking lot, Black has already disappeared from sight around the bend.

'Phenomenal car, isn't it,' Frank muses.

In thanks for that comment, he gets a push from Lara. 'Hey, that's a criminal in that phenomenal car: keep your wits about you, right Frank?' she admonishes him.

'Sorry,' he blurts out. 'This is all so unreal. It's like I'm in a movie, with the car chase and all.' And with a beautiful woman behind the wheel, he adds in his mind.

They come back to the intersection where they had just chosen the wrong street.

'Where did he go? It's not true, is it? Now we've really lost him', Lara growls. 'We'll have to rely on the roadside cameras to spot him.' She drives on with an angry expression on her face.

Frank wants to comfort her by saying that at least they now know who's behind the virus attacks. But he decides that it would be wiser to keep his mouth shut for now. That frown on her forehead doesn't bode well.

Mechelen

Lara and Frank both stare into space as they wait for the traffic light to turn green. Now that they've lost Peter Black, there's nothing else for it but to return to Evere. Frank plays out in his mind how chases usually end up in movies. Either a car crashes, or the perpetrators burst their tires on spiked chains that the police throw across the road. Their own pursuit was much less dramatic. At the Porsche garage they almost got him …. How will they ever find Black again? Frank looks out of the corner of his eye at Lara, sitting motionless next to him. It must be frustrating for her to have him slip through her fingers. You could have heard a pin drop in the car since she requested a wanted persons message and house search warrant over the phone.

The light turns green. Lara pushes hard on the accelerator, and the car leaps forward. She still hasn't turned on the Butler, and Frank hasn't dared mention this. They drive onto the motorway and he can't imagine them remaining silent as far as Evere.

'Are you okay, Lara?'

She gives him an angry sideways look. 'No, I'm not. What did you think?'

'I understand, but we still must be able to find him, right? How do you do that in other cases?'

'There aren't ten ways of going about it, Frank,' she says angrily. 'You have a wanted persons notice put out, and I've done that, just like for Larry Lane. Incidentally, this has so far yielded nothing, zero, nada. A house search is another opportunity to find out something. But for that you need a search warrant, and you don't get those just like that. I've just requested that too, and now we can only wait. We, by that I actually mean myself. Sorry, Frank, but you're not a policeman.' She bites her lip and looks straight ahead.

Frank doesn't mind that she takes her displeasure out on him. He thinks about how he could help her and has an idea. 'You know, I like to read police novels and they usually follow the same pattern. Something happens, a murder or a hostage situation. And then the inspector shows up and starts the investigation.'

She doesn't seem very interested in what he's saying, but he keeps talking anyway.

'Every time, the inspector encounters all sorts of obstacles. But he always gets his man in the end.'

'Frank, are you going to compare me to an inspector from a book?' 'No, I also know it's romanticized. But what's interesting is what that inspector does when he loses the scent.'

'And that is?'

'Going back over what he's already done. Trying to make connections. Looking for loose ends.'

She says nothing and looks at him. She sighs, activates the Butler, and turns her chair toward him. 'Okay, Mr. Inspector, go ahead. I'm listening.'

Frank is glad to have got her talking again, but now he has to go further.

'What have you already done?' he asks and then answers the question himself. 'You've interviewed the Dome employees. That's what got you the phishing email.'

'The sender of which we have been unable to trace.'

He ignores her comment and continues. 'Then there were the men from the computer department and the prison warder.'

'No results either...'

'We contacted the hackers,' counters Frank. 'That did yield something. You can't deny that.'

She nods. 'In the books I read, the inspector re-listens to all his interrogations. And in so doing, more than once he comes up with new insights. Did you record everything?' 'Yes, I always do.' She looks at him thoughtfully and then grins. 'Okay, we're just sitting here in the car. I might just as well listen to the recordings. Will you listen with me?'

Via the Butler she starts the recording of the first interrogation, that of Frank's father and the two other experts. They both listen intently, and when the recording ends, Lara shrugs her shoulders.

'I have no new insights, have you?' she says sarcastically.

'No, just do the next one,' Frank replies.

After listening to the questioning of the Dome's IT department staff and that of the murdered minister's mistress, Lara takes a deep breath. 'See, Frank, that's the difference between real life and what happens in books.'

'Hey, we're not done yet. Trust me, we'll find something.'

Reluctantly, Lara starts the recording of the conversation with the new director of the prison from which Larry Lane has escaped. Frank focuses on what he hears the lady saying and thinks back to how they were sitting there at her desk. As he listens, he ponders the connection between Black and Lane, because it must be there somewhere. How did it ever come about and grow? Maybe they can start from there.

His thoughts are interrupted by something he has just heard the director say. 'Lara, rewind, please,' he asks.

She raises her eyebrows and does as he asks.

He's no longer sure of what he heard until he hears the director repeat the phrase that had just caught his attention.

'And always the same, always one particular Beatles song, 'Penny Lane'.

One word in particular sticks in his mind: Penny. Where has he heard that before? He racks his brain to remember.

'What is it?' Lara asks.

He decides to ask her for help. 'The director mentions the name of the song Lane used to play, "Penny Lane." I'm wondering where I heard that before?'

'Penny Lane'? I don't know that song,' she says uncomprehendingly. He closes his eyes and thinks. Something pops up in his mind, but is immediately gone, like a fly seeing a fly swatter coming.

Just as he's about to confess that he doesn't know, she exclaims: 'I know. I know what you mean! 'White Penny?

'Yes! That's it!' he shouts, and has to restrain himself from grabbing her out of sheer joy.

'White Penny,' she repeats thoughtfully. 'Penny would stand for Lane and White would represent... Black. So they have a business together,' she says happily. 'We've found a possible connection.'

Frank nods, but he immediately feels the euphoria fade away. What good does this do them? When surfing the dark web, they had already looked up that company, also on the normal web. Without result.

Lara, on the other hand, has sprung into action and is angrily feeding instructions into the Butler. Frank bends over to see what she's doing. She types in 'White Penny' on a website he doesn't immediately recognize.

Suddenly she clenches her fist in jubilation. 'Bingo!' she shouts. 'Because we spoke a moment ago about an operations base, I called up the land register. White Penny owns real estate in Mechelen.'

She activates the address she found in the Butler and the car changes course to that destination.

'Property? Do you mean a house or a firm?'

'We'll find out soon enough. Frank, what's the name of that inspector of yours in that book? I'd like to meet them,' she says with a smile.

Frank leans back in his chair, feeling relieved and proud at the same time. Maybe he's helped make a breakthrough.

NATO Headquarters, Evere, Brussels

Anthony Dice stares at the photo he's holding in his hand. How happy he was then, there in Mexico two years ago. The time he spent there will probably never come back and that saddens him. How one day followed another on those beautiful white beaches, with the balmy evenings, the delicious food and not forgetting the tequila. Then he really went through life carefree. Of course, that had to do with the fact that he'd not yet taken up his current position, and therefore had more free time to spend. The colours in the photo, one of the few he's printed, have lost none of their strength. Blue, yellow, white. He realizes all too well that he's been taking that photo out of his drawer quite a bit lately. With his index finger he touches the image of the woman in the picture with him, smiling, equally carefree.

There is a knock at his door. Dice starts, quickly opens his drawer, drops the photo inside and closes it again. I look like an alcoholic quickly concealing his bottle, he thinks.

'Come in,' he shouts.

The door opens and Marguerite Weston waddles in. Every time he sees her, he wonders how that woman must feel. What it must be like to carry all that excess weight with you day in, day out. It can't be healthy, can it? He himself is not exactly slim, but Weston is without a doubt twice his weight.

'Anthony, we have a problem,' Weston says.

'A problem?' Larry Lane who has escaped and Black who turns out to be corrupt, those are real problems, he thinks.

'A major company has approached us saying that their files have been encrypted by a virus.'

'Yes, and so what? That's nothing unusual, is it? There are so many attacks every day,' he replies, bored. 'No more than a few hackers having fun.'

Weston takes the chair in front of his desk, pushes it back with great effort, and plops down onto it. Dice pities that chair for what it has to endure now. Hopefully it won't collapse.

'Anthony, this is serious. It involves a company you know well.' Now she has his full attention. 'Which company is that?' 'Genetics,' she says. Her laboured breathing doesn't escape him.

'Genetics? Oh no, indeed that's not good news,' he has to admit. He gets up and starts pacing up and down. 'If that's true, then NATO does indeed have a problem.'

Genetics has a longstanding relationship with NATO and specializes in genetics, as the name suggests. After years of research, the company is about to produce a serum that makes human genes more resistant to viruses and diseases. Ironic actually, that they are now infected by a virus attack, albeit from a computer virus.

'Do you know more?' he asks.

'No, the CEO was very angry and asked, no, demanded that you call him back immediately.'

He knows all too well who the CEO is. They are personally acquainted. Many years ago he worked together with Ronald Vandenbussche and that was not always a pleasure cruise. He is an extremely demanding man who always goes the extra mile and demands the same from all his employees. Genetics was founded by him and, despite the red figures in the accounts, has grown into a reputable company. Dice has to hand it to him, he did that very well. Thanks to his charisma, he was able to convince several large shareholders to buy into Genetics. He then deployed all that capital on researching into and developing serums and vaccines.

His progress caught the attention of NATO, which was looking for ways to protect their Special Forces from biological attacks.

'I'll call him now,' Dice says.

Weston nods, takes a deep breath, then manages to get up. 'Let me know if you need a press conference,' she says as she leaves his office.

Dice flops down behind his desk. He is dreading that conversation, but unfortunately he cannot avoid it. He doesn't want to avoid it either, because a thought starts to nestle in the back of his mind, which he puts aside for the time being. Could this also have something to do with Lane and Black? He opens the bottom drawer of his desk and takes the photo back in his hand. When he receives a call a little later, he takes one last look at the smiling Lara standing next to him on the beach, and then stows the photo safely away.

Mechelen

Lara's car takes them to the Battelsesteenweg in Mechelen. Apartment buildings and terraced houses pass by on both sides.

'Strange that Black and Lane bought a house here,' Frank comments. 'What did they have in mind?'

'Well, of course they needed a secret place for carrying out their plans.'

'Do you think it's here that they developed the virus?'

'Where else? The land register states that the property was purchased six months ago. That means Black took care of that, because Lane was still in jail at the time.'

'So Black made the virus on his own?'

'No, I don't think so. I think he built on what Lane had already used in that attack on NATO last year.'

The Butler alerts them that they have arrived at their destination, notifying them that a parking space is available two hundred yards away. Lara approves and the car takes them there. They drive past the house where White Penny is registered. At first glance it's no different from the other houses on the street. No trace of a nameplate or any advertising on the front. The car parks in the free space and also pays the parking ticket for them.

'Makes life easy, that Butler,' Frank says as they get out.

'Yes, but apparently things could be better in terms of security.'

'Speaking of security, what are we actually going to do here? Shouldn't we notify your boss?'

She looks at him and her look says enough. 'We're just going to take a look, explore a little.'

The way she says that doesn't inspire confidence in him. Surely she's not going to break into that house and try to arrest Black?

'Come on, let's cross the street,' she says, and they hurry across to the other side. 'We can observe better from here.'

They've not gone ten metres when Frank nudges her.

'There, Black,' she whispers, retreating into the foyer of an apartment building.

Frank quickly joins her and from the relative darkness of the hall they see Black on the far pavement.

'He came out of there.' She points to an open space between two buildings, above which hangs a large sign with the symbol of a tow truck. 'He probably owns or rents a garage there,' she whispers.

For him, there's no reason to whisper. They're more than twenty metres away from Black, who's also walking away from them. But so close together, in that small hall, that he finds it exciting, even a little arousing. When Black turns and looks around, she takes a step back, pinning him against the glass front door. Black can't possibly notice them from where he's standing now. Too bad, Frank thinks, if he saw us, she might kiss me to give the impression that we're just a courting couple. Of course, that doesn't happen and he realizes his imagination is running wild again.

They remain motionless for a moment, and then Lara looks around the corner very carefully. 'He's just gone in,' she says in a normal volume, breaking the spell of the moment for Frank.

'What now?' he asks.

'Time for action. I've seen on the Mechelen land register entry that this house has a garden. My plan is as follows. I'll try to get into the house through the garden and overpower Black. You stay here and watch the front door.'

'What? But what should I do if he comes out?' 'Chase him,' she says calmly.

Frank can't believe his ears and is relieved when she bursts into laughter. 'I had you there for a while. No, we're not allowed to that and we cannot. I'm calling Anthony now, others can fix this. Don't forget, I belong to the cybercrime division, not the infantry.'

As she calls, Frank takes a deep breath. He didn't like that plan at all.

'His line's busy. We'll have to wait, because I'm not allowed to call anyone else in NATO.'

After a few more attempts, she gets Dice on the phone. The conversation doesn't last long and apparently goes completely to her liking. Satisfied, she hangs up and raises her thumb.

'They'll be here within the hour. Anthony asks if we want to stay here until the drone arrives that they're sending off now. It's equipped with a heat sensor and will detect Black's presence in the house. Then we can go to Evere and follow the Special Forces raid on a big screen.'

In the same way as the US President was able to follow the raid on Osama bin Laden, Frank thinks. For him there's always been a sinister side to watching such events live. When all's said and done, sometimes people are killed or seriously injured, and that comes straight into the screen. He doesn't want to think about what would happen if those images were stolen and made public. Not only because of the emotional suffering inflicted on the victims' relatives, but also because of the impact on public opinion. How far can a government go in its actions to apprehend criminals?

'You stay here, I'll see if I can find his car,' Lara says. After fifteen minutes she shows up. 'I've received the signal that the drone has arrived. So we can leave.'

He looks up at the grey sky, but sees no drone, just a few pigeons flying by.

'Come on,' she says, and they hurry away from the house, back to her car. Halfway there she stops, and he sees her eyes light up. 'I have an idea. I just have to convince Anthony.'

She calls him again and when he hears her explain the plan, he's very curious as to how this is going to turn out.

NATO Headquarters, Evere, Brussels

'Hello, Ronald,' Dice says, trying to force a smile. Finally he's plucked up the courage to call him. 'Anthony, do I have to sue NATO?' Vandenbussche shoots directly from the hip. 'What do you mean, Ronald?'

'What do I mean? All my files are blocked, we can't do anything, nothing! Nobody has access to his mailbox anymore, we can't consult any documents on the server, everything is at a standstill!'

'Ronald, I...'

The CEO is unstoppable and doesn't let him get a word in edgeways. 'I demand that you rectify this immediately, and I mean immediately. I demand compensation of five thousand euros per hour because we can't work.'

Dice is silent, sensing that the tirade is not over yet. As he half listens, he thinks back to Lara's two calls with good news at last. If all goes well, Black will be arrested within the hour. That would be a big step forward. Black can then hopefully lead them to Lane.

'I want you to send your best people now to solve this problem. Don't forget that this is also to NATO's detriment. If we can't develop anything, your Special Forces aren't protected.' Vandenbussche is completely beside himself and takes a deep breath.

Dice sees his chance. 'Ronald, unfortunately such an attack cannot be ruled out. Companies are the target of hackers. Of course I'm going to help you, I'll…'

'But you knew this could happen and you did nothing. I find that absolutely outrageous.'

'Whoa, Ronald, what's happening in your company right now has nothing to do with the virus attacks that made the news. With you it's clearly a case of ransomware. They encrypt documents and demand money in exchange for their release.'

'No Anthony, it's not that simple. I've been told there are other problems.'

Dice thinks. 'Ronald, you need to install the antivirus we distributed this week.'

'We did!' shouts the man indignantly. 'Right after it was distributed, we installed it. Do you really think we'd be stupid enough not to? After what was in the news about the attack in Brussels and those two remote murders?'

For a moment Dice is speechless Is this an isolated case? 'I'm sending three of my best people to you at once, Ronald. They'll be with you within half an hour. We'll work it out, I promise you.'

Without another word, the CEO hangs up. Dice is left orphaned. He quickly calls Eddy Willems and asks if he could to drive out to Genetics with the two other experts. Fortunately, he is ready to do so immediately. Dice asks for a quick report and thanks him.

He thinks hard. Could Lane be behind this? Or is it just coincidence? When there is a knock on his door, and his secretary looks around the door with a frightened face, he already knows that she has brought very bad news.

NATO Headquarters, Evere, Brussels

When Lara and Frank enter Anthony Dice's office half an hour later, Lara stops. 'What's up, Anthony?'

Frank is surprised at her question. He too notices that Dice is tense.

'First, a company has been hit by a ransomware attack. Genetics, with whom we have a cooperation agreement.'

Before Lara can say anything, he continues. 'Not sure yet, but it could be related to what Lane and Black are up to. And yes, the company had installed the antivirus on time.'

Lara sits down and Frank follows suit. She frowns. 'But what we've seen so far wasn't ransomware, was it? Except for the case of the Dutch security expert, but that was a different case.'

'No you're right. But I still find it suspicious. That's why I sent Frank's father and his friends there.'

'And secondly?' she asks.

'I just received a report that three more companies have been affected. But at the moment I don't have enough information to judge whether it's the same problem. I have asked my people to clarify the matter as soon as possible. Annoying that Black is now out of the picture, because now I have to coordinate everything myself for the time being.' He looks at his smartwatch, stands up and gestures for them to follow him. 'Come on, it's almost time.'

The three of them head to a conference room down the hall. They close the door behind them and take seats in front of the big screen on the wall. Dice activates the screen with his voice and calls up a live connection. The screen splits: on the left appears a kind of infra-red image with a lot of grey and a vague orange spot in the middle.

'You are now looking through the camera of the drone circling high above Mechelen.' Dice points to the bright spot that appears not to be moving. 'That's Black. Good job locating him there, by the way.'

Lara nods and winks at Frank.

'The Special Forces are almost here. They'll enter the house through the garden. At the front there's a squad ready to intercept Black if he tries to flee there.'

'Has the plan changed?' Lara asks in surprise.

No, it's just a precaution. Just in case something goes wrong.' He calls up a second live connection and jerky images appear on the right part of the large screen on the wall. 'These are the images from the team leader's smart lenses.' The image is crystal clear and shows a high, dense fence. 'They're on a little dirt road behind Black's garden. I'm now going to give the order for action.'

He sends a message through his watch and a moment later the camera's image starts moving. As if in a movie, they see two Special Forces operatives smoothly climb over the fence and disappear behind it. Finally, the leader also climbs over the fence, giving them a glimpse of the overcast sky and then a view of the back of the house. The garden is not too big. There are bushes at the back, behind which the men hide.

Frank glances at the other part of the screen, at the orange spot that Black is supposed to represent. It is apparently still in the same place as before. How can they be so sure this is Black? It's not a pet animal, the shape is too human for that. Maybe it's his imagination playing tricks on him, but he wonders whether Black couldn't fool them by putting another human-sized heat source in the house. But he quickly dismisses that thought, didn't they see him go in?

The team leader takes a pair of binoculars and everyone can watch. 'The sergeant is now looking inside for possible forms of security,' explains Dice.

After a while, the man gestures to his two teammates and sends them forward. They gingerly take a few steps forward, parting ways, taking care to stay each on either side of the garden. There is a lot of rubbish there, like rainwater butts and piles of planks. They gratefully use this to approach the house unseen. They take their time and progress slowly. A few metres from the house, the one on the left freezes. Frank doesn't have time to wonder what's happening, because at the exact same moment the orange spot on the other image starts moving very fast.

'He's seen them!' cries Lara.

'Go,' Dice tells his watch, and they see the squad leader jump up and run towards the house. The two others now also fling caution to the winds, walk to the back door and take up position on each side.

Lara points. 'Look, Black's gone.' Indeed, there's no longer an orange spot on the image that the drone transmits.

'How is that possible?' Frank asks.

No idea. Maybe he's entered a room where the drone can't see him anymore?'

In the image of the smart lenses they see a booted foot kicking in the back door, after which the two Special Forces rush into the house in close succession. They hear them announce themselves in a loud voice, after which the leader also rushes in. He positions himself in the kitchen and begins to look around. In the background they hear the two soldiers shout 'Safe!' every time they have explored a room. Their voices are almost inaudible as they climb the stairs. Meanwhile, their chief moves into a small room set up as an office. They see a laptop on the table, which has been opened to the delight of the three spectators.

'We've really surprised him. Otherwise he would have taken the laptop with him,' Dice states happily.

The sergeant stands in front of the laptop ready to take it with him and the screen comes into view. Just as he is about to pick up the computer, Lara exclaims: 'Stop! Look at what's on the screen.'

'Stop, zoom in,' Dice orders.

The team leader directs his gaze to the screen. Two images alternate every few seconds. One shows the garden, the other shows a drone hovering high in the sky.

'That's our drone,' Lara says. 'How did he know we were going to use it?'

Dice looks bewildered. 'That's my fault,' he confesses. 'I shared a lot of information with Black. Now I also understand why he asked me so many questions about how our interventions work. He wanted to know everything in detail and in my naivety I told him a lot. I really trusted him.'

Lara looks at him pityingly and places a hand on his arm. 'You couldn't have known that, Anthony,' she says comfortingly.

Anthony takes her hand, squeezes it, then takes his hand away. 'The question now is, where is Black?'

No one in the room can answer that question. Fortunately, there is still plan B.

NATO Headquarters, Evere, Brussels

Two minutes have passed since the orange spot on the screen disappeared. The house has now been completely searched and there is no trace of Black.

'Damn, how can that be?' curses Dice. 'We almost had him. Where's he gone? He can't have left the house yet.'

'Isn't there a hidden space somewhere in that house?' Frank asks.

'What else? The heat sensor would have picked him up there too, you know. Unless he's deep underground, but for me that's unlikely.'

'Did they search the basement?'

'Believe me, those men are very thorough. No, something's not right here.'

Then a message comes in from the team leader. 'Mr. Dice, my men at the front of the house are signalling that a man has just come out of the house next door to Black's. His description seems to match that of the suspect.'

'From the house next door? How does that happen? Give me a view of the street, now!' exclaims Dice excitedly.

A second later, the image from the team leader's smart lenses disappears, replaced by that of the soldier standing guard in the street in his vehicle. All three see from afar a tall man walking leisurely on the footpath, without any hurry. He looks to be a workman, because he is dressed in some kind of overalls.

'Can't you zoom in?' Dice asks.

The soldier does as he is asked, and Lara shouts out first: 'That's him! That's Peter Black!'

'Arrest him,' Dice snaps.

The camera zooms out again and they see the soldier jump out of his vehicle and give chase. Black must have heard or seen that because he's already running with his long legs. He dives into an alley between the houses and disappears from sight.

'He's running to his car,' Frank says.

Lara nods as she continues to stare at the screen, mesmerized. Does she also binge-watch at home, he thinks. He can imagine it vividly.

'Get ready, Lara,' Dice says.

She calls someone and asks that person to hold the line. Meanwhile, the soldier now also walks into the alley, but Black is nowhere to be seen.

'To the right,' Lara says.

'To the right,' Dice repeats to his watch.

The soldier turns right and then they see Black again. He is just opening the door of one of the garages and is about to step into his electric Porsche.

'Lara?' Dice asks nervously.

She nods. 'Just a minute.'

The soldier arrives too late. Black is already in his car and drives out of the garage.

'Now,' Lara calls into her watch.

The Porsche, hurtling straight towards the Special Forces, stops from one second to the next, as if it had hit something.

'Success!' Lara crows.

The Special Forces aim their weapons at Black, who is completely surprised behind the wheel. He hadn't seen this coming. Satisfied, they watch in the room as he is handcuffed and taken away.

'Congratulations, Lara, that was a good idea,' Dice congratulates her. 'It was necessary, because he could have managed to surprise us in one way or another. How could he get into that other house? And why did the heat sensor not see him anymore?'

'There must have been a passage between the two houses,' Lara thinks. 'I suppose this will be investigated?'

Dice nods.

'I think I know why the sensor stopped picking him up,' Frank says.

Lara turns to him and looks at him questioningly.

'I've just looked it up. Google knows everything, that's proven once again. Rewind the last footage, please.'

Lara does as he asks, until he says 'Stop!'.

'Do you see what clothes he's wearing? The overalls with the hood? It's not just for disguise. I think that's fire-resistant clothing, and if you wear it, you're invisible to heat sensors.'

Dice and Lara look at each other, not concealing their admiration.

'I didn't know that,' Lara says.

'Me neither,' Dice admits. 'But very important information for our future interventions.'

Lara holds out her hand to Frank. 'We did it right again, partner,' she says with a laugh.

As he shakes her hand, his eye falls on the bracelet that has slid down to her wrist. When he sees the first name on it, it's all he can do to keep a straight face.

Genetics, Brussels

'Good day Mr Vandenbussche', says Eddy Willems when they are welcomed by the company CEO at the reception desk.

Luis and Righard also greet the visibly nervous man and follow him to his office. They enter the not too large and lavishly decorated office. A man is waiting for them there and when he sees them, he immediately jumps up.

'This is Dirk, my IT director,' Vandenbussche says.

The slender man with rosy cheeks seems even more nervous than his boss. He's probably been through a lot already. Which also makes sense, because the security of the company's computers is his responsibility.

'Dirk, explain the situation to these gentlemen,' Vandenbussche orders.

'Our entire infrastructure is blocked,' he explains, glancing skittishly from one visitor to the next as if they're about to punch him. 'All our files are encrypted, we can't consult anything, let alone change it. Everything is silent.'

'What can be done about it?' the CEO asks bluntly.

'Can you show us a screen from one of the computers, please?' Eddy asks politely.

'Use mine,' Vandenbussche says.

The IT director activates the screen of his boss's laptop and then hands over to the experts. The Three Amigos crowd around the computer. They see the classic message on the screen. 'Pay 1 million crypto to remove the encryption from your files.'

The three experts look at each other and nod. It's Eddy's task to deliver the bad news. He clears his throat and weighs his words. 'Mr Vandenbussche, criminals can use different methods to paralyse your activities. For example, they can bombard you with popups or padlock your computer screens. But in those cases your files are still safe.'

Vandenbussche already feels the storm coming, takes his chair and sits down.

'In your case, this is ransomware in its worst form. That means your files have been stolen and encrypted.'

'I repeat my previous question: what can be done about it?' the CEO asks.

It's Righard who speaks. 'Our advice is always the same: never pay. That will only provoke more attacks.'

'So?'

'There are two options. The first is a so-called *decrypter*. That is a tool to undo the encryption.

But there's not yet a *decrypter* for every type of ransomware, especially if it's a new type.'

'And the second option?'

'A full system recovery.'

In the meantime, the red has disappeared from the IT director's cheeks. On the contrary, on hearing the word 'system recovery' uttered, he turns as white as a freshly laundered sheet. 'Then we'll lose everything we started this morning! Just today we started a very important project and there are no backups of it yet', he protests with a trembling voice.

'It's very unfortunate,' Luis says. 'But there's no alternative. We can install security software that repairs everything and also removes the infection at the same time.'

'But if I understand correctly, you first find out if it can be solved with such a *decrypter*?' the CEO asks.

'Yes, but I must tell you now that the chances are small.'

'Okay, then do that. I'm putting off that other decision and hopefully I won't have to make it. Dirk, will you accompany these gentlemen further?'

The three experts follow the shaken IT director, leaving the CEO slumped in his office chair. As they wait for the lift down to the computer department, Righard wants to know if the antivirus was indeed installed on time.

'Yes, it was. I can't prove it now because everything is blocked, but we did so immediately.'

'In other words, it's another virus that got in here?'

'Yes, there's no other way. But how? Also via an e-mail with an attachment, like in the Dome?' Luis asks.

The IT director shakes his head. 'In my mind that's unlikely. The staff are trained to pay attention to this. We communicate a lot about it because we know the risk and absolutely want to avoid contamination, given the importance of our activities for NATO.'

'But how did it get in?'

'I may have an answer to that,' Eddy says and explains his theory to them.

Genetics, Brussels

Luis, Righard and the Genetics IT director are all ears when Eddy begins his explanation.

'Dirk, did your company take part in the RSA Virus Bulletin Conference?'

'Yes, like we do every year.'

'I thought so. That confirms what I suspected. I just remembered something there. Just before the explosions in the Dome, I saw a logo I couldn't identify on the big video screens. It seemed to be composed of a combination of letters. I think a W and a P or an R. At first I thought it was advertising, but what if it wasn't? What if that's the logo of the hackers who caused the explosions?'

'Why would they do that? Then they betray themselves, don't they?' Luis argues.

'If it was a well-known logo, then yes. But I can assure you, I've never seen it anywhere.'

Righard seems to realize where Eddy is heading. 'If you're right about that, Eddy, it means that—'

'... they had taken over the streaming. In other words, the connection with the companies, starting from the Dome', Eddy adds. 'And that in turn means that the virus could have spread to all companies that took part in the conference via streaming. Or it brought with it a second virus that had that function.'

There's a moment's silence when the four men realize the impact of these words.

'It's still just a theory. How can we know for sure?' Luis asks.

'Easy. By checking whether the other companies that participated remotely have also suffered a ransomware attack,' Righard says. 'We need to report this to Dice and get the names of those companies.'

The four men leave the lift and enter the computer department.

'Where can we call from?' Eddy asks.

The director leads them into a separate room and then goes to fetch them coffee and water. Eddy calls Dice and quickly gets him on the line. He presents him with the theory they discussed and asks if they can get the names of companies that are in the same boat as Genetics. He hangs up and seems satisfied with the answer he got. 'Dice will shortly send me the names: he agreed immediately. He heard me out with my theory, but I'm not sure he believed me one hundred percent.'

'He'll have to believe us if we can prove that those companies are right now also confronted with ransomware. That can't be a coincidence, can it?' Luis asks. 'We still need something else, namely the list of the Dome's participating companies. Of course they must also be listed there.'

'I don't think they're going to give it just like that.'

'I think they will,' Righard says. 'If I were the organiser, I would just put those names on the website. That's good publicity, isn't it?' The other two can only agree and when the IT director enters with steaming coffee and a bottle of water, Righard and Eddy are standing close to Luis, looking at the screen of his smartwatch. He's the only one of the three experts to have purchased a folding smartwatch. As a result, it has a much larger screen, almost the size of a small laptop screen. Luis has called up the Dome's website and all three are impressed by the tribute to the victims of the attack that occupies the entire home page.

'Terrible,' Eddy says and the other two nod silently.

Luis quickly navigates to the other pages in search of the most important companies that took part via streaming.

Righard points. 'Yes, there they are. I was right again, wasn't I guys?'

At that moment Eddy receives a message, which he immediately opens. 'Dice forwarded the names, there are four. Luis, shall I read them?'

'Yes please.'

'Intra Solutions is the first.'

Luis looks at the list and nods. 'It's on the site. And the following one?'

'Globe Computing.'

After some searching, the answer is the same. The answer also appears to be positive for the next two names.

'So we're not alone. I'm going to inform my boss,' the Genetics' IT director says and hurries out.

'Of course that idiot now hopes he'll be in the crosshairs less now that even more attacks have been successful,' Luis mumbles.

'Men, if our theory is correct, do you realize the possible consequences?' Eddy says seriously.

'All too well,' Righard replies. 'This could lead to a worldwide catastrophe.'

'True, if that virus has reached those five companies, it'll probably have found its way to the others as well. Luis, how many names are actually on that list of participating companies?'

Luis counts the names and then looks at them with a look that doesn't bode well. 'Twelve,' he says in a small voice. 'And they are all large to very large companies, operating in different sectors.'

'Then it's clear what we have to do first. Call those seven firms and warn them of what could happen.'

'Yes, but check with Dice first.'

'For me we're too late,' Righard says.

'There's only one way to find out,' says Eddy, calling Dice to obtain his approval.

The answer comes quickly, but it's not the one he'd expected.

Federal prison, Haren, Brussels

'I didn't know I'd see you again so soon,' the prison warder says to Lara and Frank, shaking hands. 'Sit down, please.'

They are indeed in her office again, but this time not in connection with Larry Lane.

'I understand you wish to question one of our new acquisitions?'

'Right,' Lara replies. 'The request was sent to you by…'

'Anthony Dice, yes, I received it. Well, no problem. Incidentally, your boss is no stranger to me,' she casually announces.

'He's not really my boss, but how do you know him?' Lara asks, and Frank hears that she is really surprised.

'We're old college classmates. At one point we were even more than that.'

When the woman catches Lara's look, she rushes to add, 'Good friends, I mean, no more than that. But we did have some good times together.'

With no response from Lara, she quickly changes the subject.

'So you want to interrogate Peter Black. He's only just checked in: apparently it's urgent?'

Lara shrugs her shoulders and the director gets the message.

'I know, I know, you can't say anything about ongoing investigations. Come along, I'll escort you there.'

They follow her out of her office and down a long corridor.

'Mr. Black has been placed in the section designated for the most serious criminals. Admittedly separated from murderers, paedophiles and the like. They are in a heavily guarded area in another building.'

For Frank, Black ought to be with those serious criminals after what he tried to do to his father.

They follow her into a large open space with a series of tables, each with two chairs facing each other.

'Are we to question Black in the visitors' room?' Lara asks in surprise.

'No, I've arranged a separate room for you. I've already had the detainee brought there. Here we are.' She stops at a room with no window and no peephole in the door. 'This room is normally used for intimate gatherings between detainees and their partners. But it's the only space I can make available at the moment. Sorry about that.'

Lara smiles, raises her eyebrows at Frank, then steps inside. The director remains outside and closes the door behind them. Behind a stainless steel table, Peter Black is waiting for them, handcuffed and with a sullen-looking guard beside him.

Frank looks around the not so large room and sees only a bed beside the table, more a single bed than a double one. Not a really inspiring environment for intimate meetings. On the other hand, he can imagine that a prisoner who spends every day in a cell measuring a few square metres, looks forward to the short time he gets to spend here with his beloved.

Lara has not yet taken her seat when she starts off in the usual way. 'Why?' she asks the man point blank.

Black looks her straight in the eye and is silent. There's no emotion on his face. Frank wonders why there's no lawyer sitting next to Black. Isn't that a legal requirement? Maybe that's why he doesn't want to talk?

Lara repeats her question and the two continue to stare each other in the eye like ruffs.

Then Black sighs and relaxes his shoulders. 'My lawyer is on his way here. I suggest we wait for him,' he says calmly.

'Okay,' Lara replies. 'But we can solve the case together now, so you don't need that expensive lawyer.'

Black smiles. 'Money's no problem.'

Frank is curious how Lara will handle this further.

'It may sound like a cliché, but if you give us the information we need, we can make arrangements for you.'

So the approach you see in police serials also happens in reality.

'I'm listening,' Black says warily.

'If you tell us how the virus works and where Larry Lane's hiding, I promise I'll do my best to get you a reduced sentence.'

Black turns to the guard, standing stoically beside him. 'What do you think of that? She promises to do her best. In other words, the result is uncertain. Would you agree to that?'

The guard, a broad-shouldered young man with impressive biceps, doesn't move a muscle in his face and stares straight ahead.

'No, you wouldn't. No one in their right mind would accept that. You can do better than that, inspector.'

Lara is not impressed and puts the dots on the I. 'Before we go any further, just a quick reminder of the facts. You developed a virus with which you carried out an attack that left twelve dead and dozens injured. That makes you a terrorist or even a mass murderer.'

She ignores Black's mock or real surprise and continues.

'In addition, you killed two people by crashing their vehicles. And finally, you committed an attack on a security expert's home.'

Black thinks about that for a moment and then turns his head to Frank. 'Are your parents okay?'

Frank is too stunned to answer, the words sticking in his throat. Lara helps him out by drawing Black's attention back to her.

'It's way too late to think about that. They could have both been dead, and you know that all too well.'

There's a moment's silence and then Black asks a question that gives Frank the impression he's going to cooperate. 'How much can I get the sentence reduced by?'

'I can't answer that,' Lara says firmly. "That depends on all sorts of factors. Don't ask me which factors, because every case is different.'

'Okay, my lawyer will probably curse me for doing it, but I'll try to answer your questions anyway.'

'Tell us about the virus,' Lara says, checking her watch to make sure the conversation is being recorded properly.

'The virus, that's Lane's work. I didn't build it myself. Lane came up with the concept and largely worked it out himself. My role was limited to giving advice.'

'Advice? You're going to have to explain that.'

'From my experience with viruses and antiviruses, I was able to give him tips on how to resolve certain operational problems. But I repeat, it's Lane who fathered the virus.'

Lara shakes her head sympathetically. 'Don't you believe me?' Black asks.

'No. I've seen it so many times that we arrest someone and then they minimize their own role. Sorry, that's something that makes us sick. At least take your responsibility!' she says angrily.

'I've done so,' Black protests. 'I warned twice that there would be explosions in the conference room.'

'Yes, you warned three of the thousand people present. Not really efficient.'

'I know,' he admits. 'But Lane wasn't aware I was sending those messages. I had to do it secretly, so I could only send it to a few people.' He turns to Frank. 'I know your father and his two friends from the incident a year ago when Lane hijacked the NATO network. That's why I chose to warn them via the access badges.'

'And the crashes of the self-driving cars?' Lara asks.

'Lane forced me to do that.'

'Here we go again,' she says mockingly.

Now it's Black's turn to get angry, and immediately the guard approaches. 'You don't know Lane like I do,' Black shouts. 'He really doesn't shrink from anything or anyone. When he asked me if I could crash self-driving cars, I was amazed by the question. At first I didn't even want to answer it. The image of pile-ups, with countless injuries and deaths, was one step too far for me. But then he threatened to kill my sister and her two children. He even showed me pictures of her, I don't know how he got them. So I did it. I doubted for a long time whether I should report him, but I didn't dare.'

'What did you really want to achieve by working with Lane?' is Lara's next question.

Black shrugs and makes a sad face. 'I wanted people to look up to me. That they would respect me because of what I'd achieved together with him. I know it smells like a cliché, but it's the truth.'

'How did you cause those crashes?'

'Using the same system you used to lock me in my car.'

'So not with a virus?'

Black shakes his head. 'Not with a virus. I've destroyed all traces of my actions. I could do that because there were no restrictions on my accesses.'

The fact that no virus was used must be a huge relief to Lara, but it doesn't show in her facial expression, which she has well under control.

'So far you haven't helped us any further,' she says reproachfully. 'I don't see why I should plead for a reduced sentence for you.'

Black grins. 'No? I think yes. You've got a lot already you can tell your boss.'

'Not enough. You can make it up to us by telling us where Larry Lane's hiding.'

'Do you really think he's going to share that with me? He may be a little crazy, but not that crazy.'

'Then this conversation is over,' Lara states firmly and stands up. 'Come on, Frank, we're off.'

'Wait a second. I said I don't know where Lane is. But I do know a way to contact him.'

She sits back down and looks at him expectantly.

'Give me your word, plus Dice's, about the reduced sentence, and I'll get back to him.'

She doesn't hesitate and calls Dice. She relays Black's request, hears Dice's reply, and has him repeat it after activating her watch's speaker.

Black nods and tells them what he needs to get into contact with Lane.

Genetics, Brussels

'What?' shouts Eddy, who is on the phone with Dice. Righard and Luis are startled by his reaction. 'Can I let my colleagues listen in, please?' he asks.

He can, and Dice repeats what he's told Eddy. 'You needn't approach those seven firms on the Dome's website. I have been informed they're all victims of ransomware, which was unfortunately to be expected. But what I didn't expect was a call from the boss of Belgium's largest drinking water supplier. He informed me their systems are also completely encrypted, bringing their activities to a complete standstill. And his company is not on the list of the twelve,' Dice says agitatedly. 'So the virus has found its way out. Damn, I was hoping to keep it within that limited group and fight it there.'

Luis and Righard, like Eddy, are perplexed and realize all too well what is happening. If the virus can spread that fast, it could infect every computer in the world within twenty-four hours. And demand ransoms everywhere to release the systems again.

'An attack of this proportion is unheard of,' Eddy says softly.

'What can we do?' Dice asks. 'A new antivirus? What do you think?'

'Sorry?' Eddy says.

'No, nothing, my secretary has just come to tell me there have been more angry calls. So the virus is indeed fast. This calls for radical measures, so I repeat: what can we do?'

Eddy looks at his two companions and they shrug their shoulders. 'We haven't had the chance to investigate the virus yet. We suspect the first virus brought along a second virus and spread it via streaming to the companies participating in the conference.'

'That's why the antivirus doesn't work, because it's a different virus,' Dice says understandingly. 'Does this mean we have to build another antivirus?'

'Yes', the three experts say in unison and Eddy takes the lead. 'I suggest two of us try to understand the virus here at Genetics. And that one of us tries to figure out how the virus spreads. Through phishing e-mail or through another way.'

'And how long will that take?'

None of the three want to answer that question because they simply don't know what they're dealing with. 'I can't say', is Eddy's honest answer.

Dice's sigh is clearly audible and there's a moment of silence. Their coffee is steaming on the table, but no one has drunk it yet. The IT director, meanwhile, has returned from his CEO and is biting his nails on the other side of the table.

'Can NATO also be affected?' Dice asks.

Now it's Righard who speaks. 'In theory, every company is a possible target. Thus, NATO too.'

Again it's quiet for a while and the experts give Dice time to think about this announcement.

'We can't afford to become a victim of some lunatic hijacking our systems again. What's the most radical way to ensure that NATO computers are not infected? Same as a year ago, in other words: pull the plug?'

'No, that will not yield anything because there is no infection yet. Besides, Lane may have learned his lesson and figured something out.'

'Surely there must be something else we can do?'

'You could ask all staff members not to handle e-mails and certainly not to open attachments. But we are not yet sure the virus spreads in this way. Moreover, it may already be in one or the other mailbox and we're too late with that measure. And it's also never certain that everyone will follow that instruction or read the relevant communication in time.'

'It's enough to drive you to despair. Surely there must be something else we can do?' Dice asks in desperation.

'Yes, there's another way to avoid the contamination, but I don't think you'll like to hear it. The virus travels via the internet, so if all NATO systems are taken offline, the virus cannot enter.'

'Impossible,' is the immediate answer. 'Then we are powerless. Are we, as the very guardians of the internet, to be cut off from the outside world?'

'We don't see any other option, I'm sorry.'

'If we cut ourselves off from the internet, that also means that we have to paralyse the management of self-driving traffic, doesn't it?'

'Yes that's correct.'

'That's exactly what the last Security Council was about. I fought not to shut it down, and now I'm obliged to. What a situation', Dice says sadly. After another deep sigh they hear him pull himself together, his voice is stronger and louder again. 'Okay, I'll discuss this further with the NATO Secretary General and keep you posted. Eddy, I'm also calling your son, because he's going to have his hands full with crisis communications, I'm afraid.'

Dice hangs up, and the atmosphere in the room is depressed.

The IT director joins them and addresses them. 'My boss was a bit angry just now and he's asking when you're done. He has an online meeting with shareholders today and he wants the problem resolved by then.'

Luis looks at the man questioningly and Eddy also doesn't understand how he can ask such a thing. Righard's answer therefore leaves nothing to be desired in terms of clarity.

'Tell your boss to get some training double-fast on how to give bad news.'

The IT director stares at Righard, realizes he means what he says, and sits down. He bows his head and continues biting his fingernails relentlessly.

Federal prison, Haren, Brussels

Just as Black is about to tell them how to contact Lane, Lara receives a call. She gets up and leaves the room. A moment later she pokes her head in and beckons Frank.

'Anthony, Frank is here with me, we're listening,' she says a little later when they're both in the corridor.

Dice tells them of the virus that has infected the twelve companies that took part in the conference via streaming and that it has now also reached other companies. He reproduces what the experts have advised him and then addresses Frank. 'Frank, Meredith Weston is standing here with me, and we've just had a meeting with the Secretary General. We want you to prepare a press conference on the topic of the recent ransomware attacks.

The message must be that there is a dangerous virus in circulation and that it is an entirely new type, a type against which there is no antivirus yet. Something like this: "NATO and Europol have joined forces to combat this unknown virus and to develop an antivirus as soon as possible. In the meantime, we advise all companies to disconnect from the internet."'

Frank is shocked by that advice and he notices from Lara's look that she hadn't expected anything like that either.

'"We suspect the virus automatically finds its way through open ports on servers and the network and, through vulnerabilities in the hardware and software, weaves its way into companies. We realize that this has a serious impact on companies' activities, but we are convinced this measure will only be necessary for a short time. Once the antivirus is available, we shall distribute it so that the threat can be contained and email traffic can resume." To end with NATO thanking everyone for their understanding. Got it, Frank?' Dice asks.

'I've recorded it,' Lara says, winking at Frank.

'Good. Any further news?'

'Yes, and it's good news,' Lara says proudly. 'The two crashes were not caused by a virus, but by misuse of the system.'

'By Black?'

'Indeed. Supposedly under duress from Lane, but I don't believe that.'

'That's good news. How is it possible I didn't see that right under my nose?'

'And something else. It was Black who sent the messages, unbeknownst to Lane. That part must be true, I think, and it argues somewhat in his favour. But more importantly, he promised us to contact Lane. If he pulls that off, we can track Lane down and arrest him.'

'Okay, do what you have to do, Lara, I'm counting on you. And Frank, I expect your texts within the hour', Dice concludes and hangs up.

'Sorry, Frank, so you won't be there when Black calls Lane. I'll let you know how it went.'

Lara steps back into the room where Black is waiting and Frank looks at it with sorrow. He would have liked to have been there. But setting up a press conference for NATO isn't exactly unpleasant either. Especially if he manages to smuggle in his communications agency's name somewhere. For example, in the background, in miniature, but still clearly visible. Yes, that would be good advertising. He heads off enthusiastically to the coffee bar, a nice espresso will give him inspiration.

Federal prison, Haren, Brussels

'Okay, you now have the word from my boss and myself, how are you going to contact Larry Lane?'

'Simple,' replies Black. 'Over the phone.'

'So you just call each other?' I find that hard to believe.'

'We'll call, but not with a regular phone.'

'On a secure connection then?'

He smiles. 'Better than that. We use a Sectra Tiger.'

'A Sectra? That's the phone used by NATO. So you stole two of them? That too!' says Lara, upset.

Black raises his cuffed hands in a defensive gesture. 'Whoa, not so fast. It's Larry Lane who got me one, it was in the house in Mechelen.'

'So one more incriminating fact. Don't you know that just calling from a device that is forbidden to the public is enough for a conviction?'

He shrugs his shoulders. 'Then add it to the list.'

'Where's that phone now?' Lara asks crossly.

'Still in the house in Mechelen, well hidden.'

'No time for riddles, Black, just tell me where the phone is.'

'It's in a duvet.'

'I hope for your sake you're speaking the truth,' she threatens and leaves the room again. In the corridor she calls a team colleague and asks if the investigating magistrate has already issued the search warrant she requested. That turns out to be the case. When she hears that a team is on its way, she cannot hide her joy. She indicates where the phone should normally be, and asks to have it flown directly to the prison in Haren by drone. That's faster than by car. She hangs up and goes back inside to tell the guard she'll be back in half an hour. Because she can't help but wait, she goes to the staff cafeteria, and who is sitting at a table writing with great concentration? She approaches Frank from behind and then taps him on his shoulder, nearly causing him to choke on his espresso.

'Lara?' 'I didn't hear you come in.'

'Hey Frank, it's going to be okay, Black is going to call Larry Lane very soon. On a phone he has hidden in Mechelen.'

'Okay, and what do you want him to say?'

'That Black wants to meet him so we can lure Lane out of his den.'

'And be present at that appointment, of course. Hopefully that will work.'

'I hope so too. Now I have to wait for them to bring me that phone. Will you keep me company for a while?'

'How can I refuse?' he says, glancing timidly at his text for the press conference, which isn't quite ready yet.

She gets them both another coffee and sits down next to him. 'Can I read?' she asks.

'Of course,' he says, sliding the iPad toward her.

Lara begins to read intently. He finds it cute how she forms the words she reads with her lips. His eye falls on her wrist, where the bracelet that he saw earlier has appeared again. However, he can now clearly read what it says: 'Anthony'. He can no longer restrain himself and the question is over before he even realizes it. 'Lara, may I ask, are you a couple, you and Anthony Dice?'

She raises her head, notices him pointing at her bracelet, then looks understandingly. 'We were a couple. Now we're just good friends. And he remains my client of course.'

'Oh, okay, sorry for my question.'

She puts her hand on his arm and smiles. 'No problem, Frank. It's normal to ask that question when you see this.' She twists the bracelet around her wrist. 'I don't really know why I'm still wearing it.'

'Did you break up recently?'

'Yes, last month. It was over, we'd been together for two years, we worked really hard all that time and that's why we didn't spend enough time together.'

'You are indeed very absorbed in your job.'

'Yes, I don't know how else I could do it. Are you like that too, Frank?'

'No, I like my job, I'm proud of my small business, which I built myself, but I have a red line for myself that I won't cross.'

'A red line?'

'Yes. Remember, President Obama? He always spoke of a red line. By which he meant that countries or terrorist organizations were not allowed to cross one strict border. For example, that was the use of poison gas, remember?'

She nods and looks at him with interest. 'I was young then, but I do remember something like that, yes.'

'Well, I have that red line too. If I feel tired or am the slightest bit stressed, I call my assistant and take a few days' break.'

'Wow, nice that you can. You should teach me that, Frank.' After a short silence, she continues. 'Wouldn't it be easier if you had a partner to help you guard that red line?'

He feels himself starting to blush, knowing she means this in general. 'Yes, it would,' he says.

She stares at him for a moment and then stands up. 'Let's see how the drone is doing,' she says and walks away.

He looks after her and doesn't know what to think about that. He takes out his iPad and tries to continue writing, but the sentences don't come. His muse has apparently just deserted him.

Sint-Jans-Molenbeek

Larry Lane emerges from one of the exotic supermarkets in his neighbourhood with a braided shopping bag full of food items. With his head slightly bowed, but not so much as to stand out, he is completely absorbed in the other people on the footpath. So far no one has spoken to him or sought a fight with him. Whenever he approaches a surveillance camera, he makes sure to walk just behind someone so that his face is not scanned. A few times that didn't work out, but then there is still his disguise that can lead the investigators astray. He can't wait to get back to his flat. He's very keen to know how many companies have already been infected by his virus. In principle, it should now go very quickly. An antivirus does not yet exist and all those companies are in constant contact with each other via multiple channels. He has read on specialized websites that NATO has distributed an antivirus that could neutralize all threats. But then they didn't know yet that the virus they found in the Dome's network was just a transport vehicle. So they'll have to come up with an antivirus all over again. What a farce; and what a stain on their reputation!

Lane arrives at the building where he is currently staying, and steps into the hall, which, as usual, stinks of urine and sweat. How happy he'll be when he doesn't have to come here anymore. Once he's achieved his goal, he'll torch his flat without hesitation to destroy all traces of his stay here. Before that, he still has a few things to take care of. For example, there is Anthony Dice, who has gradually grown into his arch enemy. He's the one who caused him to spend a year behind bars. And he's also the one who is now leading the investigation into his escape, like a bulldog that never gives up. Along with a bunch of seniors, a young pretty woman and some chump from a communications agency. He knows all this through Black, who has served him well so far. Of course he is also very well paid for it.

He steps into the lift and elbows the filthy floor button. Here, too, the smell of urine dominates and he wonders whether it comes from humans or from the numerous dogs that live here. Probably both.

Yes, Black has been a good partner, too bad their collaboration is about to end. When he found out that Black had warned people about the explosions in the Dome, Lane was very disappointed and angry. But he managed to keep his cool, which wasn't easy. He still needed Black for a while, so he didn't say anything. But now his role is almost over. He did have one last assignment in store for him, and knowing Black's greed for money he would certainly have accepted it. But he mustn't take any risks. If Black hides something from him once, he can do it again, and that's unacceptable.

Lane steps into the dingey flat and drops the bag of groceries on the table. Half an hour later, it's still there as Lane watches with fascination the carnage his virus is wreaking on the business world. A sense of triumph washes over him, and he grins his battered teeth at the thought of how the bulldog must be feeling right now.

Federal prison, Haren, Brussels

Lara hurries back with a plastic bag containing the high-tech phone to the room where Black and the guard are waiting for her. Her Europol colleague has made haste: less than half an hour has passed and the phone is already in her possession. Fortunately, Black was telling the truth and the phone was indeed hidden in a duvet. But that won't score him any points. He remains a murderer, and whether those murders were committed under duress or not is immaterial. They have promised him a chance of a reduced sentence, but she herself does not expect this. If they can grab Larry Lane by the throat now, that would be fantastic. Tracing Black's call to Lane is crucial. It wasn't easy to activate the tracking function on such a well-secured device. Fortunately, NATO also uses it, and Anthony Dice is good friends with Sectra's CEO.

Lara arrives at the room, opens the door, and then stops in surprise in the doorway on seeing Black taking a nap with his head on his chest. She storms in and slams the bag with the phone in it on the table.

Black wakes up with a jolt and looks up at her with half-open eyes and a sleepy face.

'And you allow that?' she snaps at the guard. 'That man's a killer and you just let him take an afternoon nap!'

The guard spreads his hands to indicate that he cannot or should not do anything about it.

Angrily, Lara sits down and slides the plastic bag towards Black. 'Here, call him. Now. And say you want to meet him. That you want to discuss something urgent with him. And make sure the conversation lasts at least a minute, preferably longer.'

Black rubs the sleep from his eyes and looks at the phone. Without saying anything, he raises his hands and shows his handcuffs.

'It works just as well with them on. Call him,' Lara orders implacably.

Black sighs, pulls the bag towards himself and withdraws the phone. He slowly types in a number and puts the device to his ear.

Lara keeps a close eye on Black and the guard is also wary, perhaps because he fears Black might want to use the heavy phone as a weapon. But that doesn't happen and then Black starts talking.

'It's me. Can we see each other?' Black asks, looking Lara straight in the eye.

Lane is probably asking why he wants to meet, because Black is doing what Lara asked him to do.

'We need to discuss something urgent. Very important.'

Lara is glad Black has decided not to tell Lane everything. Nor can you tell from the way he talks that he is lying.

Lane has answered something, as Black nods. 'Okay. See you there.'

He puts the phone on the table. The guard relaxes and retreats into the background.

'That was too short!' Lara shouts disappointedly. 'What did he say?'

'Didn't you record the call?' Black grins.

'I'll only ask once,' Lara says with suppressed anger.

'He's agreed to see me.'

'Where and when?'

Black laughs. 'Looks like it's going to be a tourist excursion. In an hour's time on the Brussels Grand-Place. '

'Did he notice anything? Was he behaving normally?'

'Lane never behaves normally. But no, I don't think he noticed.'

'Put the phone in the plastic bag and hand it over here,' she orders. He obeys and she takes the bag. She turns to the guard and points to Black. 'Take him back to his cell, we don't need him for now. And thanks again.'

The guard nods and Lara leaves the room. The Grand-Place in Brussels. Always full of people. Easy to arrive unseen and escape unseen. It won't be an easy task. Moreover, with the meeting due within an hour, they don't have time to make the necessary preparations, if that were even possible in such a place. Lane doesn't make it easy for them, she has to admit. But her father always said: 'Difficult also works', and her father was always, but always, right.

Les Lacs de l'Eau d'Heure, Wallonia

'Who dares?' the round-bellied guide asks the gaggle of schoolchildren who are standing in classroom mode for the first time since the start of the tour. So far they have all behaved like the schoolchildren they are. Talking, pushing each other, hiding. But now they're grouped together at what seems to them a safe distance from nothing short of an abyss.

'We're standing here at a height of one hundred and seven metres, on the largest dam in Belgium,' Maurice tells the children, thinking of pearls and swine. 'This dam was built more than sixty years ago and provides electricity for more than six thousand families.'

When showing adults around, Maurice always has people guess the number of families. But with children he gave up doing that long ago. He would get the most ridiculous answers and it was just frustrating.

'Who dares?' he repeats, taking in the grandiose view of the lakes.

'Me,' he hears someone say in the back of the group.

'Come here, I'll go with you,' Maurice says with satisfaction.

A petite girl with a heavy blond plait falling on her shoulder squeezes forward. The other children look at her with between envy and admiration. Typically not a squeak from the cocks of the roost of a couple of minutes ago. When things get critical, they are not to be seen or heard.

'What's your name, little girl?'

'Isabelle,' she says in a small voice.

'Isabelle, that's a nice name. Come on, then let's show your boyfriends and girlfriends that you have more guts than them.'

He directs her towards the Skywalk, the glass platform on the tower of the dam. 'It's not dangerous, just beautiful,' he reassures her.

He gives her a little nudge in the back and she hesitantly takes a few steps forward. They've almost reached the glass when Maurice hears the siren. Strange, it's not Thursday today, is it? Could they have changed the day for testing the siren? He hesitates for a moment, but then decides to call his boss just to be sure.

'Stay here for a second, Isabelle,' he says. 'Children, all just stand still, this is a test,' he shouts. 'I'm going to call and see what we should do.' He takes his phone and calls his boss in the control room. 'Raymond, what does that siren mean? It's…'

'Maurice, get the kids downstairs, immediately. Something's wrong with our computers, we can't get into the system any more. So take them down and then come to the control room.'

The conversation ends before Maurice can ask another question. He's shocked at the emotion he's just heard in Raymond's voice. He has worked with him for years. Raymond is always calm personified, but now he seems completely beside himself.

Maurice feels someone tug at his coat sleeve. 'I don't want to go any further, m'sieur,' the little girl utters, almost crying.

He realizes that the children are frightened by that wailing siren and takes Isabelle by the shoulders. 'Don't be afraid, girl. We're all going down now and we'll come back another time. Good?'

The girl nods and he takes her hand. He leads her to her classmates, most of whom are also beginning to look frightened. He realizes he has to put on a poker face and tries his best to force a smile.

'Come on, children, let's take the lift down, the tour's over.'

He rounds up everyone, calls the lift and then counts the number of children. Fortunately, they are all there, and a moment later everyone is safe and sound at ground level. When he's dropped off the children with their teacher, who was waiting at the bus, he hurries back upstairs. Raymond sounded really worried. Surely the dam will be okay, he wonders as he watches the floors whiz by. He feels a stab in his heart as he thinks of what would happen if it broke. His family, his friends, the houses. Everything would flood, the power of the water would be destructive. The lift doors open and before he enters the control room, he makes a quick call to Clothilde, his wife. He asks her to pick up the kids from school and drive to his parents. Their house is on the far side of the dam.

Federal prison, Haren, Brussels

Lara has gone to fetch Frank and they're now in another room for a video call with Dice and Weston.

'Frank, your texts for the press conference have been approved by everyone, thanks for the good work.'

Lara nudges him and gives him a thumb-up.

'The press conference is scheduled in an hour and a half, with the idea that we can also announce that we've caught the mastermind behind all those attacks.'

That's optimistic, Frank thinks, but says nothing.

'We need good news, folks. NATO is seriously under fire from all sides. Dozens of complaints have already been received from companies, large and small, that have come to a standstill because their systems have been blocked. This is slowly turning into a crisis and could get worse if we don't find an antivirus soon.'

Frank wants to ask if his father is involved in the development, but Dice cuts him off.

'Everyone from Europol and NATO's cybercrime division has been mobilized to help. Frank, your father and his two colleagues too, of course.'

'Is the ransom demand the same for all companies?' Lara asks.

'Good question, Lara, because yes, that's right. Every company is being asked for a million euros, even the smaller companies, who can never put that sort of money on the table.'

'Probably because the virus was already complex enough.'

'Maybe. Something else. The federal police have sent in a few hundred images from facial recognition cameras. We purposely lowered the scanning precision because we suspect Lane is disguising himself. Otherwise, he would have been noticed somewhere by now. The tips we received on the so-called tell-tale line, on the other hand, have yielded nothing. Lara, I want you to look at that footage now and see if it shows anyone who looks like Lane. In case our elite troops can't catch him on the Grand-Place.'

'Okay, send it through, Anthony.'

Now that Frank knows that Lara and Dice were a couple, he views their interaction differently. At times they are sweet with each other, but at other times it's hard against hard. Was it a passionate relationship?

'Thanks,' Dice says, and the screen goes black.

Lara wastes no time and logs into one of the screens. She doesn't have to wait long for the file with the images. 'Later' is clearly not in Dice's dictionary.

'Can I watch?' Frank asks.

'You have to watch,' she says. 'You know the *four-eyes principle*, don't you?' 'Yes, two pairs of eyes always see more.'

'Precisely. Just dig up the photo of Larry Lane and we can start.'

Lara slides another screen closer, next to the other. She searches the Europol database for the best photo they have of Larry Lane, and enlarges it until it fills the entire screen. It's a front-on photo, but Frank can't help feeling that the villain is looking him straight in the eye, just like the Mona Lisa.

'Here we go,' Lara says and the first picture appears on the screen.

To Frank's surprise, several people are depicted on it. Around the face of one man is a circle drawn by the camera software, to indicate the person concerned. The image is sharp and in colour, but Frank immediately notices substantial differences between the man in the photo and Larry Lane. Lara thinks the same, because she's already switching to the next one. With that photo too there's no doubt that it's someone else. They go on like this for a while and not once is either of them uncertain.

'How many pictures are there, in fact?' Frank asks after they've been busy for half an hour.

She laughs. 'Do you really want to know?'

'No, leave it.' In other words, they're not yet through with this.

After another ten minutes, Lara receives a call. She answers quickly, because it's Dice.

'And?' she asks enthusiastically.

Her disillusionment is evident when she hears the answer. They couldn't catch Lane.

'Okay, that's a shame. I'll continue with the images,' she says and hangs up. She looks at him sadly and shrugs her shoulders. 'We're not giving up, are we Frank?'

She clicks open the next photo and they both realize this is going to keep them busy for several more hours, with no guarantee of results.

Sint-Jans-Molenbeek

Larry Lane is angry. Can no one remain in their role anymore? He's already experienced this in previous unsavoury cases where he needed accomplices. Either they tried to cheat him, which usually ended badly for them, or they were arrested for being stupid enough to make a mistake he had already warned them about. Peter Black therefore fell into the latter category.

He'd figured it out right away when he received the call. If only because of the agreement they'd made from the start that only Lane would call the other, and never the other way around. On top of that, it was highly suspicious that he wanted to meet Lane in person. With the Sectra they could discuss everything openly, it was impossible to overhear them. He couldn't think of any reason why a physical meeting would be necessary. Maybe Black was trying to warn him, because at no point did he push to continue to speak. The call was just forty seconds long, making tracing impossible.

He can certainly no longer count on Black, but in fact that's not a problem. Everything has been set in motion and, after all, he's not alone. There is of course the virus that has entered the wide world and is currently rampaging wildly. More and more companies are becoming infected and the reports are now appearing on prime-time television and in the social media. Good news, because that's exactly what he hoped would happen. Bring on the chaos, it's to his advantage. Let them run around like headless chickens, putting out fires. There'll surely be no shortage of them. As long as they're busy with that, he can go after his real target undisturbed.

He opens his laptop and continues what he was doing. The dam. Thanks to the virus, he has gained full control over the local control room. He can imagine the panic in the computer operators' eyes when they discover that their systems are not only encrypted, but that settings are also being changed. He doesn't know what that control room looks like, but he hopes there are many meters that display the values very visually.

Very slowly he enlarges the openings in the dam through which the water can drain. They are probably now at a loss when they notice that the emergency operation is also switched off. Soon they'll be calling their director and asking to activate the crisis plan. Amusing.

He takes another look at the shabby interior of the flat and consoles himself with the thought that before long he'll be one of the most powerful men on earth.

Federal prison, Haren, Brussels

Lara and Frank have already thoroughly analysed more than a hundred photos, and have put two of them aside. Both bear a vague resemblance to Larry Lane, but they're not sure. One photo comes from a camera in the very south of the country, somewhere in the region of Arlon. The other is van Klemskerke, the other far end of the country. They both realize they have no other option than to dig further, because how else can they track down Lane?

After another half hour of routinely looking at picture after picture, Lara stands up. 'Pause,' she says. 'I'm tired of this. Join me for a coffee?'

Frank needs no second asking and they go looking for a coffee corner.

In the corridor her watch rings and she picks it up immediately. 'Yes, Anthony, tell me.'

He pricks up his ears, maybe there is news?

'Good and bad news? Okay, give the bad first, then we'll get rid of that.'

He sees her mouth fall open in surprise.

You're kidding? So it's not just ransomware.

Oh, that's not good, he thinks. So that virus is capable of more than we all thought.

'A dam?' he hears her say. 'Hell's bells, what a bastard. Are there fatalities?'

Apparently not, because she shakes her head as she looks at him. 'Anthony, that means we need a really good antivirus. Do the developers already know about this?'

Knowing Dice, Frank doesn't doubt it.

'And then the good news. I hope that it's really good, Anthony, but I'm afraid it won't be.'

There's a moment's silence and Frank wishes she'd put Dice on speaker so he can listen in. But, of course, she can't do that, as they're standing here in a prison corridor.

'Is that all? Sorry, Anthony, but that seems more like one of the thousand tips we've received in response to our search notice. Isn't it enough for that woman to be questioned by the local police?'

She retraces her steps to the room they just left. Frank has trouble following her, she walks so fast. Once inside, she turns on her loudspeaker and Frank finally hears what Dice is saying.

'Lara, I've good reason to believe that prostitute. She didn't just give a tip, she actually filed a complaint. Moreover, when the police showed her Lane's photo, she immediately recognized him, apparently without a second thought. And then there's something else. She remembered clearly the name of that thin man with the mean smile who had punched her. Apparently, she always asks for her customers' first names, like some kind of kinky signature. Very strikingly: this customer gave her both a first and a family name.'

'Yes? And what is it then?'

'Hold on tight. John Lennon.'

For once, Lara is speechless.

Shibuya Intersection, Tokyo, Japan

At Tokyo's Shibuya intersection, the busiest in the world, James Gordon, a British expatriate, is waiting to cross. Two metres tall, he towers over the Japanese like a scarecrow in a cornfield. He's been living and working here for a year now, but he's still amazed every time at the spectacle at this intersection. It's incredibly busy there, especially during peak hours. Every time the traffic light turns green, it processes about 2500 people. That's what he heard a guide say to the people he was showing around.

It's no different on this cold February winter day. The vast majority of pedestrians are walking from or to the large train station nearby. Once again, a huge group waiting in disciplined fashion to cross. No one thinks of crossing the road if the traffic light isn't green. He's long understood that this is a cultural fact for the Japanese. That's not the case for him. When he was still living in Great Britain, he made a sport of getting to the other side of the street as fast as possible, even if the traffic lights were red for pedestrians. And he was not the only one. The British sense of discipline, once the admiration of other countries, is long gone. His parents were still good citizens who queued up neatly at bus stops.

James is snapped out of his reverie as the traffic light turns green and a large crowd is set in motion. He has no choice but to go forward, propelled, as it were, by a human tsunami. He's halfway through the intersection, thinking about all the work waiting for him at the office, when he hears someone scream. He looks in the direction the sound comes from. For once he is grateful for his height, because it allows him to see immediately what's happening. He blinks because he can't believe it at first, but it really is. The traffic light for the cars has also turned green.

Because all cars are self-driving and centrally controlled, they automatically respond to the green light by entering the intersection. All these cars bear into the masses of people. To his horror, he sees several people disappear under car wheels. Before the surprised drivers, sitting behind their steering wheels working or surfing, can switch to manual control and stop their vehicles, it's already too late for many. Alert young pedestrians were able to jump away in time and James also manages to reach the other side of the intersection quickly. Fortunately, he was not on the edge of the crowd. Safe on the footpath, he surveys the chaos at this gigantic intersection. It's full of injured and dead people, and some cars have not yet stopped. Perhaps, to their horror, the drivers have not yet succeeded. James realizes he must help and walks back into the intersection to tend a Japanese woman lying on the floor, moaning. While addressing her in his best Japanese, he wonders how this disaster could have happened.

Sint-Jans-Molenbeek

'Can I really not come in?' Lara asks the sergeant.

She's standing with four other NATO Special Forces in the hall of the Sint-Jans-Molenbeek police station.

'No,' is the short answer, probably because it's the fourth time she's asked him. 'But you can listen in,' says the forty-year-old, handing her a tiny grey earplug.

'Thank you!' she says. As she stuffs it into her ear, she feels like a little girl who gets a present from her daddy after a lot of nagging.

'Team, one minute.'

She continues to regret not being able to be present at Larry Lane's arrest. That would have done her reputation good. She finds a free chair in the waiting room and sits down.

'Team, go,' the sergeant sounds sharp in her ear. For two minutes she only hears muffled footsteps, until the sergeant tells everyone to halt. The sergeant has just explained their approach to her in a few words. He's not a big talker, she quickly understood that. The bottom line is that they are going to approach the apartment building from two sides and then simply enter through the front door. A drone circles above the building, just like they did in Mechelen. However, the heat sensor attached to it is ineffective this time: there are six apartments and several residents are at home. It's impossible for the drone to know which of the orange spots is Lane. It's useful only for the camera images of the apartment building roof. They will be important in the event Lane wants to use this escape route.

'Team 1, inside,' she hears.

She actually finds this quite exciting. Not as exciting as if she were there. But now she can let her imagination run wild and imagine the hallway of the apartment building, the stairs, the lift. As they and the Special Forces together studied the photos of the old building, she wondered why Lane was hiding out there. Doesn't he stand out a mile among all those people of different nationalities? But on further thought, she understood better. It's the kind of neighbourhood where everyone minds their own business and leaves the others alone.

'Team 1 in position,' she now hears another voice say.

So they've split up. Lara now imagines a corporal who, along with some soldiers, has holed up in the hall of the building, stopping anyone who wants to enter. The footsteps heard faintly in the background now sound louder. The sound reminds her of her father's footsteps on the stairs when she was in bed as a child. Then she knew he was coming to give her a kiss, a moment she always looked forward to.

'Team 2 upstairs', and with that she knows that it was indeed footsteps on the stairs. 'Tele active', she hears.

She wouldn't have understood that if she hadn't followed the briefing. By 'tele', the soldier means that they've put an ultra-thin camera on a flexible cable under the door. They do this to get a picture of the flat and especially who is in it.

There's a moment's silence and then comes a disappointing message. 'Suspect not in sight.'

Damn, he's not going to get away again, is he? But then she realizes that the small camera can't see everything. They determined from the floor plan that it is a tiny flat, but there will be a bathroom, and a bedroom, right?

'Plastic attached.'

That was also mentioned in the briefing. She knows what's about to happen next and she wonders if she shouldn't remove the earplug. But things move faster than she'd expected, and a hard, blunt bang resounds in her ear.

'Team 2 inside!' That message, unlike all the previous ones, is not whispered, but shouted. It must give you an adrenaline rush if you storm into a flat just after the door has blown off its hinges. 'Living room okay,' she hears someone panting. A few seconds later a second message, an unknown voice this time. 'Bedroom okay.' Immediately after that the first voice again. 'Bathroom okay.'

Lara sighs and bows her head. She can already see the storm coming. 'Team 2, flat okay. Suspect not present.'

That message confirms her suspicion. Just as she is about to remove the earplug in disappointment, she hears 'Quick scan in progress'. That wasn't mentioned in the briefing. Perhaps it's standard procedure?

'Food on the table. Empty alcohol bottles on the floor. No computers.'

Despite her disappointment, she smiles at the very brief descriptions of what the soldier sees in the flat. He'll never be a poet. She begins to wonder if they are actually at the right address. Is that prostitute really sure it was this flat? If she had been drinking or taking drugs herself, she could very easily have mistaken the flat. But that theory is dashed by the last message she hears.

'Phone found. Brand Sectra.'

She angrily removes the earplug from her ear and has to restrain herself from throwing it in the nearest rubbish bin.

NATO Headquarters, Evere, Brussels

Everyone, including Meredith Weston, has reconvened in Anthony Dice's office. The atmosphere is depressed and Dice's face is set on bad weather.

'So we're nowhere,' he shouts. 'Lane has disappeared, the virus is on a world tour, causing more and more companies to come to a standstill. I have the NATO member states on my neck, urging a solution. But I have no solution. 'And neither do you.

While Lara was following the raid on the flat in Sint-Jans-Molenbeek, Frank was using his free time to plough through the social media in search of news about the virus.

'The virus has indeed already infected companies into the smallest corners of the world. As far as North Korea, but that's officially denied by the sister of the recently deceased president. And the bizarre thing is that the virus doesn't just demand a ransom in exchange for releasing the computers. It also does other things. Just think of the dam at the Lacs de l'Eau d'Heure, where all the water is gradually draining away and there is a threat of flooding. There is also the incident at that famous intersection in Tokyo, where several people were killed and many injured. The virus had taken control of the traffic lights and deliberately confused the traffic, with all the subsequent consequences.'

'The virus or Larry Lane? Can a virus do that on its own?' Weston asks.

Eddy answers this question from the NATO head of communications. 'A virus can be programmed to do various things. Ransomware is in any case the most important function in this case. Lane wants to bring in money, that's very much the primary intention.'

'Yes, and he's going to use that cash for a murky new project, and who knows what that'll be?' Luis remarks.

'Encrypting systems and asking for ransom money is indeed what we are mainly experiencing now', Righard agrees.

'But those other things, why are then happening?' Frank asks.

'To create chaos. Keeping the governments busy while his crypto bank account is getting better fed by the minute.'

'When will the antivirus be ready?' Dice asks.

'We've just had online consultations with all major players in the security industry and with the laboratory in Zemst. Everyone is mobilized and they're working round the clock.'

'How long until we have an antivirus?'

The three experts look at each other. 'One day. Maybe less, maybe more.'

Dice sighs. 'That's no use to me. I cannot communicate this to the Member States. Let alone the United States or China.'

'Let alone mention all that money being channelled through to Lane's account. Can we really not block that crypto bank account?' Lara asks.

'That's possible, but only after a European court order. The procedure for that is very tough, and we don't have time for that now.'

There is a moment's silence and then Dice returns to something he had already mentioned last time. 'Is NATO's network adequately protected against this virus?'

'To be honest, I'm afraid for it,' Eddy replies. 'At the moment, NATO is largely cut off from the internet. But maybe it's already inside and slumbering somewhere. Then it's no use. Moreover, no one will be able to work efficiently anymore. Consulting databases, meeting online, sharing documents, none of that would be possible anymore.'

'Don't forget the self-driving cars and trucks, too.' Everyone realizes this is not a solution and that no alternative is available.

Then Righard stands up and starts pacing up and down. 'What if Lane has other intentions?'

Luis and Eddy recognize the 'what if' reasoning and are curious about what their colleague has in mind.

'What if Lane doesn't just want to collect a ransom from his victims, but sees other possibilities?'

'What do you mean, Righard?' Luis asks.

'What if he gets paid and still doesn't release some companies' systems? What would happen then?'

'Those companies would get into trouble and could even go bankrupt,' Frank replies.

'Indeed, and Lane could benefit from that.'

'I get it. With their shares falling in value, Lane could buy in very cheaply, then sell them later for a heck of a lot more. There's some point in that, Righard.'

'What can we do about that?'

'I'll take care of that,' Dice responds firmly. 'I only see one way and that is to completely halt all stock market trading.'

'Well, that's radical. But you're right, Anthony,' Weston says. 'Come on, let's try to get that done.'

Dice opens the door and lets Weston go first. He turns and points to Lara and the four men. 'And you, get me an antivirus or get me Larry Lane. Preferably both. I don't care how you do it. For all I care you can break all the laws there are, but just do it.'

Sint-Jans-Molenbeek

Unaware that the door to his flat has just been blown in, Larry Lane strolls quietly down the narrow Paalstraat pavement, towards the municipal square. He' about half a kilometre from the flat he's left for good. Now there is no turning back. But that's no problem, going into hiding isn't for him anyway. That's more for cowards, for scared weasels.

The house he's heading to belongs to a Muslim he met during his brief stay in Brussels. Before contacting him, he had observed him for some time. Because Lane needs someone who doesn't ask questions, who will take his money and who will not cheat him. He has watched Farid do several things and so far he has fulfilled all three conditions. Lane wonders if that will still be the case now that he's come to collect what he's previously entrusted to him. He puts his hand in his jacket and feels the butt of the small revolver he managed to pick up. He doesn't like guns, especially when he has to use them himself. But if Farid tries to trick him, and his car is missing or damaged, he'll not hesitate to spend a few bullets on him.

Arriving at the house, he knocks three times on the brand new garage gate right next to the house, as agreed. Less than five minutes later, Lane pulls out and parks just down the street. That went smoothly. He takes his revolver, puts it under his seat and then sets the GPS. In his original plan he was not supposed to go there. But because he can no longer count on Black, he has no choice but to do the job himself. What's there in that security expert's home is too important to simply ignore. He slowly drives away and not much later leaves the Brussels Region and enters Flemish Brabant, on his way to Elewijt.

San Francisco, United States of America

'Too bad the trip's almost over,' says Belinda, resting her head on her husband's shoulder.

He puts his arm around her and kisses her tenderly on the forehead. 'This isn't our last trip together, I promise you,' he says softly into her ear.

The couple, both in their sixties and both graced with salt-and-pepper haircuts, are standing on the top deck of the *Queen of the Seven Seas*. The cruise ship, which can accommodate more than

6,000 passengers, has been their home for a wonderful week at sea, with the visit to the Hawaiian Islands.

'You say that every time, Mike,' Belinda counters.

'Now I mean it,' he says, looking into her eyes.

That's what he says every time, Belinda thinks. Their final destination is getting closer by the minute and so is the end of their holiday. She knew when she married him that he was a workaholic, and he still is. She had secretly hoped he would change as he got older, but unfortunately that was not to be.

'Come on, let's go even further forward,' she says, pulling him along by her hand.

Only when they are at the extreme point of the prow is she satisfied with the view. There they stand with their arms around each other for several minutes, until her lover breaks the spell.

'Aren't we sailing too fast to dock?' he breaks the silence.

Belinda laughs. 'Are you the captain already?' She lays her head on his chest and enjoys hearing his heart beat.

'Belinda, I mean it. Something's wrong.'

The serious tone with which he addresses her makes her open her eyes. The mainland has indeed approached very quickly and she sees dense crowds of people walking around on shore.

'This is not right. We weren't docking at Fisherman's Wharf, were we?' Mike says. 'I don't think that's even possible, given the size of this ship.'

Belinda is now really worried by what her husband is saying. All the more so because he used to have a boat himself and therefore knows what he's talking about.

'Come on, let's move back,' she says anxiously.

Mike doesn't move and stares straight ahead at the quay wall that has now come very close. He can almost make out the faces of everyone walking around, especially those who are standing on the bank and pointing to the mastodon of a boat heading straight for them.

'Run then, you bunch of simpletons, don't stand there,' he growls.

When the ship's siren starts wailing, Belinda panics. She drags her husband with her and together they run away from the forecastle. They have to work their way in between groups of curious tourists who have come innocently to take pictures of the mooring.

When they're about midships, she glances over the railing and sees the ship brushing against the world-famous and photogenic seals. As the giant ship looms beside them, they smoothly dive into the ocean from the jetties where they were napping. Moments later, above the wail of the siren, she hears a huge din as the *Queen of the Seven Seas* smashes through the moored fishing boats. A second later, the wooden jetty and the entire wharf are pulverized as the 250,000+ tonne vessel comes to an inglorious halt at the famous and historic Fisherman's Wharf.

NATO Headquarters, Evere, Brussels

'I've another question for you', Frank says.

Luis grins. 'I'd rather you had an answer, but ask your question.'

'It wasn't clear to me just now whether Lane is manually causing these disasters or if he programmed the virus to do that.'

'I think he got the administrator position using the virus and in this way took control remotely.'

'Speaking of controlling,' Lara says, glancing at her watch, 'I just got a report that a cruise ship has entered Fisherman's Wharf and crashed into the shore.'

'What? So Lane took control of that ship? That's unbelievable.'

'What could he be doing this for?' Frank wonders.

Before anyone can answer that, Eddy receives an alarm signal from his smartwatch. 'No that's impossible!'

'What's wrong, Eddy?'

Without looking up, he informs them. 'It's my alarm system at home. There's a break-in right now, right now.'

'Call the police,' Righard yells.

Eddy looks at him and seems completely upset. 'It's Larry Lane. Lane is at my house,' he blurts out.

'Are you certain?' Lara asks.

Eddy nods slowly. 'Yes, look. Since the incident with the furnace, I've had additional security installed. Among other things, a very small camera in the corner of the living space, almost invisible to the naked eye. And, very importantly, it's not connected to my home network. So if that gets hacked, it won't affect that camera. I have to go there.'

'Come on, I'm driving. Call the police,' Lara says and she's already out of door.

The rest follow her as best they can, but when she's in the car, she still has to wait a while for Eddy and Frank to get in. Luis and Righard stay in Evere to help search for an antivirus.

Lara drives out of the parking lot at high speed and heads for Elewijt, about fifteen minutes' drive away. 'I've called the police, they're sending a patrol, but they can't guarantee they'll get there faster than us.'

'Is he still inside?' Frank asks.

Eddy nods. 'Yes, I still have him in the picture. I assumed he was going to do something with my computers, but he just ignores them. He's looking for something in my desk and in my cupboards.'

'What would he be looking for there? Do you have any idea?'

'No. Not what Larry Lane's doing at all in my house.'

'It's already the second time he's targeted you personally, father,' Frank says in surprise. There has to be a reason for this.

Not for the first time they are shaken when Lara takes a sharp turn much too fast. It's clear she's ignoring all traffic rules.

Eddy keeps looking at the camera image on his watch and suddenly holds his breath.

'What is it?' Frank asks with concern.

'Lane, he... he's just taken my diskette off the wall and then he's gone out of the picture.'

'A diskette?' Lara asks in surprise. 'Which diskette?'

'That's a long story. But the bottom line is that, way back in the late 1980s, I managed to thwart the very first ransomware attack ever. That was, in fact, the beginning of my career as a security expert. I kept that diskette out of nostalgia and hung it in a frame on my living room wall. And now Larry Lane's stolen it.' Lara ignores a red light, goes full throttle and pretends not to hear the horns of the other drivers. 'How does Lane know you have that diskette?'

'I was in the news a lot with that, maybe he noticed it then.'

'What would he need that diskette for?'

'I don't know. He can't use it for anything, because it's ancient, primitive technology.'

'Diskette or not, we can't let Larry Lane escape again.'

Elewijt

After a slight turn they arrive at Eddy's house and they just see an electric Porsche Taycan speeding away.

'That's Black,' Frank shouts. How can that be? He's in prison, isn't he!'

Lara pushes the accelerator to the floor and gives chase. 'Frank, will you inform Dice and ask him if he knows Black has escaped? And wasn't that Porsche impounded?'

Frank calls Dice, explains the situation to him and says he'll hold the line. 'He's not aware of Black's possible escape, but he's calling the prison director right now.'

After two minutes' waiting, Dice comes back on the line.

'No? Okay, then it's someone else behind the wheel. Yes, we'll keep you informed.' Frank turns to Lara and his father. 'Black didn't escape, so it must be Lane driving.'

'Lane and Black may have bought two identical Porsches, hence the confusion,' Eddy concludes.

Just like the first time Lara was chasing the fast sports car, now she's also gradually losing ground. They tear through the narrow streets of a residential area and she's at a disadvantage in the many curves.

Eddy receives a call from the police, who ask him where they are at the moment. He reports their position and is promised that a drone will be sent to keep track of the fugitive.

Lara tries her best, but she's already so far behind that once Lane has disappeared around a corner ahead of her, Lane can take advantage of those few seconds to turn into a different street without his pursuers seeing. That's probably what happened when Lara screeched round a corner, landing them on an empty street at a two-block intersection. So she has to choose just like last time, hesitates for a moment and then drives into the street on the right. A new call from the police comes in with the happy report that the drone has spotted the Porsche and is currently flying above it. The officer says he'll stay on the line and names the street over which the drone is now flying. Lara is happy to see on the GPS that she just made the correct choice by driving to the right.

'Suspect has stopped,' the officer reports to everyone's surprise. 'What's he up to now?' Frank wonders.

Fortunately, the drone is filming everything he does, because they're not yet on site. 'Suspect opens car boot. There's something in it. It's a drone, a big one. He's activating the drone and it's taking off out of the boot.'

'This can't be true,' says Eddy, shocked. 'That's how he escaped from prison!'

Lara nearly squeezes her steering wheel to pulp and Frank is also frustrated.

'Suspect is hanging onto the drone and is taking off. Our drone will follow', is the police officer's dry comment. Moments later, the tone with which he reports changes. He becomes noticeably more nervous. 'Suspect is pulling something out of his inside pocket, it looks like a weapon. He's shooting at our drone. First shot missed. Second shot too. Third... the connection to our drone is broken. Probably crashed.'

'Over there!' Lara points.

Eddy and Frank follow her hand and indeed see a drone with a man below it silhouetted against the grey sky.

'Don't let him out of your sight, men,' she says grimly, continuing to speed.

Eddy and Frank do their best to steer her right or left depending on where they see the drone flying. Sometimes it disappears behind a tall building or a church tower, but luckily always comes into view again. Driving on a narrow road with fields on either side, they are surprised to see the drone stop and hang motionless in the air. 'He's stopped. Why?'

'Is this a ruse?' Eddy wonders.

Because the drone has stopped, Lara quickly catches up and they come alongside the stationary drone. She turns off the engine and jumps out of the car.

'Watch out, he's armed', Frank calls after her, but she's already run to the edge of the field.

While Eddy stays in the car to inform the police of their location, Frank also leaves the car, but somewhat more cautiously than Lara did. Like them, he cranes his neck in the direction of the criminal they've been looking for so long, and who has always slipped through their fingers.

'What now? He can start flying again any minute.'

Lara shakes her head. "No, I didn't think so. There must be another reason.'

Her words are fully out of her mouth when the drone falls like a lead weight with Larry Lane below it. Frank's gapes in surprise and

Lara also looks wide-eyed at what is happening. With a hard, sickening thump, Lane and the drone land on the ground. Lara and Frank can't believe it and look back at Eddy, who has now also got out.

'What happened?' he asks.

'He just crashed to the ground,' Frank says.

Lara enters the field through a gate and makes her way to where Lane is lying. When she's a metre or so away from him, she gestures for Frank and Eddy to come closer.

'Warning, if you've never seen a corpse, it's not a pretty sight. There's something else you should see.'

Eddy and Frank go over to her and she points to the badly damaged drone on the ground.

'Look,' she said in a dull voice.

On the drone's screen is a familiar text: 'Pay 1 million crypto to remove the encryption from your files.'

'The virus got into the drone and stopped it. Lane has fallen foul of his own virus.'

NATO-base, Zemst

The three of them are staring at the dead Larry Lane, lying on the ground in an unnatural position.

'I would have preferred him not dead,' Lara says.

'Same here,' Frank agrees, 'at least then he could then have been tried for all the crimes he's committed.'

'But that's just the way it happened. The police can arrive here at any moment and then we'll lose a lot of time answering questions. Time we don't have.'

Frank admires her rational approach, she always sees clearly in every situation.

'I suggest we take the diskette now and get out of here. I'll call the police and tell them we'll make a statement at the police station later.'

She crouches down by the corpse and searches Lane's pockets for the diskette. Nothing there, so she opens the small backpack he was wearing. She reaches in and pulls out a framed diskette.

'Bingo,' she says.

Eddy is happy to see his showpiece again. At first glance it's not damaged, because Lane fell on his stomach.

'Come on, we're gone,' Lara urges her companions as police sirens can be heard in the distance. They get in and she puts her foot hard down as usual.

'I want to come back to why Lane stole your diskette. What does it have to do with the virus?' Frank asks his father.

Eddy shrugs his shoulders. 'I've been thinking about it in the meantime. Maybe there's another hidden code on that diskette related to the virus Lane developed.'

'Wait a minute, that can't be. When does that diskette date from?'

'From 1989.'

'And when did Lane develop that computer virus? Not during that period? I don't think he was even born then.' 'Your son has a point, Eddy,' Lara says, turning into a small side street and parking the car out of sight.

'Then what's the connection with that diskette, father? And how did Lane know you had that diskette?'

'Well, the story appeared many times in the media. And it always seems to surface again, like the Loch Ness monster. It was of course a unique case at the time.'

'That does explain how he knew you had the diskette.'

'For me there has to be another copy of that diskette, Eddy adds pensively. 'And Lane owns it.'

'Yes, that makes sense. That must be it.' There's a moment's silence in the car. 'But how did Lane get it?'

'He may have received it from the maker,' Eddy suggests.

'I looked it up while you were talking,' Lara says. 'The diskette was made by a certain Dr Schultz.'

Eddy laughs. 'I too could have told you that.'

'But do you know where that crazy doctor taught?' Eddy doesn't answer immediately, so she continues.

'In Berlin. And now here it comes. Where did Larry Lane get his PhD? Right. In Berlin. That's written in black and white in his file.'

'That must be it,' Eddy admits. 'That's where they met and that doctor must have confided in him. Which is something one should never do with Larry Lane.'

'Okay, now we've solved that riddle, another question arises. How can we copy that disk so it can be analysed?'

'That diskette can't read by a modern computer, that goes without saying. So we have to find someone with a computer that dates back to that time.'

'Do you have such an old computer?' she asks. She notices on her dashboard that the range has fallen sharply, so she parks the car at the side of the road.

'No. I don't immediately know anyone who keeps such old computers. Wait a minute, yes. At the RSA Virus Bulletin Conference, I met a young man who collects old computers as a hobby. He may be able to help us.'

'What's that boy's name?' Lara asks.

'Jorgen, that's his first name, I'm sure.'

'And his last name?'

Eddy racks his brains and closes his eyes. 'It's on the tip of my tongue. Something with the letter o in it. I know. D'Hondt, Jorgen D'Hondt. That's it.

Lara repeats the name for the Butler, and fortunately there is only one search result thanks to rare first name.

'He lives in Halle.' Lara activates the route and they are off. 'I'll have to stop at a charging station, because the car battery's almost empty.'

'Then that's it. The advantage of Lane's death is that at least no new disasters will be caused now,' Frank says.

But he's badly off target here.

E19, near Wemmel

Fifteen minutes later, a lot has happened. Lara has partially charged her car battery at a public charging station, called the police and Dice, then hit the highway. Eddy in turn has called Jorgen D'Hondt, who was immediately ready to make his computer collection available. All three sense that the worst is over and a solution will soon be found for the crisis the world is currently going through.

They are racing towards Halle at a hundred and thirty kilometres an hour when a call comes through the Butler. It's Anthony Dice.

'Lara, where are you?'

'Still on the way to Halle', she says.

'Lara, you have to hurry. We've just received word that someone or something has taken control of the nuclear power plant in Tihange.'

'What? But Larry Lane's dead! Are you sure about that?'

'Yes, the message was confirmed three times from different sources. The situation is not yet critical, but we don't know how much time we have left. How long before you get to Halle?'

'Ten minutes, fifteen minutes?'

'Lara, hurry,' Dice says softly and hangs up. 'That's very bad news,' Eddy responds. 'The virus is probably equipped with artificial intelligence, which means it's constantly learning and keeps getting better and smarter.'

'So it doesn't really need Lane anymore?'

'No, it now charts its own course and will do everything it can to achieve its goal.'

'That goal was to create chaos, make companies go bankrupt and then buy their shares for a low price.'

'Yes, at least that's what we assumed, we're not sure', Eddy corrects her. 'Who knows, maybe Lane had something else up his sleeve. Don't forget he tricked us twice. First with that explosion in the Dome, which ended up being just a diversion manoeuvre Then the ransomware attacks, which we considered to be the end point of his actions. But then he starts causing disasters. He will also have planned in advance to take over control of the nuclear power plant.'

'Unless...' Frank says. 'Father, if you'll let me, I'm going to use your 'what if' reasoning for once. What if the virus is now out of control?'

'Son, I admire your imagination, but a virus doesn't just make decisions on its own. A virus is programmed by its creator to perform certain actions, and no more than that.'

Lara takes exit 21 for Halle, refusing to slow down on the bend that leads to the road. The seat belts prevent Frank and Eddy from being slammed together by the centrifugal force.

'Anyway, it doesn't matter. We just need to get an antivirus into the cloud as soon as possible to compete with that goddamn virus.'

Eddy is furious with Lane and Black, and swears in the car. Then something hits him. 'We need a cleanroom,' he says more to himself than to the others.

'What's a cleanroom?' Frank asks.

'A space that's completely sterile, where there is no sign of dust or magnetism. It's only in such perfect conditions that we stand a chance of reading the code on the diskette.'

'Where do you find such cleanrooms?'

'I know someone who owns a small company where he has installed two cleanrooms to conduct research. But that company is in the Ardennes, too far. And who knows, their systems may have been blocked by the virus.'

'Don't hospitals have those sterile rooms for patients who are not allowed to come into contact with the outside air?' Frank suggests.

'But it's not the same. I'm not convinced there isn't magnetism in those rooms because of all the devices they use there.'

'Call the AZ VUB hospital', they hear Lara instruct the Butler.

Eddy looks at Frank and shrugs his shoulders. In any event, it's better than nothing. 'I'll call Righard and Luis and ask them to join us at the hospital. We'll need all the help we can get.'

Lara meanwhile lands at the secretariat and insists rather strongly to be put through to the department where the sterile rooms are located. She gets on the phone with the responsible doctor and explains the importance of her request. After the doctor asks for Europol's telephone number to check she is who she claims to be, he gives her permission to come over. Lara then asks if all devices can be removed from the room. This is no problem either.

'Great, I'll call Jorgen', Eddy says motivated and puts his money where his mouth is.

He explains the problem of the cleanroom and the young man, in his unbridled enthusiasm, immediately agrees to put his old computer into his car boot and drive to the AZ VUB.

After another ten nerve-wracking minutes, they arrive at the hospital, report in and are allowed to drive to a parking lot close to the building where a sterile room awaits them. They are led into the room and when they enter, they find a completely empty hospital room, which makes a strange impression on them. In the middle of the room there is an area of about two by two metres, hermetically enclosed by a plastic curtain.

'A real cleanroom is equipped with an extraction system that extracts all particulate matter from the room. We don't have that here, but it's still is a very sterile room,' says Eddy, who still seems to be unsure about their approach.

There's no furniture in the room, so all three sit on the floor and wait for Jorgen. Eddy goes to talk to the nurses and then comes with some surprising news.

'Apparently this room was adapted during the corona crisis for research into the COVID-19 virus. So there is a greater chance that it'll suffice as a makeshift cleanroom,' he says happily. After five minutes, Righard and Luis arrive and Eddy immediately informs them of what has happened. After another ten minutes that seem like an hour, a doctor knocks on the door.

'Are you expecting this young man?'

'Yes, thank you, doctor.'

Jorgen appears in the doorway and Lara literally pulls him into the room.

Eddy points. 'Behind that plastic curtain.'

Jorgen, who is sweating profusely from the weight of the heavy computer he is carrying, hurries over. Frank holds the curtain open and the young man steps inside.

'Are you all staying outside?' Eddy asks. 'We have to avoid dust as much as possible.'

He closes the curtain hermetically while Jorgen plugs in the computer. Then he presses the button and the old PC starts to boot.

'Sorry, it'll take a while.'

Eddy puts a hand on his shoulder and nods in understanding. 'You don't have to tell me, young man. When I was your age, these were the only computers we had.'

After a few minutes, when all processes inside the computer have been completed, Eddy raises the diskette he took from the cover. 'Hopefully,' he says.

He inserts the diskette that has hung on his wall for years into the wide, deep slot of the more than forty-year-old computer.

AZ VUB, Jette

Two pairs of eyes focus on the greenish screen of the computer from the collection of a twenty-year-old young man from Halle. One white line after another with incomprehensible abbreviations and English terms appears, until the screen is filled with text that at first glance appears meaningless.

'That's part of the control program', Eddy explains. 'We need to try to read the diskette and then copy the contents onto another medium. You have to do a few things for that.'

'May I?' Jorgen asks.

'Of course,' Eddy replies.

Jorgen types in some instructions and after each instruction he presses the enter key. The white printed texts change and Jorgen keeps entering commands. Eddy can only admire his finger dexterity.

'I'm now trying to get the code we need out of the trash, so to speak,' he explains.

Eddy watches mesmerized and frowns when Jorgen pauses. 'What was that again?' the boy wonders. 'Oh yes, I know.'

He continues typing and Eddy hears the sound of an incoming call in the background. The ringtone is vague and Lara's voice is also distorted by the plastic screen. He can't understand what she's saying, and can only hope they're not too late. Hundreds of thousands of people live around that nuclear power plant, so if something were to happen there...

Eddy forces himself to focus on what Jorgen is doing. They need to find that ransomware code, that's their only chance to stop the virus. The memories of that TV broadcast in 2020 come flooding back. Then, in the presence of some journalists, he had attempted to bring the code to life. It didn't work then, so why should it work now? Because it has to, he tells himself. But he notices that the typing has stopped. The young man is unsure of himself and apparently doesn't know what to do next.

'Come on, Jorgen, what's the next command? Think.'

The white rectangle cursor blinks invitingly and seems to challenge him. Jorgen thinks deeply, but seems to be unable to think of anything for the time being. Eddy shows understanding for that young man. It can't be easy for him. Someone watching him closely, and four more people waiting hopefully outside the plastic screen. He's probably also thinking of all those people who are currently in trouble or who don't know what disaster is hanging over their heads.

Eddy sees Jorgen close his eyes and think deeply. Then he looks up at Eddy. 'What if it were really simple?' he says. 'No, that can't be. Or perhaps, after all. He decides to take a chance and types in the command he hadn't thought of so far. He had assumed this wouldn't work anyway.

To their mutual surprise, the blinking cursor begins to form one sentence after another, in rapid succession. Eddy reads what appears on the screen, and a weight of several tons falls from his shoulders.

'I've got it,' Jorgen exclaims with a smile, raising his fists into the air.

'We've got it!' Eddy calls to the others.

Lara immediately calls her boss to inform him. Everyone laughs exuberantly — except Eddy.

Frank is the first to notice. 'Father, what's up?'

'This is just the first step. Now we need to make a copy so that what's on it can be analysed. But I don't know how we're going to do that yet,' he says discouraged.

'Mr. Willems?' Jorgen asks.

'Call me Eddy.'

'Okay thanks. 'I have an idea. In my car boot there's another computer with a built-in CD player. Now if we copy the code to this computer's hard drive, and then connect this computer to the other with a cable, we can move the code to the other computer.

Then we copy the information onto a blank CD. Would that work?' the young man asks politely.

Eddy stands up and takes him by the shoulders. 'That's a very good idea, Jorgen. Get that computer, quick.'

The boy makes a narrow opening in the plastic screen, squeezes through and starts to run.

'What is it?' Frank asked amazed.

'It's going to be OK!' Eddy reassures him. 'We're going to make a CD, remember them?'

The surprise on Frank's face, for whom CDs are all about music, causes Eddy to burst out laughing after a delay and he feels the stress slipping away. Until he spots Lara, who is still on the phone with Dice. And she's not laughing, far from it.

AZ VUB, Jette

'Guys, another problem's come up,' Lara reports.

The rest do not believe their ears, because they thought everything would soon be all right now.

'We've just talked about Larry Lane's diversionary manoeuvres. Well, I think we now know his real purpose. Hold on tight. Of the fifteen thousand satellites that provide the worldwide internet, more than ten thousand have already been taken over by the virus.'

Everyone needs some time to process that information. 'The satellites Elon Musk once launched?'

'Yes,' Lara confirms. 'Anthony says they're being taken over by the virus at a dizzying rate.'

At that moment Jorgen enters with another computer and a long cable in his arms. He sees the serious faces and stops in the doorway. 'What's happening?'

For the second time that day, the young man is dragged into the room by Lara. 'Come on guys, hurry up,' she yells.

'She's right,' Eddy says. 'Come on, Jorgen, action.'

They go straight to work, as Lara leaves the room and starts another call. After five minutes, the other computer has started up and is connected to the first one. After another three minutes, the code is present on the PC with the CD reader and the data has been copied onto a blank CD.

'Done', says Jorgen, removing the diskette from the PC. 'Strange, it looks like there's something else on that diskette.'

Eddy hurriedly takes the CD and thanks Jorgen. 'Where's Lara? We need to get this CD to NATO as soon as possible.'

Eddy runs outside and he sees Lara standing at the entrance. 'Lara, we have to leave,' he shouts, waving the CD. When Lara doesn't move and shakes her head, the CD almost falls from his hands in surprise. The thought that she's an accomplice of Larry Lane flashes through his mind. It's not true, is it? Just when they've found the code to make the antivirus.

Eddy stops and doesn't know what to do. Then he hears a whirring sound like an electric car. But it turns out to be a drone, which slowly descends behind Lara and hovers half a metre above her. She steps aside and smiles at him. She has provided a drone! A very good idea, because that's much faster than by car. Eddy hurries over to the small machine, opens the leather case hanging below it, and inserts the CD. He closes the bag and nods to Lara. Immediately the drone takes off. In an instant it has disappeared.

Eddy calls Dice to report that the drone is on its way and that they must commence the analysis immediately. Stepping into the hospital corridor, he suddenly feels very tired. The others also look tired, only Jorgen is still full of energy and enthusiasm.

'There's not much we can do now but wait,' Eddy says in frustration, and they all return to the cleanroom.

'If we can't do anything for the time being, I suggest going for a coffee in the cafeteria. Agree?' Frank asks.

'Son, you really are addicted to coffee, you know?'

'I'm going to put my computers back in my car and then I'll join you,' Jorgen says.

'I'll help you out, Jorgen,' Frank says, and they each take up one of the heavy computers.

'What a weight', Frank puffs. 'What a difference from today's PCs.'

When the computers are in the car, they join the Three Amigos and Lara, who already have cups of steaming coffee in front of them. They talk for a while, but then there is a silence. It's clear everyone is not only tired, but also uneasy. They're all thinking of the disasters that are currently unfolding and of the satellites high above their heads, which are being taken over one by one by a computer virus. Like living cells in a human body that are losing the battle one by one.

When Lara's smartwatch rings after half an hour, they are startled out of their thoughts and immediately alert again. 'Anthony, tell me, I'll put you on speaker.'

'The diskette was analysed and the AIDS ransomware code was found as expected. But after further investigation with specialized software and hardware, we found something else,' Dice says.

All eyes at the table are on Lara as if she is going to tell them.

'What do you mean, Anthony?' she asks quickly.

'Another code was found on the diskette, and not just any one. A very nasty piece of software, which must have been placed on it by the creator of the AIDS ransomware.'

'By that German doctor Schultz?' Luis asks.

'We suppose so. Anyway, we were able to reconstruct the program and it was immediately sent on to the security industry to turn it into an antivirus.'

Lara thanks Dice and hangs up. 'An extra code on the diskette? So the ransomware was just an afterthought for that mad genius doctor.'

'So he intended much more than to encrypt companies' computers. But for some reason he didn't follow through with those plans.'

'How long will it take for the antivirus to arrive?' Jorgen asks.

'That can go quickly, especially since everyone is really working on it now.'

'Making the antivirus, that's one thing,' Eddy says. 'But getting it on the Internet is another matter.' He gets up and announces he's going for a walk so as to think in peace.

The rest realize there's no answer to that last question for the time being and remain seated at the table. All three are following the social media telling what's happening around the world.

'Did you also see this much fake news?' Lara asks Jorgen.

The young man nods. 'Yes, a huge amount, ever since the virus first hit, the most nonsensical reports have been appearing. The funny thing is that a lot of people like those messages.'

'I've also seen many messages from prophets of doom who say the end of the world is now really near. Incredible', Frank sighs.

'Yes, Anthony?' Lara says when her smartwatch finally rings.

'The antivirus is ready! I've also sent it to you. We're now going to inject it into the cloud. I'll keep you informed.

Dice hangs up and everyone is relieved. Everything seems to be returning to normal.

'Eddy, you'd probably never thought there was another malicious virus in your diskette?'

'No, not at all. To think it's been hanging on our dining room wall for so long.'

'How long have we been in the security industry?' Righard asks. 'I've never experienced this before.'

Eddy grins. 'No, you're right. Good thing, too. We're actually lucky that we deal mostly with 'ordinary' cybercriminals and hackers who want to prove themselves at all costs or simply want to make money. Sometimes we've had to deal with larger criminal organizations and occasionally there were even hackers behind them who were supported by governments, but Larry Lane was of a completely different calibre.'

'As a human being you have to be thoroughly bad to send such a virus into the world, don't you?' Luis comments.

'Maybe that's why he never married,' Lara says. The men frown at her and she doesn't understand why. 'What? It's in his file, you know.'

The atmosphere is more positive now that there is a prospect of a solution to all these problems. Half an hour later that atmosphere changes when Dice calls back with bad news.

'We can't get the antivirus into the cloud. The virus is blocking all internet access,' he says, and the desperation can be heard in his voice. 'We'll keep trying,' he adds.

'Anthony, we're coming to you. Maybe we can help.'

NATO Headquarters, Evere, Brussels

The party leaves the hospital and drives to NATO in two cars. No one knows what to say. The last few hours have been a real rollercoaster.

After fifteen minutes they arrive at the NATO main entrance. When they are in the hall, they notice that a heavy security door has closed at the security post, blocking access.

'That's the work of the virus,' Luis states, stunned. 'What now?'

Everyone starts looking for a way to open the door, but they soon have to give up. Frank drops his shoulders in disappointment. He can't believe they've come this far and are now literally hitting a wall. So is there really no way to get the antivirus into the cloud?

His eye falls on the dish that serves to scan all smart objects during access control. Of course he hadn't thought of that before!

'I think I may have found a way to get the antivirus into the NATO network,' he informs the others. 'From there, the antivirus can then spread further.'

'What are you thinking about?' Eddy asks.

Frank points to the dish and explains it to him.

Eddy nods enthusiastically. 'That could work, son. Very good idea!'

Frank approaches Righard and asks him to establish a connection between the antivirus he received from Dice and his own smartwatch. Righard immediately takes care of this. When the data has been transferred, and the antivirus has therefore also been picked up by the lenses, Frank walks to the table on which the smart dish is placed. Everyone gathers around him and looks expectantly at what he is up to. 'Genius,' Luis says enthusiastically to Lara. 'It's like this: when the smart lenses are scanned, all applications on them are read and checked for malicious properties. The antivirus is something unknown and will be opened by the system to check it. That's the chance for the antivirus to sneak into the cloud and go looking for the virus.'

With some effort, Frank removes the two smart lenses from his eyes and places them in the palm of his hand. 'Hopefully,' he says and puts the lenses onto the dish. Everyone holds their breath and for a moment nothing happens. But then a green light comes on. The little disk, which is tasked with scanning all smart objects, does its job and scans the smart lenses and all files on them.

'Yes, it works!' calls Eddy.

'Is the antivirus now on NATO's network?' Lara asks.

'Yes! Now it will spread to all infected devices right round the world.'

'To the satellites also?'

'To the satellites too!'

Everyone is relieved and startled when the heavy door slides open.

'It works!' Jorgen shouts.

'Come on, let's go to Anthony,' Lara says. On the way, she calls him to announce their arrival.

A moment later they're sitting in his office looking at the wall, on which two rows of constantly changing numbers are projected.

'Good job everyone! Will you join us?' Dice points to the image. 'The row of numbers on the left is the number of satellites still under NATO control. Until now that figure has been steadily declining. Hopefully that'll soon change now.'

Everyone looks concentratedly at the screen, but for the time being there is no change.

'How did you come up with the idea of those lenses?' Lara asks.

'It's not difficult,' Frank replies. 'A year ago, Lane gained access to NATO's network through a pair of smart contact lenses left behind by my assistant at the time. I suddenly thought of that. If the antivirus is put in the cloud in this way, hopefully it will go unnoticed.'

They look tensely at the moving rows of numbers, and they all secretly hope they were not too late with their action.

After five minutes, Lara calls out first: 'It's stopped falling!'

And indeed, the numbers are no longer going down that fast. It's like someone's resisting, but not yet strongly enough to stop the fall completely. Frank imagines that the antivirus is now fighting the virus, which is more or less the case in reality. At first the decline continues at that slower rate, but then that rate drops even more, eventually coming to a halt.

A cheer goes up in the office. They make so much noise that his secretary swings open the door and comes to look inside curiously. But everyone is so euphoric that they don't even see or hear her. They are jumping and shouting together like at a football match. Dice now shows other images from around the world on the wall and they are glad to see that the virus is gradually losing control. The situation around the nuclear power plant has been resolved, as has the situation with the dam. Disasters are also being avoided in other countries because the antivirus is now clearly winning the battle against Larry Lane's virus. One ransomware encryption after another dissolves into nothing, to the relief of the companies, who can resume their activities.

'Did we really manage to do that?' Frank asks Lara.

'Yes, partner,' she replies. 'I never thought I'd say the following sentence, but now I'm going to: we just saved the world. What do you think? Champagne?'

'Champagne!' everyone agrees in unison.

A day later, there's no sign of the virus. All companies have their systems and networks back in place and are catching up to repair the damage. Frank organizes a press conference about the virus for NATO, also the last one on that subject. Peter Black is grumbling in jail, awaiting trial, and already knows he'll be an old man if he ever gets out. That is, if nothing happens to him in prison.

Lara and Frank agree they will have a nice dinner together that evening, this time without her friends. Frank is just as nervous about this as he was on his first day of school. The Three Amigos and Frank are sitting at Eddy's house in the afternoon, enjoying a very good whiskey and now and then glancing at the diskette, which again hangs neatly framed on the wall. The world is licking its wounds and fortunately has been spared from even more catastrophes. Together they were able to contain the virus and everything turned out well in the end. The four men raise their glasses in a toast to a virus-free future.

Epilogue

Bangkok, Thailand

In a Bangkok suburb, in a large specialist rice exporting company, night watchman Charong, stands in the computer department with a tablet in his hand. His thoughts are with his wife and children. He would very much like to be home already. Unfortunately, he will have to practise patience for a while. He still has to complete his last round through the factory. Only then can he take his moped and ride home.

He runs through his list again to make sure he hasn't forgotten to check anything. All the computers are still there, he counted them. The cupboards are locked, check, and the windows are all closed, check. So everything is okay. The power is completely off, except for that little sensor, check.

Charong checks everything on his tablet, leaves the computer department and slams the door behind him. As a result, he fails to notice that the lamp, which he had mistakenly taken for a sensor, starts flashing. A dormant application has suddenly woken up and commenced its pre-programmed journey along a global highway of ones and zeros.

Appendix

Dear Reader,

You've had a lot to process in this book! Centrally controlled self-driving cars, access badges with built-in GPS, a virus that is conquering the whole world, and so on. Much of what we have enjoyed writing down has sprung from our imagination. But other things, such as smart lenses and self-driving cars, already exist. 2034, the year in which the book is set, is right now only eleven years away. During that time, a lot can still evolve in terms of technology. In the end, it may turn out that we have been too modest in our vision of the future. Especially with regard to the virus. We sincerely hope that we are wrong and that such powerful malware is hopefully never developed and then released into the world. One thing is certain: without human help, such a virus could never spread on a global scale. It always needs someone who is not attentive enough. Someone who opens a strange e-mail attachment without thinking or who doesn't update in a timely manner. It can spread only if computers are not adequately protected with good antivirus or security software. So don't give viruses and other malicious software a chance. And keep in mind Willems' second law:

CSP = TF x HF

CSP = Cyber Security Problem
TF = Technological Factor
HF = Human Factor

In other words, every cybersecurity problem is the result of the combination of technology and people. Without human naivety, curiosity, or other human shortcomings, malware wouldn't stand a chance.

Eddy Willems & Alain Dierckx

𝕏 @EddyWillems and @alain_dierckx

Authors' note

Righard Zwienenberg and Luis Corrons really exist and are actually security experts and good colleagues of Eddy. The characters Frank Willems and Nadine, Eddy's son and wife respectively, are also not made up. All other characters in the book are fictional.

Further information

Would you like to read more about the (true) story of the AIDS ransomware? And about the test to read the diskette in 2020? Then surf to www.eddywillems.be.

Would you like to read the short story (free) of Larry Lane's first exploits against NATO, a year before the events described in this book? Then surf to www.eddywillems.be.

Acknowledgement

We would like to express our heartfelt gratitude to Ulrich Seldeslachts, CEO of LSEC, a not for profit industry association focused on Information Security in Europe, based out of Belgium. Without his unwavering support and encouragement, 'The Virus' would never have been translated into English and made available to so many more readers. His faith in our work has been invaluable, and it is a privilege to share this journey with him and LSEC.

With sincere appreciation,

Eddy Willems & Alain Dierckx

WWW.LANNOO.COM

Register on our website to receive a regular newsletter with information on new books and interesting, exclusive offers.

Cover design: Bij Barbara
Cover image: iStock (front cover), Getty Images (back cover)
Translation: Michael Lomax
Formatting: Studio Lannoo
Typesetting: banananas.net

Any resemblance to actual events and/or persons is purely coincidental.

If you have any comments or questions, please contact our editorial team at: redactiefictie@lannoo.com

© Eddy Willems, Alain Dierckx, Uitgeverij Lannoo nv, Tielt, 2024

D/2024/45/564– NUR 330-332
ISBN: 9789020957099

All rights reserved. No part of this edition may be reproduced, stored in an automated retrieval system and/or be published in any form or by any means, electronic, mechanical or other, without the prior written permission of the publisher.